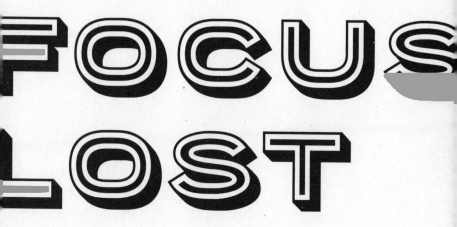

FOCUS LOST

FOCUS LOST

DOUG COOPER

A VIREO BOOK | RARE BIRD BOOKS
LOS ANGELES, CALIF.

Set in Minion
Printed in the United States

10 9 8 7 6 5 4 3 2 1

Publisher's Cataloging-in-Publication Data
Names: Cooper, Doug, 1970-, author.
Title: Focus Lost / Doug Cooper.
Description: First Trade Paperback Original Edition. | A Vireo Book |
New York, NY; Los Angeles, CA: Rare Bird Books, 2019.
Identifiers: ISBN 9781947856899
Subjects: LCSH Celebrities—Fiction. | Actors and actresses—Fiction. |
Photographers—Fiction. | Hollywood (Los Angeles, Calif.)—Fiction. |
Los Angeles (Calif.)—Fiction. | Thrillers (Fiction.) | BISAC FICTION /
General | FICTION / Thrillers / General
Classification: LCC PS3603.O58262 F63 2019 | DDC 813.6—dc23

For all those who take a bite of the apple
and want a little bit more.

CHAPTER 1

THE ROAD TWISTS AND turns away from Los Angeles. A man and girl ride inside an open Jeep. The vehicle slows and bends onto a grassy lane. Trees line both sides, connecting above, cloistering the path. Branches smack against the grill and windshield, raining leaves on the passengers, actor Levi Combs and young starlet Emily James.

A blonde ponytail sprouts from Emily's head. She rubs the debris from her bare, milky shoulders and legs and swats at the swarm of gnats swirling through the cab. "How did you ever find this place?"

"Driving late at night." Levi downshifts into first gear to navigate the uneven terrain. Strands of his black curly hair bounce against the red bandana wrapped around his head. He nudges up the black Ferragamo sunglasses resting on the tip of his nose. "You'll see, you need places like this to escape the cameras."

Even at only seventeen, Emily already knows that. She had been a working actor since she was three. Levi didn't get his break until he was twenty. "But what do you do out here?" Emily says, leaning toward the middle to avoid more of the invasive underbrush. She latches onto Levi's forearm as he continues to work the gearshift.

"Just roam," Levi says, powering the Jeep through the brush. A dilapidated farmhouse and barn appear ahead. He drives past the buildings into an overgrown orchard. Wild plants and grass extend up through the decaying branches spotted with leaves but bearing no fruit. "Solitude is your only friend in our business. Everyone either wants a share of what you have or to keep you from getting theirs." He increases speed, swerving between the dying trees. The thick weeds and fallen branches scrape against the undercarriage.

Emily clutches the safety bar. "Shouldn't you slow down?"

Levi accelerates, passing the last row of trees. "Hang on."

The weeded field drops off into a canyon fifty yards ahead. Panic seizes Emily. "Come on. What are you doing? Just stop." The space between the Jeep and the canyon decreases. Shrieking, Emily closes her eyes and curls up into a ball on the seat.

Levi stomps the breaks. The Jeep skids to a halt. Levi and Emily thrust forward. The seatbelts tighten and yank them back into the seats. The edge of the canyon appears just beyond the hood. A cloud of dust passes over them. Levi kills the Jeep. The sound of the engine fades into the fog blanketing the bottom of the canyon. Nearby rocky peaks poke through the mist like islands in a white sea. Unbuckling his seatbelt, Levi stands and looks out above the windshield. "Great view, huh?"

Emily uncoils and opens her eyes to the tranquil, majestic setting. She rips off the seatbelt and launches from the Jeep. "You're an asshole." She stomps to the edge of the canyon and stares into the emptiness.

Levi trails after her. "Relax. You weren't in danger. I told you, I come here all the time."

"But what if we had rolled over?" Emily asks, the fear revealing the young girl she never allows herself to be.

Stepping up next to her, Levi bumps his hip playfully into hers. "But we didn't."

"Still," Emily says, accentuating her pouting with a little girl's voice. "Why do you have to push everything?"

"That's funny, coming from the queen of the fast lane. You know I wouldn't let anything happen to myself. The world would be such a far drearier place without me." Levi wraps his arm around her, wiggling it to loosen her up. "There's a waterfall a short hike from here." He spins her toward him. "What do you say we go for a swim?"

"I suppose." A restrained smile creeps out through her dissipating anger. "But I'm still mad at you."

◆◆◆

STANDING ON A ROCK abutment, Gabe Adams wipes the sweat from his tanned, bearded face and closely clipped blonde hair. A black Nikon D5 camera dangles from his neck. He lifts the camera and zooms across the gorge to a horsetail waterfall that fans out and falls into a circular plunge pool fifty-feet below. He had been there since sunrise scouting and shooting the area after receiving a tip about this place from a patron viewing the photos for sale at his stand in downtown LA. Adjusting the lens, he snaps several shots, followed by more fine-tuning and clicking of the shutter.

Along the creek below, Levi and Emily hike into Gabe's shot. Emily says, "This is gorgeous. You own all this?"

Levi stops by the edge of the pool, removing his shirt. His broad shoulders and angular back glisten in the gleaming afternoon sun. "Not this part. Just to the edge of the canyon." He kneels down and splashes water on his face, rubbing it over his hairless chest and arms.

From his elevated vantage point, Gabe lowers the camera in frustration. He whispers to himself. "Jesus. Get out of there.

You're ruining the shot." He returns the camera to his eye and snaps more pictures, zooming in on Emily and Levi.

At the edge of the creek, Levi strips down to his black boxer briefs. Emily, all traces of the little girl gone, scans him up and down. "I'm surprised Mr. Paranoid isn't worried about paparazzi."

Levi plunges into the water and resurfaces. "No chance some fat piece of shit photog could've followed us. Why do you think I love it out here? It's one of the few places I feel safe and away from all the bullshit. That's why I wanted you to see it. You need to find a place like this."

Surveying the area, Emily removes her tanktop and drops her shorts. She thought he was bringing her out for another reason and doesn't want to waste any more time getting to it. Levi swims away toward the waterfall to avoid leering at her lean, developing frame. Furthering her intentions, Emily removes her bra and panties and jumps in. She buoys above the surface and blows water from her lips. "Whoa! Why didn't you tell me it was so cold?"

"Good for the circulation," he says, ducking his head under the falling water. "You'll get used to it. Don't be such a baby."

She swims to him and wraps her arms around his waist, pressing her body against his. "Come here and keep me warm."

Levi tenses. "What are you doing?" He steps back, but she doesn't let go and floats along with him. He reaches for her locked arms. "I don't think this is such a good idea."

"Who's being a baby now? I mean, why bring me all the way out to the middle of nowhere if you didn't want this to happen?" She keeps her body tight against his. "No one is going to know. You said yourself, we're completely alone."

He leans back. "Still—"

"I won't tell if you don't." Emily slides down along his body and disappears underwater. Levi's eyes widen. His lower half wiggles back and forth under the surface. Emily pops up and throws his wet briefs to shore. "That's more like it."

"Emily, we really need to—"

She clips his words with a kiss. Levi cups her shoulders, pushing her away. She presses tighter against him. He surrenders, wrapping his arms around her and pulling her close.

Up above, Gabe watches through the zoom lens. Uncomfortable with the voyeuristic direction his shoot has taken, he lowers the camera, but raises it seconds later, snapping more pictures.

In the creek, the waterfall crashes behind Levi and Emily. She climbs up on him, clamping her legs around his waist. He says, "Are you sure?"

"Absolutely." She nods and bites her bottom lip. "This is perfect." She eases herself onto him and rocks back and forth. Levi crouches down and supports her slight weight with his thighs. She thrusts harder. The water splashes between them and shoots up their stomachs and chests. Levi matches the intensity and timing of her movement, but his legs tire and ache. He walks her to the shore.

Kissing his neck, she says, "What are you doing? Don't stop now."

"Don't worry. Stopping is the last thing on my mind." Still cradling her around the waist, he spreads his shirt and shorts with his foot and lowers her to the ground. "Isn't this better?" His body covers hers. Visible only are her arms and legs sticking out each side and wrapping around him.

"Mmm-hmm," she coos. "I love feeling you on top of me."

Gabe creeps backward off the abutment into the tree line, his lens remaining on them. He knows it's wrong, but he doesn't stop. The camera clicks in rapid succession as he retreats onto the trail. A rock tumbles down the canyon wall.

It collides with others on the way down, jarring them loose. They hit with a staggered thump onto the canyon floor.

Startled, Levi pulls back from Emily. He looks up in Gabe's direction, scanning the area for movement.

Emily kisses him. "Come on, keep going. It's nothing." She tightens her thighs around him and grinds her pelvis in a circular motion.

Levi rotates with her, but he keeps scanning the canyon wall. Sunlight reflects off Gabe's camera lens, revealing his position. Levi separates from Emily. "Someone's here."

Emily pulls him back toward her. "Come on. It's just your imagination."

"No. I saw a reflection." He rocks back onto his knees and stands.

Through the lens, Gabe watches Levi looking directly at him. Gabe lowers the camera and charges off into the trees.

By the creek, Levi yanks his clothes out from underneath Emily and throws them on. Feeling deserted and vulnerable, Emily covers herself with her arms and hands. "Levi, come back down here. I'm cold. It's nothing."

Levi turns away from her and scours the rock face for the best way up. "Just get dressed and wait here."

"What?" Emily gasps. "You're leaving me?"

"I'm going to catch this loser and beat him with his camera." Levi jams one foot then the other into his shoes, not even bothering with the socks.

Emily sits up. "I can't believe you. You're being ridiculous."

"You, want to see ridiculous? Wait for the shitstorm that follows if those pictures get out." He turns and runs off along the creek.

In the woods, Gabe, cradling the camera in one arm and the case in the other, scrambles along a trail. He approaches a fork in the path. Unsure which way to go, he stops and scans side-to-side. Stuffing the camera in the bag, he opts to go right.

Levi angles away from the creek. Experienced with the terrain, he moves quickly and efficiently up a rooted trail to the woods. He weaves around, over, and under trees and branches, leaving the path, and cutting straight through the woods.

Lost in the woods, Gabe panics. His heart pounds, lungs heaving. He pauses to catch his breath and hears Levi yelling in the distance. "You better run. I'm coming for you." Gabe takes off again, still unsure exactly where he is or if he is going in the right direction.

Levi stops to get his bearings and listen. Through the trees, he spots Gabe. "I see you, asshole. You're mine." He angles to the right, calculating where to intercept.

At edge of the woods, Gabe views the canyon road through the trees and empties his lungs in relief. With the camera case cradled like a football, he pumps his arms to go faster, but his legs, heavy from use, don't cooperate. His brown Suburban sits on the side of the road fifty yards down. Darting in that direction, he lets go of the camera case and rummages through his pocket for the keys. The case swings behind him, dangling by the strap around his neck and banging into his backside as he bounds down the road. With the distance between him and the Suburban narrowing, he locates the keys in his pocket and presses the button to unlock the vehicle. The lights flash, the horn beeps.

Exhausted and out of breath, Gabe shuffles the remaining fifteen yards to the vehicle. He checks behind him again, still not seeing any sign of Levi. The camera case swings around to his left side. As he collects it in his arm, only steps from the Suburban, Levi bursts out of the woods and tackles him. They roll on the ground struggling for control. Levi maneuvers on top of him, pinning Gabe facedown on the ground. Levi drives his fists into Gabe's back and head. "How the fuck did you find us?"

Gabe fights to free himself, struggling to get out any words. "I—just—there—waterfall." Levi is too strong for him. Gabe stops fighting back.

Straddling Gabe with a firm grip around the back of his neck, Levi grabs Gabe's shoulder and flips him over. Levi studies Gabe for a moment to see if he recognizes him. "Who the fuck are you? Who do you work for?" His hesitation lowers his guard. Gabe rips his right arm free and grabs hold of the strap of the camera bag. Swinging with all his might, he hits Levi in the side of the head with the bag. Dazed, Levi falls over to the left.

Gabe kicks him off and scrambles to his feet. "I don't know who the fuck you are. I was just there for the waterfall."

Levi lunges and grabs Gabe's right leg. "I need those pictures."

Gabe delivers another blow with the camera bag to free himself. Disoriented, Levi scrambles to get up but stumbles, sliding headfirst across the stones.

Gabe yanks open the Suburban door and leaps inside, immediately activating the locks and starting the vehicle.

Levi, on his hands and knees, shakes off the wooziness and lumbers toward the Suburban, which roars to life. He yanks each door handle as he passes along the driver's side. Banging on the window, face to face with Gabe, Levi says, "You're mine, motherfucker. There's no place to hide. Nowhere to go that I won't find you." Gabe shifts the vehicle into drive. Levi slides around to the front and backs into the middle of the road. "What are you going to do now? You're going to have to go through me."

Gabe pulls off the side of the road, spraying stones behind him. He drives directly toward Levi, who holds his position in the middle of the road. Gabe swerves at the last second into the other lane. Levi slaps the side of the Suburban with his hand as Gabe speeds by. "Fucking coward!"

Gabe angles the Suburban back to the right lane. In the rearview mirror, he watches Levi shrink in the distance. The camera case strap twists around his neck and heaving chest. He untangles it, his hands shaking, and tosses the case on the seat next to him.

Still standing in the middle of the road, Levi removes his phone from his pocket and dials his agent. "Eva, it's me. You still got that contact at the LAPD? Good. We have a bit of an issue. I need you to have him look up a license plate. Three-apple-prince-rainbow-one-four-four... Yep, that's it... I'll explain later. We're still on for six at the Polo Lounge, right? Of course, I'll be on time. Okay, I'll see you then." He returns the phone to his pocket and heads back into the wooded area.

Following the path on the way back, he winds through the forest to the waterfall and climbs down to the creek. Emily sunbathes in her bra and panties, using her shirt and shorts for a blanket since Levi took his.

Levi walks up and stands over her, casting a shadow. "Come on. Hurry up and get dressed. We got to get back to the city."

She cups her hands over her eyes, her stomach muscles tightening as she tilts her head up at him. "About fucking time you got back. Did you at least catch him?"

"I did but he got away." Levi turns, kicking a rock into the creek. "I got his license plate though. Eva's going to track down who the piece of shit is."

Emily remains reclined on the ground. "Let her deal with it. That's what we pay them for."

Levi glances over his shoulder, noticing Emily is not moving. "No, I need to meet her anyway. She said she has some good news to share."

Emily sits up, pressing her finger into her bicep to check how much sun she got. "So, you brought me all the way out here and now we're just going to turn around and rush back? Un-fucking-believable." Levi walks away from her. She slaps her hand on the stones next to her. "At least come and help me up."

Levi spins around and plods back to her. Looking up at the waterfall, he extends his hand to help her up. "Believe me. You don't want those pics getting out any more than me."

"I'm not ashamed of my body." She puts one hand in his and holds up the other for him to grab hold. "Everyone thinks we're doing it anyway."

"Come on, hurry up. Every minute is critical." He scoffs, reaching over with the other hand and pulling her up in one forceful motion.

Continuing her momentum, she falls into his chest. "You sure we can't just take a break and finish what we started?" She drags her finger down his nose and across his lips.

He steps back, looking past her up at the waterfall again. "Are you nuts? Let's deal with one problem before we create another."

"Ugh. You're such a buzzkill." She turns away and bends over to pick up her clothes, intentionally presenting her ass in his direction. "Just because you play my dad in the movie doesn't mean you have to act like him." She slips on the shorts and tanktop and slides into her sandals.

Levi shakes his head. "You're fucking twisted, you know that?"

She shuffles over to him, cupping her hand on his crotch, leaning up, and kissing him on the cheek. "That's what you love about me, Daddy."

CHAPTER 2

FILM AGENT EVA FLOREZ waits alone at a round table for two in the Polo Lounge at the Beverly Hills Hotel. Her silken black hair curls around her ears, falling to the middle of the charcoal jacket that matches her skirt. In any other city, she would just be another attractive woman waiting for a business colleague or maybe a lover, but in this town, everyone knows her as the one who turned Levi Combs from an unknown college student into a Hollywood leading man. Draining her last swallow of white wine, she glances at the polished steel Baume & Mercier watch that Levi had paid for. Now she couldn't even get him to be on time.

A handsome male server approaches. Like most service industry people in Los Angeles, he is a this-slash-that-slash-this with two of the identities being actor and model to go along with the server role he is currently fulfilling. He, similar to the rest, believes all he needs is a break. "Another white wine, Ms. Florez?"

Eva slides the empty glass to the edge of the table, tapping her silver-tipped nails against the table. "Might as well. Never know when he'll show up."

The server nods and departs. Eva picks up her mobile phone to check for messages.

In the Jeep, Levi, still wearing the bandana, T-shirt, and shorts from earlier, drives off Sunset onto Hartford and around to Glen Way to avoid the lobby and enters through the service entrance in the back. A half-empty fifth of Tito's sits in the passenger seat. To help calm down, he had replaced Emily with the bottle after he dropped her off. He parks in a spot marked for deliveries only. Taking off the bandana and tossing it next to the vodka, he runs his hand through his hair and checks the mirror for any marks on his face before slugging more Tito's and exiting the Jeep.

A few steps away, a paparazzo, immediately snapping photos, surprises him from behind the trash dumpster. "Slumming it today?" he asks, referring to Levi's casual attire and the Jeep, since Levi rarely drives it out in the city.

"Fuck off," Levi says.

The paparazzo, wearing wrap-around sunglasses and having a similar size and build as Gabe, stays in front of Levi, walking backward, taking pictures. "What do you think about the Oscar buzz your new movie is getting? Will you be taking Emily James to the ceremony?"

The mention of her combined with the excess alcohol he has consumed triggers his rage. He steams toward the paparazzo. "Why are you asking me about her?" He rips the camera from the photographer's hand. "Was that you at the waterfall?"

The paparazzo backpedals a safe distance away. "Cool down, man. I'm just making conversation." He takes out his phone and starts recording a video.

Levi studies him for a moment, his vision cloudy from the vodka. He recognizes that it's not Gabe, but he still spikes the camera. Plastic and glass smash against the concrete. Levi grinds his heel into the camera. "You're all fucking scum.

Let's see how many pictures you can take now." He kicks the pieces off to the side and steps toward the paparazzo, who is still recording the video with his phone. Levi darts toward him. Having ample footage, the paparazzo tucks the phone in his pocket and runs off. Already late, Levi stops and hurries toward the back entrance. A group of hotel staff gather outside smoking. Levi passes them with a nod and weaves through the kitchen and out into the dining room.

Seeing Levi make his way across the distinctive green and pink carpeting, guests percolate with excitement. Most of them have come for the chance to see a celebrity of Levi's stature. All eyes follow him. He stops at a table to sign an autograph.

Eva knows Levi is wasted because of his eagerness to interact with the fans. He's only nice when he's drunk anymore. He strolls over and bends down to kiss her on the cheek. Her body stiffens, barely acknowledging the greeting. "You're late…again."

"You know how the fucking paparazzi are," Levi says, waving and smiling at a couple pointing at him from across the room. "They make it impossible to be on time."

"Suppose they got you drunk too?"

The server arrives with Eva's glass of wine and two menus.

Eva says, "Thank you, but we'll just be having drinks."

Levi pushes out his bottom lip. "Don't be like that. I thought you said we had something to celebrate."

The usual warm emerald pool in Eva's eyes frosts to icy green. "I have better things to do than sit here and wait for you."

The server shifts uncomfortably, not sure whether to stay or go. "Something to drink then, Mr. Combs?"

"Macallan twenty-one, neat," Levi says.

"Right away, sir." The server nods and charges away.

Eva's phone buzzes on the table. She turns it over and reads the notification, immediately accessing the phone and opening the message. Her eyes widen then constrict. She shakes her head and slides the phone toward Levi. "It seems you've been busy today. Guess that explains why you were late."

Unsure which story has made the news, Levi says, "What is it now?"

"The fucking photographer you assaulted outside." Eva says, gesturing toward the phone.

"Jesus, that was fast." Levi glances down at the article with the video titled *Camera-Stomping At The Polo Lounge*, referring to the tradition of spectators repairing the divots at halftime of a polo match. Levi shakes his head. "It just happened five minutes ago. The douchebag was hiding behind the trash dumpster and surprised me. Just take care of it and spare me the fake outrage."

Eva leans to the center of the table, lowering her voice but increasing the emphasis on her words. "I assure you, this isn't fake. You just don't seem to get it. The next six weeks are the most important of your career."

Levi turns at an angle in his seat, crossing his legs and looking up at the ceiling. "I know, I know. You've made it painfully clear over and over."

"Then why do you keep pulling these stunts?" Eva asks. "I had to promise TMZ an exclusive to make the last one go away."

The server delivers Levi's scotch, hesitating for a moment. Receiving no acknowledgement from Levi or Eva, he simply nods and leaves. Levi gulps half the drink. "That fucker deserved it. I mean, get into my business as much as you want, but if you start digging into my mama's past, that's where I draw the line." His Southern accent creeps into his speech. Eva had worked him hard to suppress the drawl, but anytime he gets drunk or talks about his past, especially his mama, it resurfaces.

Exasperated, Eva picks up her wine and slides back in her chair. "But you know better than that. They're just fishing for a reaction to generate clicks."

Levi raises his glass for a toast. "There's no such thing as bad publicity, right?"

Eva reluctantly touches her glass to his. "Times have changed, Levi. It's not just about what you do on the screen anymore."

"I know, I know," Levi says, weary of the same, tired argument. "Enough of this bullshit. What's the good news you have to share? I need to hear it before you rip me for why I needed that license plate."

"Always fucking something with you." Eva leans to the middle of the table, speaking in a whisper. "I've heard from a few different sources that *For Love* is going to get nominated for best picture."

Levi doesn't react. "That's good news but hardly a surprise with the other buzz and award recognition it's received."

"That's not the good news," Eva says, letting go of her anger and lighting up. "There'll be another nomination." She sits back in her chair, just smiling and nodding.

Levi jerks forward. "But how? I didn't think we had a chance. The other groups snubbed me."

"Apparently the Academy feels differently," Eva says. "Congratulations, Mr. Oscar Award Nominee."

Resplendent optimism replaces his regular rife-with-rancor response, but it retreats rapidly.

Eva says, "What's wrong? I thought you'd be happier. Regardless of if you win or not, this is going to help so much with the new movie."

"No, it's great," Levi says. "It's just that other thing we need to talk about could have a bigger impact than I thought."

Worry tightens Eva's face. "Wait, you're actually concerned about something? Mr. Don't-Give-A-Fuck-About-Nothing. This can't be good."

"It just happened before I called you. Could be nothing but if not, maybe we can get out ahead of it." Levi gulps more Macallan. "I took Emily out to my orchard today like I told you I wanted to, and we hiked to that one waterfall you and I found. Some photog was there and got pics of us together."

None of this is surprising to Eva since she's the one who orchestrated it. Walking to her car after a lunch meeting one afternoon, she noticed some of Gabe's other waterfall shots on sale at his stand downtown. She didn't stop and never really thought about it until Levi mentioned he was taking Emily out to the waterfall on his property. Even then, she didn't approach Gabe herself. Over the years, she learned it was best to use intermediaries and keep her distance from these things. She could've sent one of her usual paparazzi, but they were too unreliable. Too many times she had given people access, only for them to sell the photos to the highest bidder. She wanted someone she could control, someone from outside the business. Of course, there was a chance Gabe would miss Levi, or Levi would change his mind. But a missed photo nobody sees is better than an uncontrolled one everyone does. "So what?" Eva says, sowing the seeds of her plan. "That actually works for us. You and the film are getting nominated. You're hanging with your costar. Maybe you two should go together to the ceremony. It'll show you as a friend, a mentor."

"These pictures won't," Levi reveals. "When I say together, I mean to-*gether*."

Eva closes her eyes, waving her head back and forth slowly. "No. Please tell me you didn't." Even though she hadn't expected this, she isn't shocked either. With Levi, she knows anything can happen. It's another reason she wanted to use an outsider. She still has time to get out in front of it, and at a cheaper cost. Paparazzi would shop the photos around and drive up the price. She steadies herself with a calming breath. Although it's not what she had planned, in the end, the negative photos will just be more leverage she'll have over Levi. After all, it isn't just the money and success she has brought him over the years that keeps him a client.

"It's not my fault," Levi says. "She came on to me. It shouldn't be a big deal, right? I mean, we're both consenting adults."

Eva clenches her jaw, continuing to play her role and direct the performance. "No, you're a consenting adult. She's a seventeen-year-old girl."

"Seventeen going on thirty," Levi says, swallowing another mouthful of scotch. "You should've seen her. She knew exactly what she was doing."

"It doesn't matter, Levi. If this gets out, the public, the awards committees, and the advertisers won't look the other way. Not this time. This isn't like when you passed out in a pool of your own puke on the Museum of Tolerance's steps."

Levi finishes his scotch. "I thought it was funny. I was making a statement on the lack of compassion in our society."

The server returns, quieting both of them. "Another twenty-one, Mr. Combs, or perhaps you'd like to try the twenty-five?"

"Or maybe you'd like to go the other way," Eva says. "Maybe the fifteen, or better yet, the twelve?"

The server hesitates, looking back and forth between them, confused. Levi says, "Just bring the twenty-one, please."

The server scurries away. Levi looks at Eva. "If nothing has come out yet, we might still be able to fix this. The license plate I gave you was the photographer's vehicle. I chased and caught him by the road, but he got away. It was a brown Suburban."

Eva accesses an email on her phone even though she researched everything about Gabe before she sent him out there. "My guy said it belongs to Gabe Adams from out in West Covina. I got his address and did some checking. Doesn't seem like a usual paparazzo. He has a landscape photo stand down on Gallery Row and an exhibition starting at a gallery over on Traction. Maybe we can work out some kind of arrangement before these things get out. I'll go over to his show tonight and take care of it." She lifts her eyes to Levi. "Just promise me one thing?"

"I know," Levi says. "Steer clear of her unless you're there."

Eva interlocks her fingers, holding her hands in front of her as if praying. "At least until she's eighteen. After that, do whatever you want."

CHAPTER 3

G ABE, HIS WHITE T ripped from the V in the neckline down to his mid-abdomen and covered with dirt, views pictures of the waterfall on a laptop in the garage-turned-studio of his three-bedroom ranch house on Lolita Street in West Covina. Mounted and framed photographic prints of coastal and mountain landscapes surround him.

He scrolls through the photos on the screen.

Levi and Emily standing by the creek

Close-up of Levi's face

Close-up of Emily's face

Levi removing his T on the shore

Emily dropping her shorts with Levi in the water watching

Levi and Emily facing each other in the waist-high water in front of the waterfall

Levi and Emily kissing with the waterfall pouring behind them

Barebacked Emily mounted on Levi, her legs wrapped around his waist.

Gabe's sixteen-year-old sister, Abbie, her blonde ponytail swaying side to side, rushes into the garage swinging a pressed white dress shirt on a hanger. Her appearance resembles Emily's—obviously a fan—but her face is rounder with green eyes instead of Emily's spurious blue. "What are you doing?

Don't you think a shower would be a good idea before the biggest night of your career?" She stops, taken aback by his ragged appearance. "What the heck happened to you?"

"No time to clean up. Had a little run-in during the shoot." He nods toward the screen.

Abbie walks over behind him. Scrapes and cuts cover the back of his neck. Abbie picks off pieces of gravel ground into his skin. Gabe jerks forward, wincing. "Some couple hiked into the shot, totally ruining it. The guy spotted me and freaked out. Chased me all the way back to the truck. Barely got away. Total freaking whacko."

Abbie's eyes widen with disbelief, leaning toward the screen. "Are you effing kidding me?" She pushes his hand away and swipes through the images forward then back.

"I know," Gabe says, sitting back in the chair. "I waited aall morning for that light."

"No," Abbie says. "You do realize who this is, right?"

Gabe looks again at the faces on the screen. "No clue. Looks a little bit old for her."

Abbie stops at the picture of Emily mounted on Levi and zooms in. "That's Levi frickin' Combs and Emily James."

"Is that supposed to mean something to me?" Gabe removes her hand from the touchpad and closes the picture application.

Abbie rolls her eyes and scoffs. "Remember that show *Funwalla* that I used to be into in my early teens? That's her. Now she's playing his daughter in that movie *For Love*—the one getting all the Oscar buzz."

Gabe looks again, shaking his head. "If they're both so famous, they should be more discrete." He stands and takes the shirt from her, walking toward the house. "I'll delete them later."

"Are you crazy?" Abbie trails after him. "These things are worth a fortune. She's like the biggest teenage star and is only seventeen. He could win an Oscar. You gotta sell these."

Walking through the kitchen, he takes off his ripped T and tosses it in the trash. More scratches and scrapes from rolling in the gravel angle across his narrow back and shoulders. "No way. I'm not a paparazzo."

"Oh, that's right. I'm sorry. You're a photographic artist." Abbie tears off a paper towel from the roll on the counter and wets it underneath the sink. "Come here. Let me clean those scratches before you put that white shirt on and ruin it." Gabe stops next to their four-person, round kitchen table next to the sliding patio door that leads to the backyard. He pulls out one of the wooden ladder-back chairs and sits down. Abbie shuffles over behind him. "This might sting a little."

Gabe tenses as she dabs at the wounds. "I don't want to be known for celeb photos. Those people are toxic."

"Let me get this straight, you finally have pictures worth thousands, and you're just going to throw them away?" Abbie asks, pressing the dampened towel more firmly into the cuts.

Gabe turns to face her. "Hang on, you said she's only seventeen?"

Abbie puts a hand on each shoulder and spins him back around. "I know for sure because she's a year older than me, except for the two months after my birthday when we're the same age, until hers in November."

Gabe is quiet, considering the new information. "Hmm… if she's underage, maybe we should send these to the police."

"Like the cops would do anything other than jack off to them." Abbie folds the wet paper towel to a clean spot and wipes the dried blood from the last of the scratches.

"Watch your mouth. What did I tell you about your language? This is serious. If we have proof of a crime, we're obligated to turn it in." He removes the shirt from the hanger and slips it on, hurrying down the hallway to his bedroom.

Abbie trails behind, talking to his back. "But you saw her. She was obviously loving it, right? It's not like he was forcing her."

"Still. The law is the law." A gray suit jacket and pants dangle from a hanger on the door of his bedroom. Gabe lifts up the suit, holds onto the pants and tosses the jacket and hanger on the bed. He turns and motions for Abbie to turnaround in the doorway.

Facing away into the hallway, she says, "Look, if you really want to get this exposed, bypass the cops and go to a tabloid. That way you can bank some coin too. We could probably use it."

Gabe kicks off his jeans and slips on the pants. "I'm not going to the media. It's just not right to benefit on something like this." He tucks in the shirt and fastens the pants. "Someday you'll understand."

Abbie turns back around, nodding, approving of his transformation. "I doubt it, but I still love ya."

Gabe struggles to button the right cuff. Abbie strides over to help. He just extends his wrists and smiles. Abbie stares affectionately at him, calmly fastening one then the other. Sadness weighs down her eyes. She says, "Mom and Dad would be so proud of you tonight."

Gabe folds his arms around her. "Hey, don't think about that. Tonight is a happy night."

The unhappy night was in the spring of 2006. The six hundred seniors of Gabe's West Covina High School graduating class sat in rows spread out between the fifty and twenty yard lines facing the south end zone of Bulldog Stadium. Family members and friends filled both sides of the bleachers. Mexican fan palms alternated with the banks of lights circling the perimeter and extended toward the blue sky spotted with clouds.

Screams and cheers from the students and spectators drowned out the final words of the principal as she formally introduced the new graduates. The seniors flipped their maroon tassels to the other side of their hats and tossed them skyward. The marching band seated to the right of the stage played the alma mater. Students sang along, officially barking out the words for the last time. "Alma Mater, we praise you. Your strength makes us born anew…"

In the bleachers on the home side, seven-year-old Abbie stood with her and Gabe's parents. As the students began to scatter on the field below, their dad lowered the video camera that had been pressed to his eye for the previous hour. "Come on. I told Gabe we would meet him by the south goal post."

"Give me your hand," their mom said to Abbie. "I don't want you getting lost in this crowd."

Abbie scrunched her nose, reluctantly extending her arm. "Fine, but I get to ride with Gabe to the restaurant."

"That's up to him," their dad said. "He may want to ride with us."

It was their mother's turn to respond with a crinkled face. "We'll be lucky if he still wants to eat with us."

They descended the bleachers and weaved through the crowd toward the goal post. Gabe was posing for pictures with classmates. His long, shaggy hair flapped in the wind. A pair of gold wayfarer sunglasses, similar to those of his classmates, covered his eyes. Their dad exchanged the video camera in his hand for a digital camera in the bag dangling around his neck.

Abbie broke away and ran up to Gabe, jumping into his arms. He caught her and twirled her in a circle like a helicopter. Beaming, she pleaded for him to stop, but would've been upset if he had. Their dad circled around them, rapidly snapping pictures.

"Okay, put her down," their mom said. "You'll make her sick. You know how dizzy she gets."

Gabe brought her in for the landing. Abbie staggered in the grass catching her balance, squealing with laughter.

"Let's get a few of the graduate alone," their dad said. He directed Gabe in a variety of shots and poses, then brought in their mom, and Abbie. As everyone grew weary and started to complain, he showed one of the other parents how to operate the camera and lined up several more family shots.

Their mom looked at her watch. "If we're going to make our six o'clock reservation, we better get a move on it. It'll take us about an hour to get to Seal Beach, depending on the traffic."

"Do you want to ride with us?" their dad asked.

"No, I better drive my own car," Gabe said. "I have a bunch of parties to hit after. Do you think I can take the camera? I want to get a few shots of some friends in the parking lot."

Abbie, fighting back tears, clung to their mom's leg.

Their mom said, "Somebody was hoping to ride with you."

Gabe crouched down to make eye contact with Abbie. "You want to keep me company on the way there?"

Abbie's head popped up. She charged over to Gabe, jumping on him again, this time knocking him over. He swallowed her up in his robe.

"Enough already, you two," their mom said. "Get up off the ground before you ruin the gown."

"It's not like I'll need it again," Gabe said, lifting up Abbie and setting her on her feet. He stood up, brushing the grass off his maroon robe and picking up the mortarboard lying in the grass next to him.

"You want to follow us?" their dad asked.

"Nah, I know the way." He took Abbie by the hand. "We'll meet you there."

Their dad said, "Take the Ten to the Six-oh-five. Will save you about fifteen minutes."

On the way, curling around the ramp to the 605, Gabe noticed Abbie turned away from him to stare out the window. She hadn't spoken since they got in the car. He reached over and shook her leg. "Since when are you so quiet?" A tear streamed down her face. He said, "Hey, hey, hey. Why the tears? We're supposed to be celebrating."

She buried her face between the seat and the door.

Gabe said, "You know what I'm going to have at the restaurant? Maybe some crab…" He reached over and grabbed her thigh again. "…legs."

"Stahhhhp!" She jerked her leg away.

"Or maybe some lobster…" He pinched her butt. "…tail."

A giggle squirted out. She pulled her lips into her mouth, fighting to hold in any further squeals.

"No, I know what I want." He lifted his hand, hovering it above her. A smile crept on her face as she anticipated his next move. "I think I'm going to have some…" He dropped his hand to her rib cage, tickling her. "…ribs. Nom, nom, nom."

"Stop it," Abbie chortled. Gabe dug his fingers deeper into her midsection. She said, "You better stop or I swear, I'll pee all over your seat. You know I'll do it, too."

Gabe lifted his hand but kept it floating above her. "Fine, I'll stop—but only if you tell me what's wrong."

She pushed her lips out. "I'm mad at you."

"Me? What did I do?" Gabe asked, guiding the car along the San Gabriel Freeway by the California Country Club golf course.

"You're leaving," she said, the frown returning. "Why do you have to go so far away to Chicago?"

Gabe faked an attack with his hand, instantly transforming her sadness to a smile. "I have to go. The Art Institute there has one of the best photography schools in the country. I can't pass it up. It's only four years though. Plus, I'll be back for Thanksgiving and Christmas and summers."

She looked at him skeptically. "You promise?"

"If I'm lying, I'm dying," Gabe said, rubbing her head and mussing up her hair. "You can't get rid of me that easy."

The rest of the ride, Gabe turned up the music, and they belted out the lyrics to some of Abbie's favorites, like Gwen Stefani's "Hollaback Girl," Black Eyed Peas' "My Humps," and The Killers' "Mr. Brightside," with her doing some of her best passenger-seat dancing. She loved when Gabe played the music loud and encouraged her dance moves, which amounted to her acting out what she thought the lyrics meant. It was more entertaining than the actual song.

Off the freeway, they navigated the local streets and the small stretch of the Pacific Coast Highway to Walt's Wharf on Main Street, Gabe's favorite restaurant. He didn't recall why or when it had become his favorite. It just always had been. He used to come down with his mom and dad as a child before Abbie was born and go to the beach and play on the playground by the pier. They would spend the whole afternoon swimming, watching the surfers, and collecting shells. Every trip ended with a meal at Walt's. Gabe would always ask the server, "Is the fish fresh?" to which the server would always respond, "If it was any fresher, it'd still be swimming." A tradition that he had passed on to Abbie, and one she tortured the servers with like it was the first time they had ever heard it.

At the restaurant, the attractive college-aged hostess informed them that they were the first in their party to arrive. She walked them to a table by the mural of a fisherman on a pier with his two dogs that covered the wall of the main dining room. The hostess said, "I understand we're celebrating a graduation tonight?"

"Yep, he just finished high school," Abbie said beaming with pride. Gabe cowered, casting a glare at Abbie, slightly embarrassed to acknowledge his youth in front of their beautiful hostess. "What?" Abbie said. "You did."

"Yes, that's correct," Gabe admitted. "West Covina."

"Congratulations. I just finished my sophomore year at Cal State Long Beach," she said, placing the menus on the table. Gabe didn't know what to say next. He just nodded. She said, "Enjoy the meal. Your server will be right over." Gabe watched her walk away.

Abbie said, "Ooh, you got a crush on her. You want to go out with her, don't you?"

"Just sit down and stop embarrassing me," Gabe said, sliding into one of the seats facing the mural. Abbie just stood by the opposite chair. He said, "What are you waiting for? Have a seat."

Abbie glanced over her shoulder at the flamingo propped on the post behind her in the mural. "I can't sit here with that thing watching me."

He said, "It's just a painting, Ab." She shook her head. He pushed back in his chair. "Do you want to switch?" She shook her head again. He reached over and slid the menu to the seat next to him. "Just sit here then. It doesn't matter."

"I don't want to upset your girlfriend," Abbie teased.

Gabe patted the chair. "Just sit down and quit being an idiot."

The server came over and took their drink order. Abbie fidgeted with the table settings, whining, "What's taking Mom and Dad so long? I'm hungry."

"I can't believe we beat them," Gabe said. "You know how Dad is about traffic. Thinks he always knows the best way."

Another fifteen minutes passed. Gabe ordered some appetizers, so they didn't have to wait until their parents arrived.

The food came before their parents did. The server said, "They might be a while. We've had several calls from diners with reservations who are stuck in traffic. I guess there was an accident up on the PCH. They're probably caught up in that."

Another twenty minutes passed. Abbie peppered Gabe with questions. For every minute that went by without their parents' arrival and with Gabe having no new answers, she became more upset. After another fifteen, Gabe said, "Stay here. I'm going to go to the hostess stand and use the restaurant phone to call Dad's cell."

"You just want to talk to that girl," Abbie said. "Let me come with you."

"Not now, Ab," Gabe snapped, worry hanging on his face. "I'll be back in five minutes." He was back in three. "It went right to voice mail. Their phone must be out of juice. You know how Dad always forgets to charge it. Probably why they didn't call."

After another half hour with the restaurant filling up, the server stopped at the table. "They should be coming now. I heard from another table that the roads are clearing."

But another hour passed, and they never came. Abbie was scared and crying. Gabe had run out of excuses. He probably would've left earlier, but he didn't have enough cash to pay the bill. The restaurant manager, also concerned, told Gabe to just come back with their parents another time and settle up.

As Gabe drove back up Main Street toward the PCH, he already knew what had happened. He just didn't know how bad it was. Abbie still hadn't gotten to that point yet. She said, "Where could they be? They know Walt's is your favorite."

"Probably just some car trouble," Gabe said. "We'll head home and check the messages."

Turning left onto the PCH, they didn't have to go all the way home to find out. On the left side of the road, barely recognizable because the front was smashed into the back seat, sat their dad's white Subaru Outback. Glass and oil coated the pavement. A red jack-knifed semi with a smashed passenger-side cab still blocked one of the lanes.

Gabe attempted to distract Abbie before she noticed the car. "Looks like it was a trucker."

Abbie craned her neck looking at the semi and scanning the accident scene. "Looks bad. Do you think Mom and Dad were—" Her eyes fixated on the car. "Pull over, pull over." She shook his arm. "That's Dad's car."

Gabe switched lanes to the outside to move farther away. "No, that's some other white car."

Abbie flung off the seatbelt, kneeling on her seat, then scrambling into the back to get a better view. "It's his. I'm sure of it. I can see my purple dance school bumper sticker on the back. You have to stop. They're probably here."

Gabe angled the car to the side of the road. "Okay, I'll go check, but you have to stay here."

"No, I want to go with you," Abbie pleaded.

"This is not a discussion," Gabe said. "I'll go talk to the police and check what happened. I need you to stay here."

Abbie protested, her fear turning to tears. "But what if they're hurt? I want to see them."

"If you really want to know, then stop fighting with me and let me go find out." Gabe unhooked his seatbelt and exited the car. The rubber-necking traffic crawled by. He weaved through one lane at a time. The smell of burning oil hung in the air. He walked to the edge of the yellow tape blocking off the scene. The uneasiness in his stomach swelled. He could see that the inside of the mangled car was charred. Water used to extinguish the fire dripped onto the street.

A California Highway Patrolman stopped him from entering the scene. "Son, you're going to have to stay back. We're not quite finished here."

Gabe's legs wobbled. Dizziness filled his head. He squatted down, steadying himself with his hands on the pavement. He looked up at the patrolman, gathering the strength to straighten his body. "That's, uhm, that's my parents' car." The vertigo returned. He fought through it, knowing Abbie was watching. "Are they okay?"

The patrolman came over. "Vickie and Paul Adams are your parents?" Incapable of speaking, Gabe nodded. The patrolman lifted the tape. "Why don't you come over here and sit down, son?"

Gabe followed the patrolman to his car and sat in the front seat facing out with his feet on the pavement. Abbie sat in the driver's seat of Gabe's car, her face pressed against the window.

The patrolman said, "Their car had just rounded the bend and was heading southeast on the PCH."

Gabe delayed the outcome by interrupting the patrolman. "They were coming to meet my sister and me for dinner at Walt's."

The patrolman said, "The semi was traveling the opposite direction and attempted to make a turn on Marina Drive. He says he never saw the car."

Gabe latched on to the patrolman's comment, squeezing out any potential hope. "So they're all right?"

The patrolman shook his head. "I'm afraid not. Only the driver of the truck survived. Your parents' car collided with the passenger-side of the semi. I know it probably doesn't help much, but they didn't suffer."

Gabe dropped his head into his hands and sobbed. Again remembering Abbie was watching, he straightened up and looked across the street to his vehicle, but she was no longer in the window. The door was open and she was running across the street toward him. Cars screeched to a halt. He leapt from the seat and charged toward her.

She jumped into his arms. "Tell me what happened. They're okay, right?"

He squeezed her, pulling her head into his chest. "I'm sorry, Ab. There was an accident."

Standing in his room, remembering that day, Gabe hugs Abbie and rubs the back of her head. She regains her composure and pushes back from him. "Tonight won't be so happy if you're not on time. You better get a move on it. You're not famous enough to be fashionably late."

Gabe snags the jacket from the bed and angles toward the door. "You'll be there later?"

"Of course." Abbie walks to the dresser. "Gabe?"

He stops in the doorway. "Come on, Ab. I'm already late enough. What is it?"

She picks up a bottle of Giorgio Armani cologne from the dresser and sprays some at him. "You stink."

Gabe steps into the lingering fragrance and kisses her on the cheek, then hurries away.

Abbie follows him down the hallway to the front door and watches him through the bay window in the living room as he backs out of the drive and speeds off. When the Suburban is out of view, she turns and walks back through the kitchen out into the studio.

At the computer she swipes her hand across the touchpad. A dialog box prompting a security password appears. She enters Gabe's password, which she knows from using his computer for homework, and logs in. With several finger movements and button clicks, she maneuvers the pointer to the menu and emails copies of the first five pictures to herself. A notification dings from the phone in her pocket. She pulls it out and confirms the pictures were received, then deletes the record of the transmission on the computer to erase the trail.

CHAPTER 4

MARCUS AMBROSE, A DEPUTY district attorney for Los Angeles, stands in the middle of the empty spare bedroom of his eight-hundred-square-foot Lake View Mansion apartment in Westlake. There's no lake, and it's no mansion. His apartment is on the backside and doesn't even overlook Lake Street. Marcus has called it home for over thirteen years, dating back to the five years he attended Golden Gate University, the three years at Loyola Law School, and the five years he needed to work his way up to deputy district attorney from his starting clerk position. The rootedness was never planned. It was more just coincidence and good fortune that his undergrad, law school, and first job were all within a few miles of one another. He considered moving with each new beginning—thought he would have to at some point—but he really couldn't afford much more until his deputy DA promotion. But each time it came to deciding, he concluded it would've been more of a distraction than a benefit. At first it was his schooling and now it was work, but most of all it would've taken away from what was taped and spread across the wall and the floor.

Looking down at his phone, Marcus watches the video of Levi and the photographer outside the Polo Lounge. He switches back to the article and sends it to the printer, which immed-iately whirs and shakes, churning out the content. Walking to the printer, he slides the phone into his pocket. His high fade haircut accents his long face and narrow, angular head. His eyes sag from not sleeping and his midsection swells on all sides, pushing over his belt. The page in the printer tray has a still image of Levi stomping the camera embedded in the text.

A headshot of Levi occupies the center of the beige-painted wall to his left. Three strings of blue, red, and green yarn extend from the picture, each end pinned with a tack. The blue thread is labeled alcohol/drugs; the red, women; the green, violence. An assortment of photos and articles branch off from each of the colored strings. Marcus bends over and removes a green tack from a plastic container on the floor and walks over to the same-colored string and pins the new article to the wall, adding another leaf to the densely populated violence branch.

Marcus has been following Levi's career for almost twelve years at this point, well before anyone knew who Levi was. But it wasn't until Marcus got the job in the district attorney's office after law school that he delved into the level of detail spread on the wall before him. Over the years, his focus has changed from patient observation to comprehensive tracking to hunting. Every one of Levi's missteps found its way to the media hangs on the wall. Marcus is just waiting for the right opportunity to nail Levi and get himself out of the endless cycle of pornography cases he has been prosecuting in the valley.

Looking at the wall, Marcus knows the time will come and is approaching rapidly. The frequency of Levi's public solecisms has been increasing. Marcus steps closer to the wall, starts at the center and reads the string of events, looking for a pattern or anything he can use to expedite his pursuit.

He releases a stunted sigh, reaffirming that soon he can finally do something about what happened to his big sister, Tamara, and fulfill the entire reason he became an attorney.

Growing up, Marcus had always looked up to Tamara, who had been more of a mother to him than his own. Not that his mother was a bad mother. She, like their dad, was just always working. They really didn't have much choice. They had gotten pregnant during her senior year, and they were parents the following October, never able to catch up, let alone get ahead. They both worked multiple jobs, which collectively, barely covered the cost of their three-bedroom apartment. When their father died of a heart attack at forty-two, it only put more pressure on their mom, and she was around even less.

What Marcus idolized about Tamara more than anything was that she was always out pursuing some dream. At first, she wanted to be a singer, then a dancer, then a painter, and eventually a makeup artist. It wasn't like she was unsuccessful at what she tried. She was actually quite good at everything. She would just lose interest. But as one ambition faded, another one would always spring forward and take her in a new direction.

The makeup gig seemed like it was going to stick when she worked her way into a job on a popular TV show. Marcus, then all of fifteen, used to wait up until she got home to hear about whom she had worked on and what had happened on the set each day. But as she settled into the job, the stories transitioned from work to more about her drama-filled dating life than anything else. The boys had always been fond of Tamara. She had thick, coily hair flowing out and down to her shoulders like a halo. Her full lips always seemed seductively pursed, drawing people in, while her penetrating stare kept them at bay.

Every dating story followed the same script. The relationship started strong and fast. An immediate, intense emotional attachment led to a deeply felt, although usually superficial attraction that too often was centered on sex. After a few weeks, she would start to feel trapped or bored or smothered, or something, and would focus on the new guy's shortcomings and disengage. The guy would then pursue, which would turn her off even more. Eventually she would either sabotage the relationship beyond repair or push the guy away enough that he gave up. If he did get frustrated and end the relationship, it would usually reinvigorate her for a few more weeks until the cycle repeated enough that there was nothing left worth saving. Once it finally ended, she would swear off men for a while until the next emotionally unavailable guy came along, and she would jump right back in.

It didn't take long for Marcus to hate hearing the stories and seeing her go from one ill-fated relationship to the next. But she had done so much for him, he felt that listening and comforting her was the least he could do to support her. Every time she came home all excited about some guy, he held out hope that it would be different, that the new guy would be the guy, and they could go back to talking about what was happening around her rather than to her.

Levi Combs was supposed to be that guy. At the time, he was relatively new to Hollywood, which meant polite and full of hope. It didn't take long for the shallow, self-serving environment he was dropped into to change that. Before being cast on Tamara's show, he had only done modeling and a few bit parts here and there. But it didn't take long for the offers to start outnumbering the rejections. He was quickly becoming the new, shiny toy.

Once cast on Tamara's show, she and Levi hit it off from the second he first sat in her chair. Different from the other guys, he jumped into the relationship with the same intensity as her. For once, neither person blinked nor pulled back. Passion met passion and exploded into an all-consuming blaze. For weeks, everything was Levi said this, and Levi did that. He even came over to the apartment, something none of the other boyfriends had ever done. Levi was the first one Marcus had even met, and was his first TV star.

From their first interaction, Marcus was as charmed with Levi as Tamara was. If their father hadn't died suddenly, meeting Levi might have done it anyway. Not because Levi was a TV star, but because he was white, and not just white, but pretty-boy white. He had Hollywood everything: hair, nose, teeth, body. It was like Tamara had opened up a magazine and pulled him out of a fashion advertisement. And Levi's actions matched his flawless looks. During one of his visits, he had turned to Marcus and said, "Do you like surfing?"

Marcus shrugged. He had never even really thought about surfing. It sounded cool, but despite living close to the beach, he had been there only a few times and didn't even know how to swim. He said, "Like in the ocean?"

"Of course, my man." Levi flashed the smile that was garnering so much attention. "Where else do people surf?"

"I know," Marcus stuttered. "I'm not stupid. I guess I just never really had the opportunity."

"Let's go one of these Saturdays," Levi said. "I can show you. Actually, maybe I shouldn't. I'm pretty horrible. But I know some people who can give you some lessons."

Marcus just shrugged again. "Okay. Sounds pretty cool, I guess." Levi always invited Marcus to whatever Levi and Tamara had planned: to the movies, restaurants, or drives along the coast. It was one of the reasons Marcus liked him from the beginning. This time, just like the others, Marcus glanced at Tamara when Levi offered, and her glare communicated there would be no surfing, just like all the other events, in his future. He didn't care though. He just liked being included and seeing his sister so happy.

Then, just like everything else, it changed as quickly as it had started. Levi stopped responding to her texts and taking her calls. At work, he would tell her that he would meet her after, then would not show and have an excuse the next day for what happened. He had been sick, had fallen asleep, had to meet his agent, it was always something. The more Levi resisted, the more Tamara launched into full-on stalker mode. Eventually Levi requested that she be reassigned from the show. When that didn't deter her, she was let go.

After losing her job—the best job she had ever had—Tamara didn't leave the house. She would be in bed when Marcus left for school, and in the same place when he got home. Then, just like her relationships, everything suddenly changed. She went from being a shut-in to always being out, except to shower and change her clothes. Something was different about her too. Marcus picked up on it right away. The previously perennial possibility in her lips plunged into a perpetual frown. Her arresting gaze waned to a lifeless stare. The kindness and comfort she had always treated Marcus with were gone as well. Her behavior was erratic. She would be angry one minute and in a dream-like stupor the next.

One morning Marcus got up for school to find the bathroom door locked. He pressed his ear to the door and could hear the shower running. Marcus knew it had to be Tamara. Their mom was never home before her night shift at the diner ended at nine. He was hopeful that things were changing for Tamara again, that she was up early and heading out to find a new job, or better yet, maybe she already had one and hadn't told him yet. He waited fifteen minutes, then twenty, and thirty. The only sound from inside was the steady stream spraying against the back of the tub. He finally knocked on the door. "Mar, you in there? I'm going to be late for school." No response. Just the consistent spray against the hard surface of the tub. Steam floated out from underneath the door. He banged harder. "Mar, is everything okay in there? I have to brush my teeth."

After another five minutes of no response, he got a paperclip and straightened it like she had taught him in order to pick the lock. When he opened the door, through the thick steam, he could see her lying on the floor curled around the toilet. He dropped down, rolling her on her back. The rubber tubing tied around her right bicep flopped across her body. A needle with a half-full plunger of blood-clouded liquid stuck out from her forearm. A corroded spoon, a lighter, and an empty sandwich baggie were next to a makeup bag containing additional needles on the back of the toilet.

Marcus tapped the side of her face. "Mar, come on. Can you hear me?" She didn't respond. He lifted her eyelids. Her eyes were fixed in a blank stare. Shaking her, he yelled, "Mar! Don't do this." He felt for a pulse, then pressed his ear to her chest. Both revealed nothing. He propped her up against the tub. Her head lolled back into the fanning stream. He shut off the water and rummaged through her purse for her phone. Minutes later, paramedics arrived confirming what he already knew. Tamara had died of an overdose.

Initially after her death, Marcus, as expected, was quiet and despondent. He moped around the house, moving from the couch to her bed, then overwhelmed with emotion, back to the couch. But at the funeral, it all ruptured into anger. He expected the day to be difficult and probably the worst day of his life. He had always thought the day of his father's funeral was the worst day he could remember, or maybe he had just heard his mom and sister say it enough that he believed it. Actually, though, he really didn't remember much of his father's death. It was just a blur of his mom and sister crying and standing by the door shaking the hands of a bunch of people Marcus didn't know as they came and left.

For Tamara's funeral, Marcus expected to know a lot of the people, or at least be able to finally put faces with the names of the people who he had heard so many stories about over the years. But none of those people came. Not one single one. Most visibly absent was Levi. Marcus knew they were all aware of the services because he had texted everyone in Tamara's phone the details. A few had responded with curt condolences, but no one came. He never understood that, and he most certainly never forgave it. Typical Hollywood bullshit was what he would learn it to be. Not really that uncommon at all. Just selfish acts from people concerned only with promoting themselves rather than helping anyone else. Time has done little to change or heal how he felt.

Standing in front of the article from today, Marcus taps the picture of Levi with his index finger. "Come on. We're so close. Just a little farther. I only need a bit more, and I can do the rest."

CHAPTER 5

WELL-DRESSED ATTENDEES CROWD THE Art on Traction Gallery in a repurposed auto repair shop downtown on Traction Street. The two in-ground lifts from the previous tenant extend six feet above the floor. The silver hydraulic pistons shine and glisten like decorative columns. Framed photographic prints hang on all four sides of the lift-decks and on the surrounding walls. The old automotive customer counter in the left corner has been repurposed into a bar. Visitors float in and out through the open garage doors.

Just to the left of the bar, Gabe views a picture on the wall of an elderly couple. In the shot, the sun peeks above the mountains, which descend into a pasture. The thick, wild grass transforms to a beach that disappears into an active ocean. Surfers frolic in the water while cows wander on the beach.

Gabe says, "This is one of my favorites. I think it captures the essence of California—the mountains to the east giving way to a pasture that turns to a beach and fades into the ocean."

An elderly man admires the picture. His left arm crosses over his body, holding his right at the elbow and extending up to his chin. He taps his index finger across his lips while he speaks. "I love the cows on the beach watching the surfers."

"Cultures colliding," the elderly woman says.

The gallery owner, a lean woman in her mid-forties with round, white, oversized eyeglass frames and long, curly red hair falling on both sides of her shoulders walks over. "Excuse me, but may I steal him for a moment?"

"Absolutely," the elderly woman says. "We've monopolized enough of his time."

The man continues staring at the picture, taking a step back then forward for a closer look. "Consider this one sold."

"Thank you so much," Gabe says, shaking the hand of the elderly woman while the man's focus remains on the picture.

The gallery owner affixes a small, round yellow sold-sticker to the placard underneath the picture and plucks a card from the corner of the frame. "Just take this to the cashier, and she'll ring you up and set up delivery."

The woman snags the card and tugs the man by the arm toward the cashier. "Come on. You'll have plenty of time to obsess over this at home."

After the couple leaves, the gallery owner speaks in a whisper to Gabe. "We have a bit of a situation with one of the waterfall pictures."

"I don't understand," Gabe says. "What's the problem?"

"Two people want it," she says with a smile.

Gabe relaxes. "That's easy. Just give it to whomever made the first offer."

The gallery owner removes her glasses. Bags circle under her eyes and deep creases angle along the side. Using loose fabric around the middle of her green silk maxi dress, she cleans her lenses. "But the other person is offering a fifty percent markup on the asking price."

Gabe shakes his head. "First offer, first sold. I'm not bumping someone just for more money."

Eva, wearing the same charcoal suit she had on at the Polo Lounge with Levi, strolls up drinking a glass of champagne. Her jacket drapes over her forearm, revealing lean brown arms through the sleeveless black blouse. She studies the picture the elderly couple just committed to buying.

Putting her glasses back on, the gallery owner sizes up Eva then nods at Gabe, acknowledging his decision and offering her approval for Eva at the same time. "Very well, then. I'll let you get back to the guests."

Gabe slides alongside Eva. "That was taken just outside of San Simeon."

Eva scans the placard for the information, pretending she doesn't know who Gabe is. "How can you tell? Have you been there?"

Gabe turns toward her. "Because I'm the one who took it."

Eva's eyes remain on the picture. "Beautiful. How much is it?"

"Unfortunately, it just sold." Gabe points to the sticker on the corner of the frame. "But I can show you some others that I think you might like."

Eva turns, redirecting her gaze on him. She assumes the pictures haven't been released yet since she hasn't heard anything. Either he doesn't know what he has, is in negotiations, or doesn't plan to do anything. Not wanting to push him in any direction, she decides to feel him out. "That's all right. I don't want to keep you. I'm sure I can manage." She sips her champagne, her eyes never wandering from him.

Feeling the strength of her stare, Gabe shifts his weight to the other foot. "Why is everyone so worried about taking up my time tonight? That's why I'm here." He notices the low level of champagne in her glass. "But first, let's refresh your drink. My work, much like me, is more interesting with alcohol."

"Only if you'll have one with me." She finishes the rest of her glass. "It's rude to let a girl drink by herself."

"Very well. After you." Gabe extends his arm toward the bar, falling in behind her. At the counter, he takes her empty glass and slips behind for two fresh ones. "Having your name on the flyer does have some perks."

As Gabe and Eva toast, Abbie strolls up with a female friend. Both wear similar black, long-sleeve trapeze dresses. The only difference is Abbie's has an off the shoulder neckline and her friend's is a V-neck. "Don't forget us," Abbie says. "Whatever you're toasting to, we'll drink to that."

Gabe looks at his watch. "Thought you were going to be here thirty minutes ago."

Abbie lifts her friend's hand above her head and spins her in a circle, rotating herself afterward. "This magic doesn't happen on its own. How about that champagne?"

"Nice try," Gabe says. "Better not let me catch either of you drinking."

"No worries. We'll make sure you don't catch us." Abbie tilts her head and smiles playfully. "Who's your friend here?"

Gabe looks at Eva, embarrassed he hasn't asked her name. Eva extends her hand to Abbie. "Actually, we just met. I'm Eva...Eva Fuentes," she says, almost slipping and revealing her real name.

"I'm Gabe's sister, Abbie. This is my friend Gwen." Arms zig and zag as they all exchange greetings.

Eva says, "What's it like having a famous photographer for your brother?"

"Puh-lease," Abbie says. "Don't inflate his ego any more than it already is. He's difficult enough to live with."

"With good reason, from what I can see," Eva says, looking around the room. "I think others agree."

Gabe says, "Or maybe they just heard there was free food and booze."

"I'll give him credit when we can stop peddling pictures at that street stand." Abbie crinkles her nose and sticks her tongue out at Gabe. "Come on, Gwen. Let's go check out the spread." She grabs Gwen's hand and leads her toward one of the handsome, young male servers circulating with a tray of hors d'oeuvres.

Gabe yells after her, "Remember what I said about the champagne." He drops his head forward, shaking it. "I just keep telling myself, I only need to make it through the next few years and get her into college."

Eva sips some champagne. "She said that you live together?"

"Yep, just the two of us," Gabe says, watching Abbie fondly. "But enough about us. You came here to see some art, not to hear me blather on about me and my sister." Gabe turns to walk toward one of the lifts. "Let's start over here."

Eva reaches over and touches his arm, causing him to stop. Their eyes connect. She says, "I'd love to hear more. Maybe we can have a drink when things wind down?"

Gabe curls his lips into a smile pulling his eyebrows, which had risen from surprise at her forwardness, down to their normal level. He looks around the room. "I suppose I better get busy so all these people get out of here on time."

Gabe leaves Eva and works his way around the room stopping at each picture telling its story. Eva mingles with other guests, spending most of her time in the vicinity of the bar. Abbie and Gwen entertain themselves as long as two sixteen-year-olds can at a gallery showing. She waits for Gabe to find his way back to Eva before attempting her getaway. Joining them by the bar, Abbie, with Gwen at her side, says, "Seems like a great opening night."

"I haven't got the final tally yet," Gabe says. "But we definitely made some money."

Abbie holds out her hand, rocking back and forth on her heels. "Do you think I might be able to get a little of that cheese? Gwen and I want to go check out the new Levi Combs movie, *For Love*. It's showing over at the Regal on Olympic at nine forty-five."

"The one with Emily James," Gwen chimes in.

Hearing their names, Eva looks away but catches herself and joins the conversation to avoid suspicion. "I hear it's very good."

Abbie says, "Rumor has it that he might get an Oscar nod for the role."

"Didn't realize you were such an Oscar buff." Gabe looks at his watch. "I don't know, Ab. Kind of late for a movie. With previews, it'll probably run past midnight."

"I promise, we'll come straight home," Abbie says. "Twelve thirty at the latest." She glances over at Eva. "Might even beat you home."

Gabe scans the three faces staring at him, all wanting the same answer, although for different reasons. He removes his wallet and thumbs through the bills. "Okay, not one minute past twelve thirty."

"Thank you, thank you." Abbie kisses him on the cheek, noticing him pulling out a twenty. "Don't forget money for snacks."

"Hold on a second." Eva digs into her silver Brunello Cucinelli tote. "I have a couple movie passes you can use."

"No, no. We can't accept those. You keep them," Gabe says. "Abbie can pay me back working in the studio or at the stand."

Eva says, "It's no trouble. I get them for free all the time through work and never go." She extends two passes to Abbie.

"Please, use them. I think there's also a ten dollar concession voucher with each one."

Abbie hesitates, looking at Gabe, who nods his approval. She takes them from Eva, handing one to Gwen. "Thank you so much. Very kind of you."

"Too nice," Gabe says. "Hope you'll at least let me buy the drinks."

"Deal," Eva says, her eyes again connecting with Gabe's.

"Eww," Abbie says. "I think that's our cue to leave." She kisses Gabe on the cheek and extends her hand toward Eva. "Really nice to meet you. Hope to see you again soon."

"Me too." Eva ignores her hand and leans in, kissing her on each cheek. "Two for luck."

"Thank you and congratulations on the show, Mr. Adams," Gwen says. "Promise, I'll have her home on time."

"Remember, young lady," Gabe says to Abbie. "Twelve thirty sharp. Not a minute after."

Abbie straightens her body and salutes. "Yes, sir." She lowers her arm and grabs Gwen by the hand as they hurry toward the door.

The rest of the evening Gabe meanders through the room, checking back with Eva periodically. When the owner shuts down the bar, guests linger finishing their drinks, eventually leaving. Gabe, Eva, and the gallery owner are the only people remaining. Outlines of blank spaces show where the sold pictures had hung. Gabe retrieves a bottle of champagne from the ice bin behind the counter and joins Eva on the small couch in the sitting area.

The gallery owner leans back in a taupe oversized lounge chair, kicking off her open-toed heels and putting her feet up on the matching ottoman. "What a night. I forget how much work these events are."

Gabe pops the bottle of champagne and pours three glasses. Handing one to each of the ladies, he proposes a toast. "To a successful opening."

They touch glasses. The gallery owner says, "Seven sales the first night. Think it's safe to say you have arrived."

Eva holds up her glass. "I'll drink to that."

Gabe drains half of his champagne. "It's a nice place to visit. Let's hope I can stay."

"The waterfall pictures created quite a stir," the gallery owner says. "Do you have any more?"

Gabe says, "Actually I found another great one today but unfortunately got interrupted…or maybe I interrupted."

"Uh-oh," Eva says. "Sounds like a bit of a story there. What happened?"

Gabe tops off their champagne. "Ah, nothing. Just a misunderstanding. Some people hiked into my shot and didn't know I was snapping photos. I'm going to have to go back to get new ones."

"You may want to hurry," the gallery owner said. "Based on the feedback I got tonight, we're going to get some good press. If you have any other pieces ready to go, you may want to bring them by tomorrow to replace what has sold. We can also review the accounting for tonight and transfer the money to your account."

"Sure thing," Gabe says. "You want me to stay and help clean up?"

The gallery owner shakes her head. "No, you two run along. The cleaning crew will take care of this."

Gabe turns to Eva. "Walk you to your car?"

Eva puts her hand on his. "That'll be a good start."

Gabe picks up the bottle of champagne they've been drinking and holds it toward the gallery owner. "Mind if we take one of these?"

She extends her glass. "Just a splash more for me then it's yours. Feel free to grab a full one on your way out. I'm not ready to get up yet. Today was too long, and this chair is too comfortable."

Gabe whisks behind the bar and snatches another bottle from an open case. He tucks the one they've been drinking under his arm and offers the other to Eva. They bid goodnight to the gallery owner and shuffle across the concrete floor to the exit.

Outside on the sidewalk, Eva points down the street to the right at a white Mercedes parked on the opposite side underneath a flickering streetlight. "That's me down there."

The heat from the day still radiates from the sidewalk, trapped between the thick, low ceiling of clouds. Eva nevertheless burrows into his arm like she's avoiding a chill. Gabe swigs from the open bottle of champagne and offers it to Eva. "More bubbles?"

"Don't mind if I do," she says. "But this wasn't the drink I was talking about earlier. I'm not letting you off this easy." She gulps several mouthfuls and passes the bottle back.

"Of course not. We can go anywhere you want. I just need to be home by twelve thirty to make sure Abbie gets there on time." He drains the rest of the bottle and drops it in a nearby trashcan.

Arriving at her car, Eva sets the unopened bottle of champagne on the roof and leans back against the driver's side door. She looks up at Gabe, her eyes narrowing from the flickering light above. "Why don't we just go there?"

Gabe misses the obvious implication of her suggestion. "We can do that, but I don't keep much alcohol in the house. I'm sure we can come up with something though. We still have one full bottle left."

"That's fine by me. I'm not really that thirsty." She purses her lips, pulling one in then the other to moisten them. Gabe bends down to kiss her. Eva pulls back. "I meant, I want to see more of your work."

Gabe lurches back, embarrassed. "I'm sorry. I thought—never mind. Of course, I'd love to show—"

Eva grabs Gabe by the shirt and pulls him close. "And you, of course. I want to see more of you." She puts her lips on his in a long, soft embrace. "Hop in. You can punch your address into my GPS, and I'll drop you off at your car."

CHAPTER 6

ABBIE AND HER FRIEND Gwen sit mid-row in the back of a dark movie theater. A bucket of popcorn balances between them on the inside corners of their seats. The screen shows a prison visiting room with white floors, walls, and ceiling. Steel screens cover the windows. Levi, arms and legs shackled, wears an orange prison top and pants. Emily sits across from him at a rectangular metal table. She looks much younger due to her tartan skirt, white blouse, and her hair in pigtails.

Levi says, "I didn't want you to see me like this."

Rocking back and forth in her chair, Emily squints, sniffling to hold back the tears. "I don't understand, Daddy. Just let me tell them what really happened."

He leans forward. "Sh-sh-sh. Remember, we said we were never going to talk about it."

Emily scampers around the table to hug him. He lifts his arms to respond but can't due to the restraints. She buries her face into his neck. "But they're going to kill you for something I did."

"No! Something I did." Levi fights to hold back his own tears.

"No way," Emily says. "I can't let you do this."

Levi rests his head on hers. "You have to, pumpkin."

The emotion flows from the screen into the theater, flooding the viewers. Gwen leans over to Abbie. "He's totally going to win for this."

Abbie grabs a fistful of popcorn. "He's good, but I wouldn't be so sure. Never know what could happen."

After the movie on the way out of the theater, Gwen checks the time on her phone. "Look at this. Should get you home with plenty to spare."

"Let's stop for a coffee then," Abbie says. "I want to show you something." She had been debating all night what she was going to do. Seeing how happy Gabe was at the opening and how well he did, she thought it best to keep quiet and didn't even tell Gwen. But watching Levi and Emily in the movie got her excited and fortified her resolve. She knew then she couldn't let the opportunity pass. She would have to do something. Gabe deserved to catch a break for once.

Gwen pulls her toward the car. "Come on, Abbie. You heard what Gabe said. If we're late, he won't let you go next time."

Resisting, Abbie stops on the sidewalk in front of the entrance on Olympic. The other pedestrians weave around them. She strokes the fabric of Gwen's dress around her midsection. "Come on. We look too good to go home this early."

"Fine, you win. But we're only staying fifteen minutes." Gwen interlocks her arm with Abbie's, and they walk to the Starbuck's a block away, behind the Yardhouse at the LA Live complex. "I hate when you make me the responsible one."

"Get, used to it," Abbie says. "Because I'm about to do something really crazy."

They each get a sugar-free caramel macchiato Frappuccino and an iced lemon pound cake to share and sit at a two-top by the window. Abbie takes out her phone and accesses the pictures she sent from Gabe's computer. "Check out these pics.

See anyone familiar?" She turns the screen toward Gwen and swipes through the photos.

Gwen cuts the pound cake lengthwise, glancing at the screen. On the third photo, she drops the knife and grabs the phone from Abbie. "Holy shit! Is that?" She expands the photo, stretching it with her fingers. "Oh my god. It totally is. Where did you get these?"

Abbie breaks off a piece of the cake and pops it in her mouth. Mumbling while chewing, she says, "Gabe took them earlier today. And get this: he didn't even know who it was." She sits back in her chair, sipping her drink. "It was a total accident."

Gwen swipes back and forth between the photos, stopping on the last one. "I mean they're totally doing it, right? No doubt about that." She looks up at Abbie. Her eyes bounce with excitement. "What are you going to do with them?"

"These are too juicy for the gossip sites. I'm going straight to Forbidden Fotos." Abbie slides her chair around the table next to Gwen and takes the phone. "Let's see what they're worth." She accesses the Hot Tip form on the site. Her thumbs work in tandem to quickly fill in the information.

"Shouldn't you just let Gabe do this?" Gwen asks.

Abbie moves her thumb over the submit button. "You know Gabe. No way he'd go through with it, but he totally deserves some good to happen, and we need the money. He's sacrificed so much for me. This is my way of paying him back." She taps the screen. "There. The faster they call us, the more money we can demand."

Gwen squirms in her seat. "I don't think this is such a good idea. He's going to be so mad."

"He'll get over it." Abbie takes another big bite of the yellow cake. "What's the worst that can happen? If they're not interested, he is none the wiser, or if they are, he makes money. No risk at all."

They both stare at the successful submission message on the screen, a two-line thank you followed by a large paragraph of legal disclaimers in smaller print. Gwen says, "How much do you think you can get?"

Abbie dims the phone and sets it on the table. "I don't know. A thousand, five thousand, maybe more."

Gwen slides back from the table. "Come on. We should probably go." Abbie stands, pushing her chair around to the other side and follows Gwen toward the door. Gwen says, "You really think that much for five pictures?"

Abbie says, "I'm telling you these things are worth at least that." A flash emanates from her phone followed by her Taylor Swift "Fearless" ringtone. Abbie looks at the screen, showing the unrecognized number to Gwen. Answering the phone, she says, "Gabriel Adams Photography... Yes, please hold." Abbie lowers the phone pressing the microphone into her chest. "It's totally them." They hurry through the Starbucks and find a quiet place outside away from the smokers milling around the front. Abbie lifts the phone to her ear. "Hello, this is Abbie, Gabe's assistant... Yes, that was me... There are five pictures of Levi Combs with Emily James taken at a waterfall recently... Two on land and three in the water... I think the content speaks for itself."

Gwen, now on board with the plan, bounces up and down, excitedly, whispering. "Ask for an offer. Ask for an offer."

Abbie waves for her to be quiet. Into the phone, she says, "Could you make an offer, please? I have several other media outlets interested... Between five hundred and fifteen hundred dollars depending on the quality and content... I was thinking more around ten grand for all five... Yes, I can do that." Abbie motions to Gwen for a pen. Scavenging through her purse, Gwen locates one and hands it to Abbie. "Go ahead," Abbie says. She writes an email address on her hand. "Got it. I'll send them right over... One more thing: we'll need Gabriel Adams Photography listed with the photo credit... I don't care if that's not your usual policy. You'll need to change it if you want these photos... Yes, I'll send them over right away. We look forward to hearing from you. Thank you." She lowers the phone, joining hands with Gwen, and squealing with excitement. "Holy shit! They totally agreed. Ten grand! I just have to email them the pics, and as long as they are what we say they are, they'll wire transfer the money to whatever account I want."

Gwen grows solemn. "Don't you think you should at least tell Gabe first?"

"I will...once I have the money." She leads Gwen by the hand. "Let's go. I'll send the pics to them on the way home."

◆◆◆

Across town, Gabe pulls into his driveway. The motion-activated beam above the garage sprays light across the front yard. He steers the car to the right, making space for Eva to pull in next to him. She does a U-turn in the street and parks on the opposite side, two houses up.

Gabe waits for her in the driveway. The neighbor's dog barks, pawing at the living room bay window. Eva's kitten heels clack against the concrete as she angles across the street toward him. He says, "You should've just parked in the driveway. Plenty of room."

Walking up the driveway, Eva squints into the light. "I wanted to leave enough room for Abbie when she gets home."

"Gwen's dropping her off." He motions to the space in front of the house, his keys jingling in his hands. "You could've at least parked in the front. You planning to sneak out and make a fast getaway?"

"Don't be silly." Eva interlocks her arm with his. Gabe leads her up the brick path from the driveway to the house. She says, "Between that light and the dog next door, no one is sneaking anywhere."

Gabe slides the key into the door, hesitating before opening it. "Please excuse the mess. I wasn't expecting guests."

"I bet you use that on all the women. Kind of like a woman not shaving her legs. Guaranteed to meet someone when you don't." Gabe flips on the light, glancing down at Eva's smooth shins and calves. She says, "Don't worry. You're lucky I wanted to wear a skirt today."

Several photographs of younger versions of Gabe and Abbie, alone and with their parents, hang on the wall. The décor in the living room to the right is twenty years past its zenith. White drapes outline the front bay window with a blue and white-striped couch and a glass coffee table resting on a brass base. A mahogany entertainment center covers most of the opposite wall. A chair matching the sofa and a glass end table fill the space to the right. A framed print of Monet's "Water Lilies" hangs behind.

Gabe notices Eva studying the decor. "Would you believe we're into vintage furnishings?"

Eva nods toward one of the photos of Gabe and Abbie with their parents. "I love the family photos, but I thought you said it was just you and Abbie."

"It is. This is their house," Gabe says. "Abbie and I just never got around to redecorating." He walks toward the kitchen, motioning for her to follow. "Studio's back this way."

Eva trails after him. "I'm sorry. I didn't mean to pry. The pictures really are cute. I keep a picture of me and my mom and dad from when I was five on my nightstand."

"It's fine," Gabe says. "I wanted to take them down, but Abbie would crucify me. She likes things exactly as they were."

"Did something happen to your parents?" Eva asks.

Gabe sets the full bottle of champagne he brought from the gallery on the counter and removes two stemmed glasses from the cabinet. With his back to Eva, he pops the cork and fills the glasses half full of champagne. "No sad stories tonight." He retrieves the orange juice from the refrigerator and tops off the glasses. "Tonight is a night to celebrate." He hands one of the glasses to Eva. "I'm glad you're here."

Eva moves closer to him, placing her hand on his arm. "Me too."

Gabe leads her toward the studio. "Let me show you the work I have finished."

They walk from the kitchen through the door into the garage studio. Gabe flips on the light. Milton casts a sleepy stare in their direction from his sprawled-out position on top of the closed laptop on the desk. He rolls over onto his back, curling up his legs and arching his back to present his belly. Eva separates from Gabe and goes to Milton, sinking her hand into his furry midsection. "Look at this chunky baby." Milton writhes and purrs with contentment. Eva kneads the doughy feline flesh. "You like that don't you?"

"No mystery with Milton. A belly rub and a spoonful of tuna now and then, and you have a friend for life." Gabe walks over to a framed picture on the worktable.

"Typical man," Eva says, leaving Milton to join Gabe. "A little physical gratification and a treat, and they're clay in your hands." She reaches down to pick up the picture, looking at Gabe for approval. "May I?" Gabe nods and steps back to pick out a few more from the finished ones leaning against the wall. Eva stands the picture on its end. A barn-like white church with two tall pointed arch windows and a single spire glows in the moonlight against thick, grayish black clouds. A shadow from the gabled entrance angles across the front, concealing the bottom half of the pointed arch window on the left. Two dark circular windows—one above the entrance and the other in the base of the spire on the roof—stare back from the picture. Behind the church, headstones reflect fragments of moonlight. A black oak creeps into the picture on the left, extending above the top of the spire, which has the dark outline of a cross at the peak resting ominously, almost floating on its own. Eva says, "Wow, this is amazing. Calm and peaceful, yet foreboding. You're drawn in but feel like you should stay back at the same time."

Gabe walks up next to her. "Isn't it cool how the tree is higher than the cross? Could be interpreted so many different ways."

"Like God is neither above or below but in all things," Eva says.

Gabe draws a circle around the branches with his fingers. "Or maybe all things flourish in the presence of God."

Eva lifts her hand to Gabe's and presses down, slowly lowering the picture to the worktable. She pulls Gabe toward her, placing his hand on the small of her back. Rising up on her toes, she presses her lips against his. He moves his other arm around her and locks his fingers, pulling her closer. Soft moans mix with their caressing lips under the hum of the fluorescent lights. Gabe lifts her up and sets her on the worktable. Eva gasps in surprise and excitement at the sudden, strong move. She reaches behind her and slides the picture farther down the table. Leaning back, she pulls Gabe on top of her. He struggles out of his suit jacket and drops it to the floor. Her hands move to his neck, loosening his tie and unbuttoning his shirt. He reaches down between her legs and works the fitted skirt upward. Her legs spread wider as it climbs, eventually revealing no other layers underneath. His hand slides up the inside of her thigh. Murmuring approvingly, she unbuttons his shirt and continues down to his waistline. With a few quick pulls and tugs, she unbuckles his belt and drops his pants to his ankles.

Yanking his boxers down, she slides to the edge of the worktable and guides him inside her. He moves back and forth at the urging of her hands on his hips. With each forward thrust, she pulls him with more force. The table creaks, coalescing with their cooing. Sitting up, she wraps her arms around his neck and delivers a deep kiss, forcing her entire weight into him. Their breathing intensifies, building then suddenly stopping for several seconds before beginning again in full, deep gasps as Milton jumps from the desk to worktable, purring and rubbing his head into her side.

"Uh-oh," Gabe says, shooing Milton away with his hand. "Looks like I'm not the only one who's smitten with you."

"Just another smitten kitten." Eva laughs, reclining back on the table, moving her hands from Gabe to Milton. "At least he waited until we were finished."

Gabe steps back from the table, reassembling his clothes. "Better him than Abbie." He glances at his watch. "She should've been home twenty minutes ago."

Eva, still flitting her fingers over Milton's head and spine, extends her legs, just able to hook Gabe with her feet and urge him toward her. "If I stay, will you promise to go easy on her."

Gabe moves toward Eva, leaning over, propping himself up with his arms on the worktable. "You want to stay?"

Her voice quivers. "I mean, if you want me to." She moves her hands from Milton, gently stroking the back of Gabe's forearms.

"Of course I do," Gabe says. "I'm just surprised. I didn't think you wanted to."

She grabs the front of his shirt and pulls him down to her, so they're nose to nose. "Is that the kind of girl you think I am?" She follows her words with a kiss, trapping his bottom lip between her teeth.

"Not at all," Gabe says, holding his jaw still. "I just figured, since we weren't planning this, you weren't prepared for a slumber party."

Eva releases his lip, kissing him softly. "The best stuff is always unplanned. How does the saying go? When we make plans, God laughs."

Gabe's phone rings in his pocket. He removes it and shows the screen to Eva. "Speaking of that, here's the queen of not planning." He puts the phone to his ear. "What is it this time? Flat tire, stuck in traffic, stepped in gum and stuck to the sidewalk?" Eva scoots off the table, adjusting her skirt and collecting her shoes. Gabe, still talking to Abbie, says, "Lost track of time, having a coffee after the movie, huh? At least that sounds believable. How long?… Okay, not a minute longer, but make sure to be quiet. We're going to bed… Yes, I said we… That's none of your business… That's enough. Just get home. If I don't hear you home by one, I'll be up waiting for you. Neither of us want that… All right. Okay, I will. Goodnight." He slides the phone back in his pocket. "Abbie says, 'hi.'"

Wearing part of their outfits and carrying the rest, they walk toward the door to the house. "Probably a good thing she was late," Eva tousles her mussy hair. "That could've been awkward."

Gabe shuts off the light as they leave the studio. "God would've definitely been laughing at that one."

In the bedroom, Gabe and Eva continue where they left off in the studio, only this time it is Gabe on his back. When they hear a door close down the hall, Eva catches Gabe stealing a glance at the clock, which displays 12:58. Eva stops, both her arms extended on Gabe's chest. "Do you need to go check on her?"

Gabe takes her wrists and spreads his arms, lowering her to him so their bare chests merge. "No, she's fine. I'll talk to her in the morning. I'm not going anywhere."

Eva breaks his grip on her wrists, maneuvering her hands into his. She interlocks their fingers and pins his arms above his head. "That's good because I wasn't going to let you, anyway." Their playful banter fades to fevered thrusting until silence followed by soothing whispers and eventual snoozing.

Eva untangles herself from Gabe, careful not to wake him. Certain that he is still asleep, she slides from the bed, slipping on Gabe's white dress shirt from the floor. She pries open the door and creeps down the hallway through the kitchen into the studio. Not turning on the light, she feels her way to the desk and sits down in front of the computer. Milton leaps from the worktable onto the desk, landing with a thud, startling her.

"Jesus Christ, cat. You trying to kill me? Not all of us have nine lives." Milton paces across the desk in front of her. His purring vibrates low and deep. She pushes him away. "Not now. Go lie down." Milton turns around and comes back, dropping down in front of her. She reaches over him and opens the laptop. "Okay, I guess we'll do it this way." She rests her wrists on him and works the keys with her fingers. The screen lights up, casting a glow on her. The security dialogue box appears. She types a-b-b-i-e. It fails. She tries the same password with a capital A then by adding numbers. It still fails. Looking around the room through the faint light from the computer, she sees one of the waterfall pictures and tries w-a-t-e-r-f-a-l-l. No luck. Milton pushes his butt in the air up by her chin, forcing her hand off the keys. She says, "You don't give up, do you? I bet you know this stupid password."

Suddenly, bright light fills the room. Eva jerks back into the chair. Milton scrambles from the desk to under the worktable. Gabe stands in the doorway. "Actually, he should. It's Milton."

Eva, her eyes adjusting to the light, squints at Gabe. "Between you and him, I think you're both trying to see who can give me a heart attack first."

Gabe, wearing only a pair of gray sweatpants, walks toward the desk. "The password is Milton, all lowercase. What do you need the computer for?"

"Oh, nothing." Eva shuts the laptop. "I couldn't sleep and started thinking about work. I didn't want to wake you, so I came out here to read some email." She holds up her phone. "My battery is almost dead. I thought I would try your computer."

Gabe stands behind her and rubs her shoulders. "Go ahead if it will help you sleep. I can keep myself busy until you're finished." He walks around to the worktable, picking up the picture of the church, which has smudge marks smeared across the glass from earlier. "I can start by cleaning this."

Eva rises from the desk chair and shuffles up next to him. "Don't be silly. You should go back to bed. Don't stay up because of me." She touches the side of his cheek. "I should probably get going anyway. I don't think I'm going to be able to sleep after all."

Gabe leans down and kisses her. "I can think of something better to do than read emails."

Eva pulls back from him and walks to the desk, fetching a piece of paper and a pen. Meticulous precision replaces the inviting warmth from earlier. "As nice as that sounds, I have an early day tomorrow, or rather today," she says, looking at the time on the computer. She scribbles down her fake name and number on a scrap of paper and hands it to him. "Tonight was great though. Here's my number. Give me a call, and let's get together again this week sometime." She motions toward the house. "I'm just going to get dressed." Gabe steps toward her to follow. She says, "I can manage. Be back in a flash."

Gabe nods, confusion furrowing his brow. "No worries, I guess. Whatever works. I'll just wait here."

Eva returns moments later, fully dressed. She stops by the back door. "So I think I have everything. Does this lead around to the front?"

Gabe looks up from the worktable and angles toward her. "I can walk you out."

"No, don't be silly. Keep working. I'll find my way." She turns toward the door and places a hand on the doorknob.

Gabe reaches her before she can open the door. He stands behind her and slides her thick black hair to the side, kissing the back of her neck. "Is everything okay? You can totally stay." Eva relaxes, the warmth from earlier returning. Gabe rubs the sides of each arm, moving down to untuck her blouse and rub her stomach. "This work can wait."

Eva bristles at the mention of work. "But mine won't, I'm afraid." She rotates to face him and pushes the bottom of her shirt back into her skirt. "I'll see you this week sometime." She rises on her toes and kisses the end of his nose. "I still need to pick out my pics before you get all famous and the price goes through the roof." Gabe leans down to kiss her. She gives him a quick peck and turns back toward the door. "I better go, or I'm going to be late."

Gabe releases her and lifts his arm above her to guide the door as she walks out. "To be continued then. Thanks for an amazing…" His voice trails off because she's already down the walk and around the corner. "…night." He shakes his head, unsure of exactly what he did to chase her off. Milton saunters over, figure-eighting between his legs. Gabe looks down. "You saw the whole thing. Want to tell me what just happened?"

Milton meows his response and walks toward his empty food dish.

CHAPTER 7

Eva steps off the elevator on the thirteenth floor of the Roosevelt Lofts downtown in the financial district. She plods down the hall to her three-level penthouse. She's moved three times in the past five years as business with Levi has improved, but all were within the same building. She could afford to live in a fancier building or more posh zip code like most of her colleagues, but she had promised herself she wouldn't get sucked into that life. Instead, each time she opted to move up to a higher floor and bigger place rather than to a new address. The first two she rented, but the penthouse is all hers. It's the first property she has ever purchased, and outside of a car lease, the biggest financial commitment she has ever made.

Inside her apartment she trudges up the steps to her bedroom and master bath on the top level, leaving a trail of clothes. She turns on both showerheads and steps inside the etched glass enclosed rectangular space. Steam swarms around her. She sits down on the stone bench and reclines against the slate and tumbled marble walls, allowing both of the hot streams to pelt against her face and chest. The realization of what she had attempted and failed to do settles in. Worse yet, she has no clue what her next move should be. She gave him a fake name and number, so even if he tries to get in touch with her, he won't be able to. Feeling the steam open up her pores, she wipes her hands down her face over her chest to her thighs where Gabe's hands had been only hours before. Slumping her shoulders forward, she leans down, cradling herself, sobbing.

It had been a while since she had had sex and even longer since it meant anything to her. Most of her encounters were brief interludes. She would meet someone, bang once or maybe a few times if he didn't irritate her, then she would push him away and be celibate for a while. After some time passed, she would feel obligated to try again and pick someone new. They would go back to his place or car or once even in the bathroom of the bar where they met. But she never felt good afterward. It was always more obligation than pleasure. Tonight was no different. That's why she usually avoided it. She never trusted pleasure. She had never learned how to feel good.

It all went back to when she was a young girl. At the time she never thought of it as abuse or even punishment. It was just something that happened and kept happening for almost a year. After the first few times, she looked at it as a responsibility more than anything. She was eleven years old and in sixth grade. Her mom had been dead nearly four years. She and her dad lived in a two-bedroom apartment in West Adams only a few blocks from their old house. He had tried keeping the house after her mom died, but without her mom's teacher salary and him being out of work for almost two years, there was no way.

At first when her dad was out of a job, Eva didn't really understand what was going on. She wondered why all her friends' parents went to work and her dad never did, but she didn't really question it. She just thought she was lucky to have him home all the time. She knew they weren't rich, but there always seemed to be enough to get by. She didn't know the money they did have was from the insurance. Eventually that ran out, and she remembered things slowly disappearing. First it was appliances, then furniture. Finally, one day she got home from school and all her stuff was packed in trash bags. Her dad had borrowed a pickup truck from a friend, and they loaded their remaining stuff in three separate truckloads and took it to their new apartment. Before they left with the last load, her dad put the keys in the mailbox. She had said, "But if you leave the keys in the mailbox, won't anyone be able to go in the house?"

Her dad said, "It doesn't matter. It's the bank's problem now."

It didn't really bother her though. She had never really felt comfortable in the house after her mother passed anyway, and she was excited to be moving so close. It meant she wouldn't have to change schools or get new friends, and there was a pool. Unfortunately, she never got to swim in it after she found several used needles at the bottom. Anytime she asked to go to the pool, her dad told her to just take a bath. That was her own private swimming pool, he said.

After her mom died, her dad never slept in a bed or even a bedroom again. The mattress, box springs, and headboard her parents had used were one of the first things he got rid of. He kept his clothes in the room but only went in to change. He always just slept on the couch or in the recliner. That's where she would find him in the mornings, and when he started working third shift at the food packaging plant, he would be there in the late afternoon when she got home from school. He would usually get up around five in the evening, make them dinner, which was usually breakfast, then help her with her homework.

Afterward, they would watch whatever old movie they could find on TV until it was time for her to go to bed. That's where she got her love and appreciation for film. There weren't too many movies made before 1980, the year her dad said everything turned to shit, that she hadn't seen. If she hadn't seen it, she could probably at least tell you why it wasn't worth watching.

At first, when her dad started working the third shift, he had a friend or family member stay over while he was at work. She really couldn't tell anyone was even there though. Her dad would tuck her in, head off to work at some point, then be home in the chair sleeping when she woke up. But when he let Roy, one of his coworkers and friends, who worked first shift, move in to the bedroom her dad never used, he didn't need anyone to stay and look after her. Roy was her live-in babysitter.

The new arrangement seemed to work for everyone. Her dad finished his shift at six in the morning and got home by six-thirty as Roy left to start his shift at seven. Once Roy was gone, her dad woke her up and got her ready for school and saw her off, then slept most of the day until she got home. Roy knocked off at three but rarely came home until nine or ten at night. Days passed without her even seeing him.

Most importantly, for the first time since her mom died, her dad was relaxed. The additional income from Roy staying with them combined with her dad not always needing favors from people or having to pay others to stay over relieved a lot of pressure, and he wasn't as sad and serious all the time. He laughed and joked with her like he used to with her mom. That was how she always remembered her mom and dad together. He had a way of always making her mom laugh, which would then make him smile.

One night after her dad had tucked her in, just as she was falling asleep, she heard a light knock on the door and the latch open. She assumed it was her dad wanting to say good night one last time before he left. But as the light from the hallway filled the room then faded when the door closed shut again, she knew from the smell, it was Roy. He always reeked like stale beer and Bengay. She said, "Roy? Is everything okay with my dad?"

"Shhh, he's fine. Go back to sleep." Roy crept over and sat on the edge of the bed. The wintergreen and menthol aroma swirled around her. He stretched out on the bed next to her. His body felt hot through the covers. He was breathing heavily. Scooting away, she moved toward the wall. He wrapped his arm around her and pulled her against him. He said, "Just lie still. You know I really like you. Right now I just need to be close to someone." He pressed against her. She could feel him poking her in the small of her back through the covers. He rocked back and forth slowly. Terrified, she started to cry. He kept moving back and forth. "Now, now, there's nothing to be afraid of. Don't you like having me here? I know your dad does." His breathing intensified. "That's why you can never say anything. If you do, your dad will be upset, and I'll have to leave. He'll be all alone on his own again." He moaned softly, his body pressing more firmly into hers. "All you have to do is not say anything when I come in to visit. Can you do that?"

Nodding, she whimpered, "Yes."

"That's a good girl," he said, rubbing his hand up and down her leg as the movement quickened until his body tightened and he rolled on his back, gasping and growling in pleasure, shaking the mattress. She remained still and silent. He slid off the bed. Before leaving, he whispered, "Remember, not a word."

And so this continued, for almost a year. He didn't visit every night, but he was there more often than not. Eventually there wasn't even any talk. He would just come in, lie next to her, stay for five or ten minutes and leave. Sometimes she would be asleep and wake up with him under the covers next to her. Others she would hear him lumbering down the hall and dig her nails into the mattress, praying that he would keep walking.

But as much as she hated Roy's nightly visits, she didn't want to upset her dad or cause him any stress. She convinced herself that Roy wasn't hurting her. It was her way to help her dad. She just pretended it was a bad dream and scooted as close to the wall as she could after he left and closed her eyes, hoping not to wake up until her dad came into her room the next morning.

Then one day it just stopped, or rather Roy was gone and never came back. She asked her dad what happened. He just said, "Roy moved out." And he never spoke of him again, which was fine with her. She never mentioned him again either, not to anyone. She stuffed it all in a box and stuck that box on a shelf in some dark corner of her mind that only seemed to open on occasions like this.

In the shower, she reaches up and turns off the water. The drops bead and cascade down her smooth skin. She collects and wrings her thick, black mane and throws it over her shoulder. From the back of the door, she snags her white Turkish cotton robe and wraps it around her in a tight embrace. Her wet feet smack against the Carrara marble tile on her way to the bedroom. The clock on the nightstand displays 5:05 a.m. Ten minutes before she usually wakes up. She crawls onto the bed and curls up on her side toward the middle. Her body tremors with loneliness. She pulls her arms and legs in tight. Her eyelids squeeze shut pushing the painful memories away until the next time.

◆◆◆

GABE SITS HUNCHED OVER a bowl of cereal at the kitchen table. His bare feet tap nervously against the vinyl flooring. Other than donning a clean white V-neck, he wears the same gray sweatpants from the night before. His open laptop rests on the table next to the bowl. He works the touch pad with his right hand and the spoon with his left, keeping his eyes on the screen as he flips through a cascading stream of photographs.

Abbie shuffles sleepily down the hall, reading messages on her phone. Her white ribbed scoopneck tank top has the message *Stay Calm and Sleep On* in pink block lettering on the front. She glances at Gabe. "Where's your friend?"

Gabe says, "She left."

"You didn't even make her breakfast? That's classy," Abbie says, picking up the empty carton of almond milk. "And thanks for saving me some milk."

Gabe drops the spoon into his empty bowl. "She had to work this morning, and there's more in the fridge." He stands up and takes his dish to the sink, noticing her skimpy top and polka-dotted shorts. "What did I tell you about your outfits? If you're going to wear that stuff around the house, you have to wear a housecoat. You're not ten years old anymore."

"Relax. I wear less than this at the gym." Abbie scoops out a handful of the multigrain cereal and eats it dry.

"That doesn't make me feel a whole lot better." Gabe gets a clean bowl from the cabinet and takes it to her. "And don't be eating with your hands out of the box. I swear, I don't know what's gotten into you lately, but you won't be leaving the house if you don't straighten up."

Abbie empties her hand into the bowl and adds more from the box. "Geez. For someone who got laid last night, you sure are cranky. Thought you would be in a chipper mood this morning. You had a great opening at the gallery, but better yet, you closed the deal at home. Can't recall you having a better day than that in a while."

Gabe returns to his seat across from her. "Maybe if I had some help around here and you came home when you were supposed to, I could actually enjoy myself."

"I'm glad you said that." Abbie sits up in her chair, wiggling her shoulders proudly. "Have you checked our bank account today?" She accents her remark with a nod toward the computer.

"No. Why would I?" Gabe swipes across the touchpad, clicking buttons and maneuvering the pointer to access the account in the browser. "What did you do?"

Abbie says, "Promise me you're not going to be mad. I know how hard you've worked and how much you've had to sacrifice for me over the years."

His eyes widen, looking at the screen. "Where on earth did you get ten thousand dollars?" He stares across the table at her. "Tell me right now what you did."

She moves her hands up and down in a calming motion. "Easy does it. Don't have an aneurism. It wasn't anything illegal."

Gabe says, "Then tell me exactly how a sixteen-year-old girl gets her hands on that kind of money."

Abbie scoops a spoonful of cereal into her mouth. "I sold those pictures."

Gabe shoots up from the chair. "You what?"

In between chews, she says, "I said, I sold the pictures of Levi and Emily for you. I knew you wouldn't do it, so I did it for you. You're welcome."

"No, no, no," Gabe says, pushing his hands through his hair. "Please tell me you're joking. It's from something else, right? You won a scholarship or grant from school or something, right?"

Abbie ignores his outrage and continues eating. "Check for yourself. Should be up by now."

Gabe drops his hands to the keyboard and types furiously. Stories, images, and videos from various media outlets populate the screen. His face fills with dread. "Jesus, Abbie. What did you do?"

Abbie says, "Go to Forbidden Fotos. They're the ones who bought them."

Gabe clicks on the link. The five photos appear under the headline "Who's Your Daddy?" with the article:

Costars Levi Combs and Emily James took time from their busy promotional schedules as father and daughter in the their critically-acclaimed film For Love *to enjoy a family trip to a clandestine waterfall in the California countryside. Bath time apparently came early as the two can be seen disrobing and swimming in the creek. Perhaps it was a snake in the water that prompted Ms. James to mount and cling so close to Mr. Combs, but one thing for sure, the kiss they are engaged in is no goodnight kiss.*

Neither party nor their representatives have responded to our requests for comment. Stay tuned as details unfold.

Gabe pushes the laptop to the side and springs up from the chair. "Now the police will get involved. What were you thinking? You had no right to do this."

"Don't treat me like a child." Abbie stands from the chair to face him. "You said yourself that because she was underage you had an obligation to go to the police. Remember? You said, 'The law is the law.'"

Gabe frowns at her quoting his words back to him. "I'll stop treating you like a child when you stop acting like one. They were my pictures. It was for me to decide. And you didn't go to the police. You went to the media."

Emotion overwhelms Abbie. Her voice escalates to a high pitch. "I'm just tired of watching you work so hard and get nothing in return. You gave up everything for me and deserve to catch a break. I knew you wouldn't do anything because you think you always have to set a good example for me. The only person who did anything wrong in all this was him. I don't care how famous he is. That's just gross. Let the cops decide what to do. Plus, think of what this will do for your gallery show. Did you see your name? I made them put that there. You couldn't ask for better publicity."

"Come here." Gabe curls around the table, opening his arms. Abbie relaxes into his chest. He says, "I didn't give up anything. Other than having Mom and Dad back, I wouldn't trade these years for anything. I just don't want to be known for these types of photos. I want to make it on my own with my art. If that takes longer, then so be it."

"I'm sorry," Abbie says, looking up at him. "I didn't mean to upset you. I really was just doing what I thought was right."

"From now on, let me decide what is right when it comes to my career, okay?" He strokes the back of her nodding head. "I guess they're out there now. We can't take them back. No sense getting upset. We'll just have to see what happens."

Abbie hugs him, peering over his shoulder at the computer screen. "Hey, isn't that a picture of Eva?" She slides around Gabe and sits at the table in front of the computer. "Right here. In this other article about Levi." She clicks on a link and opens a news story about them at the Golden Globes.

Gabe steps up behind her. "No, it can't be. She never said anything when we were talking about the movie."

Abbie scrolls down the page, scanning the article. "Oh my god. She's his fricking agent. No wonder she had those movie passes. Why didn't she say anything?"

Gabe leans forward, taking control of the pointer and scrolling back up to the picture. He reads the caption aloud. "Hollywood power agent Eva Florez and her client Levi Combs work the red carpet at the Golden Globes for his nominated film *For Love*." Gabe clicks on her name and pulls up a list of articles and pictures. "She said her name was Eva Fuentes." He accesses the slideshow of pictures, flipping through one after the other.

Abbie puts her hand on her brother's. "I'm sorry. I fell for it too. I really liked her. What a bitch, huh? I just don't get it though. If she knew you had the pictures, why not just ask you about them?"

"No reason to pay for something you can get for free." Gabe pushes away from the table and paces in the kitchen. "That explains why she was in the studio last night when I woke up. She said it was to check her email. The sad thing for her is, I would've totally given the pics to her if she had just been upfront and asked."

"I'm happy I sold them and they're out there now. That's just shady." Abbie stands and walks toward Gabe. "Serves them right. Are you going to call her? Let's do it right now." She bounces on her toes in excitement. "Screw 'em both. Tell her you got more pics and if she doesn't want them released, they better bring a suitcase full of money. Nobody crosses the family." She waves her hand in front of her, delivering the line.

Gabe stops pacing. "Easy there, Godfather. Let's just sit tight. The damage is done. We'll wait and see what happens next."

CHAPTER 8

IN A VIVARIUM AGAINST the wall in Levi's bedroom of his Point Dume home, a water python slithers out of a small pond and coils around a suspended tree limb. Levi sleeps naked facedown diagonal across his elevated platform king-sized bed. The black satin sheet twists across his back under his left hip and out between his legs. The silver duvet lies in a ball at the foot of the bed. Through the disappearing walls of glass of his second story master bedroom, the lap pool, spa, and fire pit are visible across a rolling lawn that extends to the edge of a cliff and drops off to a field of treetops with the occasional roof poking through. Just beyond the trees, the Pacific Ocean glimmers in the morning light.

Eva barrels in with a tablet computer tucked under her arm. Shaking her head at the state of the room, she walks over to the nightstand. A pair of lavender panties hang from a half-full bottle of Jameson sitting on top of a note, which reads, *Call me—310-555-2172.* She picks up one of the throw pillows from the floor and hits Levi in the head. "You just couldn't help yourself could you?"

Levi stirs, pulling the sheet from his back over his head. "What the fuck? Enough with that shit."

Eva presses and swipes the screen of the tablet a few times and tosses it next to him. The screen displays the "Who's Your Daddy?" article with the pictures of Levi and Emily at the waterfall. Pretending to be too angry to face him, Eva walks to the glass wall and stares out across the lawn at the ocean. "All you had to do was get through the Oscars and the upcoming new movie premier. Just stay out of trouble for two weeks. That's it."

Disoriented from the sudden intrusion and hangover from the previous night, Levi picks up the tablet, squinting and blinking at the screen. "You know how sexy you are when you're mad?"

Eva spins back toward him. "And of all girls—America's sweetheart—the one who played your daughter."

"Why are you so worked up? I told you about this. I take it you weren't able to locate the pictures." Levi tosses the tablet on the bed and walks naked to the vivarium.

"I located them all right," Eva says. "I just wasn't able to secure them. I didn't think they would be this bad. I mean, it's like you were posing for them. I don't think they could be much worse. Actually, I'm surprised that he acted this quickly. Didn't seem like the type. Not even a paparazzo."

Using a pair of tongs, Levi removes a dead rat from a small refrigerator on the floor against the wall next to the vivarium and pushes the rat through a feeding hole. "You met him?"

Eva turns away. "Actually, I was at his house. I went there with him after his show at that gallery on Traction. Lives out in West Covina."

"Really? I'm sorry. Did you have to show your passport to go that far out there?" The snake slithers to the jiggling rat and snaps it from the tongs. "You must be losing your touch because whatever you did, it sure didn't work. But fuck it.

Gotta keep your name in the headlines. Isn't that what you always say?"

"I don't think you realize how bad this is. It's not just about damage to your image. You've done quite well destroying that all on your own. Have you forgotten? Regardless of how she acts, Emily is only seventeen, which makes you a criminal."

Levi puts down the tongs on the refrigerator and picks up the bottle of Jameson from the nightstand. "Fuck it. Like I said, it was consensual. If anything, she raped me."

"Can you put some fucking clothes on?" Eva snags a pair of shorts from the floor and throws them at Levi. "You better hope the DA thinks so."

Levi drinks from the bottle of bourbon, allowing the shorts to hit his chest and fall to the floor. "It's not like Emily will say otherwise. She has nothing to gain by being a victim in this. She probably doesn't even care."

Eva walks to the control panel on the wall and presses a button to make the glass wall slide away. Fresh sea air fills the room. She says, "Her people do. They want a meeting today."

"Good. Since you obviously don't believe me, you can hear straight from Emily that it was all her doing." Levi picks the shorts up and slips them on. "At least we now know what we're dealing with. The pics really don't show all that much. It could be a lot worse. Way more than that happened. Right now we can just say we were swimming. We just need to get the rest of the pics before they come out. You think you can get to him before someone else does?"

"I told you I can handle him," Eva says. "Just let me do my job and try not to stir anything else up.

Levi shuffles across the bamboo floor next to Eva, extending the bottle to her. "To the Oscars?"

Eva takes the bottle and gulps a mouthful. "You can probably kiss that goodbye."

"That's a bit of an overreaction, don't you think?" Levi walks out onto the terrace.

"God, Levi," Eva says, following him. "She played your daughter in the film for Christ's sake."

"Hello, it's a movie." He leans on the edge of the terrace wall, looking out across the lawn to the ocean.

Eva slugs more whiskey. "Not to the public."

"They're fucking stupid."

"Those stupid people are the same ones you need to go to your next movie—the one you financed."

Levi flops down onto one of the chaise lounge chairs angled along the terrace. Fresh scratch marks are visible across his chest. "It'll be fine. I'll have a good showing at the Oscars and it will all blow over by the time the new premiere releases."

Eva motions at the marks on his chest. "Jesus. What the fuck happened there? Were you with an alley cat last night?" She pauses, running her hands through her hair. "Please tell me those aren't from her. You know what? Better yet, don't tell me. I don't want to know. I hope you realize there's no way you can go with her to the Oscars."

"Who am I going to take then?"

Eva doesn't hesitate. "I'm going with you."

"Ah, so now the truth comes out," Levi says. "Is this business or personal?"

Eva scowls at him. "Don't flatter yourself. It'll help with the media, you fucking egomaniac. For once listen to me and just stay away from her."

Levi lowers the bottle and nods exaggeratedly. "Yes, boss. Whatever you say."

She pads toward the door. "Just stay here today. Don't go anywhere else until it's time to come to my office at four p.m... preferably sober...and take a shower. You smell like sex."

Levi wobbles his head back and forth mocking her. "I'll see what I can do. But the 'no alcohol' thing may get in the way of the drinking I had on the agenda."

◆◆◆

MARCUS LINGERS IN FRONT of the desk of the Head Deputy of Sex Crimes's assistant. Approaching from behind, a woman in her early forties with a heather cardigan hanging from her shoulders carries a mug of tea. "You're hovering. What do you need?"

"Is the head deputy in?" Marcus asks, pulling on the lapels of his wrinkled, maroon suit jacket. He always wears stylish suits, but they are usually in need of freshening, much like him. The four hours of sleep he got last night, and gets most nights, shows on his face and his shoulders, which are perpetually slumped forward. "I got something big to run by him."

"I'm going to need more than that." She looks at him, lifting one eye and pushing her lips to the side. "He has a meeting with the bureau director in ten minutes."

"Are Levi Combs and Emily James enough?" he asks, nodding his head.

She sits in her chair, dipping the tea bag in and out of the mug of hot water. "I heard about that. I would say that classifies as big enough. You have to be quick though."

"In and out, I promise." He straightens his gray cotton tie and proceeds around the desk to the office.

The head deputy, his elbows planted on the blue pearl granite top of his mahogany desk, reads a thick legal brief with a highlighter. He has on a white shirt with a burgundy tie and matching suspenders. A navy suit jacket hangs over the back of his leather chair. His eyes flash from the document to Marcus. "Deputy Ambrose, nice to see you. What can I do for you today?" He motions to the two chairs in front of him.

"I know you have a meeting in ten minutes, so I'll be brief." Marcus strides to the desk but does not sit down. "I'm not sure if you saw the news this morning, but there are some compromising pictures of Levi Combs with his seventeen-year-old costar Emily James that have showed up online. I'm thinking we might want to look into it. I know underage sex crimes are becoming a hot button topic and this could really send a strong message."

The head deputy motions toward the seat again. This time Marcus follows the suggestion. The head deputy tosses the highlighter on the desk and leans back in his chair. "Well now—Levi Combs, huh? That is a big one. What have you got so far?"

"Just the pictures that were posted," Marcus says. "Like I said, they are compromising but nothing really definitive. I don't know if there are more, or any of the other details. I didn't want to start anything until I got your approval."

The head director tilts his head back, looking at the ceiling. "Thanks for coming to me first. It's an election year, so we need to be sure before going after anyone so visible. These people have a lot of resources and influence. A misstep can be costly, to both the city and to us professionally. What's your plan?"

Marcus angles forward bracing his hands on his knees. "I'll track down the photographer and find out exactly what he saw and if there are other pictures. I can also reach out to the representatives of both parties for comment and the website that broke the story."

"Hold off on contacting the reps and the site." He stands and puts on the jacket from the back of the chair. "Let's see what you get from the photographer. I'll bring it up in my meeting with the bureau director. I want to make sure she is behind us on this one." He walks from around the desk, prompting Marcus to rise and follow him.

"Understood," Marcus says. "I'll let you know what I find out and wait for your direction."

The head deputy stops at the door, patting Marcus on the back as he exits. "Good work. I like the initiative."

Marcus nods, breezing past the assistant waiting with a folder to get the head deputy ready for his next meeting. Encouraged by the outcome, Marcus heads toward his desk in the open area with the other deputy DAs, clerks, and paralegals. He had wanted to seem eager but not overly ambitious and come across as desperate or even worse, that he has another motive for going after Levi. He knows the likelihood of anyone, even Levi, connecting the two of them through Tamara is miniscule unless he screws up. It was so many years ago. He doubts Levi would even remember her, let alone him. There had been so many women for Levi since Tamara—so much of everything—that she had probably been discarded like lines of a bad script after the role was done. Marcus still knows better than to risk it. He only has one shot. If at any point, anyone does make the connection, he'll be removed from the case, or if he tries and loses, he can't come back with other charges no matter what Levi does. Levi is too high profile and can afford too competent of lawyers. A second attempt will only appear like someone in the DA office has a vendetta against him. No one wants that spotlight on them, and that's exactly what Levi's attorneys would do. They'd turn things around and cast Levi as the victim. After everything Levi has done over the years, no way Marcus is going to give him the satisfaction of being the victim.

Sitting at his desk, Marcus pulls up the Forbidden Fotos article with the pictures of Levi and Emily and finds Gabe's name in the credits. With swift key strokes, he switches applications. A legal search database comes up on the screen. He inputs Gabe's name into the search box to find an angle or leverage on Gabe if he won't cooperate. His criminal record comes back empty but several legal and news entries appear. Marcus clicks on the articles, first reading about Gabe's parents' crash and their obituaries, then the legal entries pertaining to the settlement of the will and his appropriation as Abbie's legal guardian. Armed with the information he needs, he scribbles down the address on his notepad and heads for the door.

◆◆◆

LATER AT THEIR HOUSE on Lolita, Abbie leads Marcus through the doorway to the kitchen and into the studio. Gabe assembles a wooden frame at the worktable. Abbie says, "Gabe, sorry to bother you. Marcus Ambrose from the District Attorney's office is here to see you."

Marcus separates from Abbie and goes straight toward Gabe, the back of his side-vented jacket flapping from the swift change of direction. Extending his hand, Marcus says, "Sorry to bother you at home…or is it work?"

Gabe rubs his hands together. "Both." A trail of sawdust flutters to the floor. Shaking with Marcus, Gabe says, "No trouble. Just getting some stuff ready for my gallery showing." Gabe notices Abbie lingering to see what Marcus wants. "Thanks, Abbie. Don't you have some homework to finish?"

Abbie remains by the door watching. "I can do it later." Gabe motions with his head for her to go into the house.

Rolling her eyes, she says, "Fine. Would you like something to drink before I go, Mr. Ambrose?"

Marcus turns back toward her. "No thank you, Ms. Adams. I'll only be a moment." He looks back at Gabe, dropping his eyes to the picture on the worktable. "Very beautiful. I'm guessing celebrity photos are not your main focus?"

"More the exception than the rule," Gabe says. "What can I do for you this afternoon?"

Marcus says, "Yes, of course. You're probably not aware, but as a result of your photos the DA's office is investigating Levi Combs for his involvement with Emily James. For far too many years, we have looked the other way in these types of cases. I've been given the authority to make sure that doesn't happen again."

Gabe bends down, assembling two of the edges around the picture. "Have charges been filed?"

"Not yet," Marcus says. "We're hoping you could help influence that decision."

"Not sure what more I can tell you." Gabe moves around to another corner of the frame. "You saw the pictures. They pretty much show what I witnessed."

Marcus follows him. "Nothing else happened or stands out?"

Gabe says, "I didn't even know who it was until later, when I showed my sister the pictures and she told me."

"And the pictures published are the only ones?" Marcus asks, leaning on the worktable toward Gabe, who doesn't answer, focusing his attention on the frame. Marcus says, "Mr. Adams, if there are other pictures, you are obligated to turn them over. If you refuse, I can obtain a court order."

Gabe works his way around the table. "What you saw is all I have. I was pretty far away, and once I realized I was interrupting a private moment, I stopped. There's really not much more I can add."

"But surely you can help fill in some gaps. For example, from your vantage point, could you see if they were engaged in intercourse?" Marcus doesn't follow Gabe this time and holds his position, standing across from him.

"You'll have to ask them," Gabe says. "From where I was, I couldn't really tell." He snaps the final corner in place.

Frustration swells inside Marcus. He increases the intensity of his questioning. "This just doesn't make sense to me. Why didn't you turn the pictures over to authorities? You say you're not a celebrity photographer, yet you went to the media first."

Gabe doesn't falter, continuing to work on the picture while speaking. "At the time the relationship seemed consensual. I didn't think it was a criminal matter." He stands the picture up on its side, blocking the sightline between the two. "Is this something I should have a lawyer present for?"

Marcus shuffles a few steps to the side. "No, this is just a friendly visit. I thought you might be able to help, and now seeing you have a sister about the same age as Ms. James, I assume would want to help."

"I just want to be done with it," Gabe says.

Marcus nods. "Of course. Would you at least be willing to testify in court to what you saw?"

Gabe dusts off the top edge of the frame and places it back on the table, making eye contact with Marcus. "As I said, I'd really prefer not to be involved. As you can see, I'm quite busy and have my sister to think about. I don't want to expose her to the media circus and all the other nut jobs that are sure to come along with this. The pictures tell more than I could. I was a significant distance away, a fact I'm sure the defense would feast on."

Marcus counters Gabe's indifference by elevating his tone. "You do realize we can issue a subpoena and force you?"

"I hope that's not necessary," Gabe says, ignoring the threat. "But if you do, I'll just say what I told you. I was too far away to really see anything."

"Mr. Adams, I did some research on you before I came to see you. Can I just say that I think it's admirable that you took on the responsibility of raising your sister after your parents died? I know how hard that must've been. My sister, who pretty much raised me, died when I was young. She had been my primary caregiver while my parents were at work before I was old enough to look after myself. Losing her devastated me, but at least, I still had my mother."

"How fortunate for you," Gabe says in a stilted cadence. "I'm sorry for your loss."

"Thank you. It was a horrible time for all of us." Marcus pauses to emphasize the past tense. "That was about twelve years ago. She would've been a few years older than you are now."

Gabe picks up the finished picture and walks away from Marcus toward the others stacked against the wall. "That is terrible. But, and please excuse my forwardness, is that supposed to create some type of bond between us because we both have lost someone close to us? If I could help you, I would. I just can't. I'm sorry."

Marcus' frustration escalates to annoyance. "Don't you at least get tired of these entitled Hollywood types being able to do whatever they want? It's like there are two sets of laws. One for them, and one for everybody else. What if that were your sister?"

"I don't feel there are two sets of laws," Gabe says, not taking the bait. "I have full faith in your office to uphold the same ones for everyone. As far as Abbie, I would expect her not to put herself in that situation. This is starting to feel like harassment, Mr. Ambrose. I've told you everything. If you have additional questions, please bring me in so I can have a lawyer present."

Marcus removes a business card from his breast pocket and passes it to Gabe. "I don't think that will be necessary for now, Mr. Adams. Thank you for your time and cooperation. I'll be in touch if there is anything else."

Gabe tosses the card on the worktable. "I suggest you pay the ones in the pictures a visit. They have the answers you're looking for." Concerned that Abbie might reveal it was her who sent the photos to the site, Gabe motions to the back door. "I can show you out this way."

CHAPTER 9

CONSTELLATION PLACE RISES BETWEEN Avenue of the Stars and Century Park West in Century City. Formerly MGM Tower, the building was the first high-rise completed in Los Angeles in the twenty-first century and served as the headquarters of Metro-Goldwyn-Mayer until 2011, when they moved to Beverly Hills. Now it's the home of several real estate, banking, and entertainment corporations, including Eva's TV & film agency. While she could avoid playing the game where she lived, to stay relevant and grow the business, she had to be visible and interact with the right people.

On the twenty-ninth floor, Eva and Levi sit at a rectangular walnut meeting table across from Emily and her agent in a conference room. The other eight high-backed leather chairs, tucked underneath the long conference table, sit empty. Eva says, "We've, all seen the pictures, and I think we can agree that while they're not completely damning, they're pretty bad. The only wiggle room we have is that compromising does not mean incriminating. Just because you can infer what is happening, doesn't mean anything actually did."

Emily says, "I still don't understand how this photographer just so happened to end up there."

"Really? It's a public place," Eva says.

"Out in the middle of nowhere," Emily's agent, a thirty-year Hollywood veteran, says. "Pretty big coincidence." There are many tiers of success in Hollywood, and Emily's agent is definitely on the upper one. He has the awards, financial trappings, and longevity that elevate him above most, but what really sets him apart is that in a town obsessed with physical appearance, he let his go years ago and doesn't seem bothered by what anyone thinks. Regardless of the occasion, he wears only velour tracksuits, donning a blue one today, to accommodate his expanding frame. His only remaining hair grows freely on the sides and in the back, especially flourishing above his eyes and from his ears. He has seen every scheme and manipulation in his career, and knows that for an industry built from on-screen coincidences, there are very few offscreen. Everything happens for a purpose, or more specifically, for someone's gain.

"Not really," Eva says. "He's a landscape photographer doing a series on waterfalls. That one's on all the maps."

Levi says, "But it's on private property and not the easiest to get to."

"Who else knew you two were going there?" Emily's agent says.

"I didn't even know where the place was, so I couldn't have told anyone," Emily responds in a high-pitched defensive tone.

Levi looks at Eva then stands and walks over to the windows gazing out at the panoramic view of Century City. As much as she gets credit for building his career, it was he who really launched hers. Without him, she never would have been able to leave her publicity job at USC and break off on her own thirteen years ago.

The first time Eva saw Levi she was standing at the thirty-yard line watching the opening football game between USC and Virginia Tech at FedEx Field in Landover, Maryland. Publicity staff didn't usually travel to the games, but the 2004 USC team wasn't an ordinary team. Experts had ranked them number one in the country to start the season, making them the favorite to win the national championship, which meant way more than bragging rights to the university. It brought recognition, notoriety, and money—a lot of money. From spring football to the last of the bowl games, the administration wanted all conversations of college football to include USC. That meant wherever the football team went, the publicity team went with them.

Eva had worked in the PR department since her junior year and stayed on after graduation. The pay wasn't much, but the job gave her access and exposure, the two most important things in publicity. Both of which she needed to achieve her five-year plan. With the talented athletes and high expectations for the team, she knew the agents and national media would follow. She planned to either stay on with one of the stars as they went to the pros or sign with a sports agency or media company. At that point the money would come. Before the season even started, she had already received offers from several agencies that a job was waiting. All Eva had to do was bring a star.

Eva believed quarterback Matt Leinart was going to be that star. During the opening game versus Virginia Tech, USC was behind 14–10 in the third quarter. She knew a loss in the opening game would derail all their plans. But that changed quickly with 1:55 left in the third when running back Reggie Bush moved from the backfield and lined up as wide receiver. At the snap of the ball, he blew by Jimmy Williams, Virginia Tech's best defensive back, and Leinart lofted a perfect over-the-shoulder throw for a fifty-three-yard touchdown and the lead, which they never relinquished. USC went on to win the national championship that year and Leinart received the Heisman, but that wasn't what changed things for Eva. It was what happened at the end of the long touchdown play. As Bush caught the pass and raced across the goal line, the stadium video operator flashed the camera to the Virginia Tech student section. A shirtless student with the angled VT logo painted in maroon on his chest filled the screen. The heartbreak that the score brought to all the Hokie fans hung on his chiseled face. Maroon lines of sweat streamed like tears from the bottom of the letters on his smooth, sculpted chest along the protruding ridges of his abs. The camera stayed on him. The weight of the moment froze him. His hands were interlocked behind his head with his elbows pulled back. Eva couldn't take her eyes off him. It was more than his sadness. He was vulnerable yet strong at the same time.

Eva scanned the stadium to locate the Virginia Tech section to see where she could find the student on the screen. In between the third and fourth quarters she left the sidelines to seek him out. Her cardinal polo shirt with gold USC lettering on the left breast elicited jeers from the hostile crowd. The field pass dangling around her neck encouraged them more.

"Go back where you came from!"

"Trojans suck!"

"University of Stupid Cunts!"

Ignoring them all, Eva located Levi in the fourth row, about a third of the way in. She worked her way down the row and filled the open seat next to him. Leaning over, she said, "I saw you on the video screen." Levi was as captivating up close as on the screen. She admired the curve of his carved calves and narrow waist fanning out into a wide back up to his broad shoulders. The furrows and ridges formed by his protruding stomach muscles undulated as he reacted to each twist and turn in the game. She shouted at him again. Still no response. Despite being right next to her, with the score 14–13 and USC in the lead and over ninety thousand in attendance, he either didn't care or really couldn't hear her. But when Bush got loose again in the secondary and Leinart connected with him for another touchdown with 5:35 in the game, making the lead 21–13, Levi, disappointed and dejected, flopped down onto the bench. She repeated her line one more time, drawing an indifferent stare from Levi, making her think he had heard her before but just chose to ignore her.

Levi's words oozed a Southern twang. "You fixin' for a fight comin' in these parts, ain't ya?"

His accent made her cringe. She knew that would be the first thing she'd have to fix. Reaching into her pocket, she fished out one of the plain white business cards, which she had developed with just her name, the title "Talent Scout and Publicist," and contact details, and handed it to Levi. "I represent an agency in LA. Ever thought about doing any modeling or acting?"

Levi took the card, looked at it then at the people around him. "All right," he said. "Which one of you jokers put her up to this?" Everyone glared back with the same blank stare that he had given Eva when she first sat down. "Why would USC want to help me get a job?" he asked her.

"No, this is not for USC. I work part-time for another Hollywood-based firm. I think you have a look they would be interested in. Do you currently have representation?" Levi shook his head, twisting the card in his fingers. His sincerity and authenticity, even in such a chaotic environment, connected with something deep inside her. She continued her pitch. "I'm assuming you don't have any headshots then either?" Levi responded with another side-to-side answer with his head. She said, "That's no problem. We can do all that when you come visit. You ever been to LA?"

Levi said, "Farthest west I've been is Oklahoma."

"How would you like a free trip?" Eva asked.

"I don't know," Levi said, shaking his head at the idea. "My mama in Knoxville is pretty sick. I don't like to be too far away from her in case she needs something."

Eva said, "It'll only be for two days, three tops. You could leave on Monday or Tuesday and be back by Thursday. If anything happens, we'll fly you back right away."

Levi was still skeptical. "What about classes?"

Eva tilted her head, her face filling with disbelief. "You mean to tell me you never skip class? At least this time it will be for a legitimate reason. What do you say? I'm offering you the opportunity of a lifetime. No obligations. If you don't like it, you come back and return to whatever you're doing."

Levi looked at the card again, which was crumpled and bent from him wringing it in his hands. "Let me ponder on it, and I'll give you a call."

Eva took out a fresh card and pen from her pocket, writing down two more phone numbers on the card. "That works for me. I leave tonight, but here's my home and office number. The one on the front is my cell. Call me if you have any questions or when you're ready for a visit."

Once Eva had returned to LA, she had just about given up on Levi when her house phone rang at 6:30 in the morning the following week while she was still in bed. "Ms. Florez?" he said. "This is Levi Combs, from the football game. I hope it's okay I called you at home. I tried the other numbers, but I got your voice mail."

"It's fine," Eva said. "That's why I gave them to you. You just caught me getting up."

Levi mumbled through his words. "Oh, I'm sorry. I thought it would be okay if I waited until after nine. You want me to call back later?"

"No, let's talk now," Eva said pushing off the covers and sitting up in bed. She didn't want to know if he had just forgotten about the time change or if he really wasn't aware there was one.

Levi said, "I thought about your offer and talked it over with my mama. She wants me to do it. But there's just one condition."

Eva pumped the arm not holding the phone into the air and extended her legs, kicking her feet in silent celebration. "Sure. What is it?"

"My mama doesn't want me to miss any school. I'll have to leave after class on Friday and come back Sunday night. Can we do that?"

Eva not only did that, she had Levi booked for three modeling jobs by the time he left. Despite his tepid interest, firms were hot for him. He returned to LA two weeks later, mostly at his mother's insistence, for four days and continued that pattern every month until the end of the school year. By that time, opportunities for casting calls and screen tests were rolling in. Eva told him that the only option to see if it could really become a career was to leave school and move west.

Again it was Levi's mother that encouraged him to go. She said, "School will always be waiting, but opportunities rarely will." What she didn't tell him was that she couldn't wait either. Her cancer had worsened. The doctors told her she had six months at the most. She knew if she told Levi, he would never go, and his life would become nothing more than watching her suffer and fade away.

As fast as the cancer moved, his career accelerated even quicker. The modeling led to working as an extra on several

TV series to a reoccurring role on the number one rated Thursday night show, which is how he met Marcus' sister Tamara. It was during the taping of the season finale that he got the call that his mother had passed. Actually Eva got the call. She had convinced Levi's mother that it was best if all news funneled through her. That way Levi could stay focused and not be distracted with all the ups and downs of the cancer. As her health had worsened, Levi had no idea because Eva had stopped telling him anything. Levi would ask, and Eva would just say, "She's tired of the treatment but still fighting. The doctors are encouraged by her progress."

When that final call came, Levi hadn't talked to his mother in over a week. The last time, all she had said was that everything was fine, and she was looking forward to seeing him. He was planning to take some vacation and go see her for the first time since he had gotten to LA five months earlier, just as soon as the filming for the season was over. That's also when Eva was going to tell him how bad things had really become. Since nothing could be done about it anyway, she didn't see any reason to burden him at such a crucial time in his career, which had really become their career.

What Eva didn't account for was that it would be too late. Levi still went back as planned, but it wasn't to visit, it was to put his mother to rest. He never even had to change his flight from the one she booked for him a month earlier. He was never comfortable with that. Eva kept reminding him there was nothing he could've done, that it was in God's hands. But to Levi, it seemed like there was plenty he could've done if only he had known. That was the last trip he took back to Tennessee.

When Levi returned to Los Angeles after the funeral, Eva sensed he blamed her, his work, the city for keeping him from his mother, but he never said anything. All he did was work more—nonstop as a matter of fact. He went from the recurring role to a series regular to starring in a drama the network created for him. The same vulnerability and strength that Eva saw on the screen at the football game resonated with viewers. Movie offers followed, and Eva was there to receive and benefit from them all, riding the opportunities from that end zone seat in the student section to this twenty-ninth floor conference room where they are meeting with Emily and her agent.

Levi turns his stare from out the window back to the room. "I don't understand how a photographer ended up there either. I've been there countless times and have never even seen anyone anywhere close to there. Eva, you're the only one that even knows I own that place."

"How he got the pictures is irrelevant," Emily's agent says, exchanging a look with Eva. He knows there's more to the story but also that she probably had good reasons for whatever she had done. He had watched her too over the years and grown to respect her as a shrewd and unyielding operator, which is as gracious of a compliment as he could give to a colleague. "More important is what do we do now that they are out?"

"We do nothing," Eva says, ignoring Levi's insinuation that she had anything to do with the predicament. "As long as there are no witnesses coming forward and neither of you say anything, we just take our lumps until this all blows over."

Levi sits down on the window ledge that runs the entire length of the glass-enclosed corner room. Positioned directly behind Eva, he speaks over the back of her head, facing the others. "What about the photographer? What if there are more photos? What if he talks?"

Eva turns in her chair to face Levi. "He won't do anything. I'll make sure of it."

"How well do you even know this guy?" Levi asks. "You didn't think he would sell the ones that are out now."

"We can't take any risks," Emily's agent says. He looks at Emily then at Levi. "You two, under no circumstances, can see each other. If advertisers get spooked, we'll lose all our endorsements."

Levi says, "Advertising? That's what you're worried about? I'm facing potential jail time and all you can think about is losing some endorsements?"

"What I mean," Emily's agent says, "is that we need to contain the damage."

Levi springs from the windowsill to the table, leaning across and pointing at Emily's agent. "You don't give a fuck about us. It's just about the money, isn't it?"

Emily's agent fires back. "Grow the fuck up. Like you were thinking about Emily's best interest taking her there in the first place?"

"It was your fucking client who came on to me. Tell him, Em."

She looks down at the table, tracing her finger in a circle. "He's right. I was the one who started it. He tried stopping me. I made it happen."

"I'm sure he put up quite the fight," her agent says. "All hundred and five pounds of you just overpowered him."

"Fuck you." Levi bangs his fist on the table. "Like it even matters to you. All you blood-sucking pimps care about is protecting your fifteen percent."

Eva pulls a chair out, suggesting he sit down. "And your eighty-five."

Emily looks up at Levi. "They're right though. We can't take any chances with this. There's too much at stake."

"Wait, you're siding with them?" Levi asks. "If we do nothing and hide, we look guilty as fuck. You were the one who initiated it. How can you want to walk away now?"

Emily says, "It's not personal, Levi. It's just business."

"Unbelievable." Levi forces the chair back under the table and walks around toward the door. "I risk everything to spend time with you, you seduce me, and now you're telling me it's not personal."

Emily stands to intercept him. "Levi, wait."

He stops in front of her. "Don't make the same mistakes I did and let these maggots turn you into a product." He steps around her and stomps off. She follows after him.

Eva shakes her head, emptying her lungs. "Don't worry, I'll handle this."

Emily's agent gathers the papers from the table and slips them into his leather attaché. "You better. If we lose one endorsement deal, I'm holding your client responsible. I'll go to the police myself."

CHAPTER 10

A BBIE LIES ON HER stomach, propped up by her elbows, on the pink comforter covering her bed. Headphones buried in her ears, she scissors her legs, bent at the knee, to the beat. A calculus book is spread open in front of her as she scratches through a problem in a spiral notebook. Clothes litter the floor and assorted makeup covers the top of the desk positioned against the wall to the right. The whiteboard on the wall above her bed displays a quote attributed to Jennifer Lawrence: "Teenagers only have to focus on themselves—it's not until we get older that we realize that other people exist."

Gabe stands in the doorway watching her. "I'm sorry about before." Abbie doesn't react. Her legs maintain the same rhythm, and her pen scribbles furiously in the notebook. He navigates the piles of clothes and sits on the side of the bed.

Feeling his weight, Abbie removes the left ear bud, the music audible through the tiny opening. She pauses the song on her phone. "Hey. Sorry, I didn't hear you come in. I know, I have to clean my room. Promise, I'll do it right after I'm finished with my homework."

Gabe picks up the photo of her and him with their parents on the day of his graduation from her nightstand. "Doesn't seeing this every day make you sad?"

She takes out the other ear bud and rotates on her side, her head held up by her hand and elbow planted on the bed. "Of course I miss Mom and Dad, but the picture also reminds me how lucky I am to be here." Both of their eyes drift back to the photograph on her nightstand. She places her hand on Gabe's. "If you hadn't let me come with you, I'd have been with them. I just feel like sometime maybe you would be better off if I had been. You'd be off in Chicago or New York or somewhere with this great photography job, not home raising a moody, teenage girl."

It had been much tougher than Gabe ever thought it would be. But it wasn't the Abbie stuff that was so difficult. While that was trying at times, they always seemed to find a way through. It was the financial side of everything. At first, between the insurance money and their parents' savings and retirement investments, they had more money than they knew what to do with. That's why he started the photography business in the first place. He thought that even if it took a few years to get going, they would be fine. But then the bills started rolling in and the income didn't. Even though each year at the stand had been a little bit better, they were still operating at a loss, and now the reserves were just about gone.

Selling the shots of Levi and Emily wasn't the first time the debate about celebrity photos had come up between Gabe and Abbie. Anytime another big story broke with accompanying photos, Abbie chastised him for not focusing on more lucrative subject matter. But Gabe had always been adamant about steering clear of what he thought was shallow, opportunistic work, which really didn't make sense to her because he repeatedly whored himself out doing family portraits, senior pictures, and weddings. To Abbie, celebrity photos seemed much easier and worth a lot more.

Gabe's plan to promote and market his business was to open the street stand downtown around Gallery Row to sell prints of all different sizes until he could land a gallery show. People kept telling him that he would have more success around Venice Beach or the Santa Monica Pier, but he knew there would be a lot more competition there, too. He also wanted to be close to the galleries and not just peddling post cards to tourists. While it sounded simple, it took him over six years to land this first show. On the day that it finally happened, Gabe had paraded into The Box Gallery downtown to make his standard pitch. As usual, he was pumped up for a positive outcome but prepared for another disappointment. A nylon portfolio case dangled from his shoulder. The stark white walls contrasted with the bare whale gray concrete floors. The open, minimalist space pushed the attention to the artwork spaced across the walls.

A female in her mid-thirties with a short blonde pixie cut, which was pushed forward and swept to the left, wiped the front of a framed picture hanging on the wall with a microfiber rag. A bottle of cleaning solution hung from her other hand. She rubbed the glass covering with several broad strokes then stepped back from the picture to analyze the result, moving back in for more swipes with the rag.

Gabe strolled up behind her. "Are you the manager?"

Her eyes traveled the length of Gabe, first to the top of his head then to the bottom and back up. "I'm the owner."

"I'm sorry," Gabe said. "I'm surprised—"

"That I'm a woman?" She straightened her body, further sizing him up.

Gabe slumped in his shoes. "No, it's not that at all. Just surprised that it's you who's cleaning. Figured you'd have someone for that."

Her face softened and shoulders settled, slowly opening to him. "Got to fill the dead time somehow. What can I do for you?"

Gabe lifted the portfolio from the floor, shaking it back and forth. "Are you accepting submissions for any new shows?"

She switched the rag to the hand with the bottle of solution and waved Gabe to the seating area in the middle of the gallery. Two white S-shaped chairs sat on one side of an acrylic coffee table facing the door. "Let's see what you got."

Gabe unzipped the portfolio case, spreading it open on the clear table. He sat down in the chair next to her. "I'm a landscape photographer. All these are photos of mine from California."

She placed the rag and solution on the floor next to her and leaned forward, flipping through the prints. "These are good."

"Thank you," Gabe said, bending toward the table to align his body with hers. "I also have a street stand over on Gallery Row."

She turned to the last print and eased back into the chair. "But not quite right for me."

Gabe hesitated for a moment, surprised by the abrupt decision. Replaying the conversation in his head, he closed the portfolio and zipped it back up. "I see."

She picked up the rag and solution and stood back up. "You can leave your info though. I'll call if something comes up."

Gabe removed a card from a pocket in the portfolio and handed it to her. "Do you know of any galleries looking for local landscape shots?"

She walked toward the door, prompting Gabe to follow. "Sorry, I only stay up on galleries with work like mine."

Gabe slung the strap over his shoulder, stopping at the door. "Thanks, for the consideration. Sorry for taking up your time."

She held the door open. Gabe slid out onto the sidewalk. Propping the door open with her foot, she sprayed the glass with the solution and wiped it down with the rag. "Good luck. Hope you find a home for those. They're too good to not be on display somewhere."

Dejected, Gabe slogged down the sidewalk back toward the stand. At the corner, he stopped and took out a paper and pen from the side pocket of the portfolio. A list of twenty galleries filled the front. All but three were crossed off. He drew a line through the *The Box Gallery* then walked to his retail stand on the corner of Sixth and Spring.

Rows of matted, nature photographs covered a rectangular folded table. More eight by ten and four by six framed pictures hung from a display. Abbie, the sleeves of her T-shirt pushed up around her shoulders, slouched in a folding lawn chair next to the table. Strands of her blonde hair stuck out from the backward Lakers baseball hat sitting on her head.

Gabe plodded up to the table. "Thanks for minding the store."

She looked up at Gabe, cupping her hand over her eyes to block out the sun. "How'd it go?"

"The usual—another big fat no."

"I'm sorry." Abbie said. "Next one will be the one. Don't give up."

"I probably should've years ago, but I'm not smart enough to quit. Still have a few more to try. Any luck here?" Gabe gestured to the inventory on the table.

Abbie said, "Not much other than my tan and some lewd propositions from carloads of teenage boys."

Gabe unfolded a lawn chair and sat next to her. "Maybe we need a new location."

"I keep telling you, you should let me get a job to help out."

"If you work somewhere else, who will fill in here when I go take the photos?" Gabe asked. "Besides, I want you to focus on school."

"Just dip into my college money if we need it. I don't even know if I'm going."

Gabe sits up, his voice filling with authority. "You're going, young lady. You know that's what Mom and Dad wanted."

"What they wanted was for both of us to go. It's just not fair. You were so excited to go. Now you're stuck here selling your photos on the street and begging for opportunities with stuffy gallery owners."

Gabe rubbed her back. "Don't worry. I'll still end up in the same spot. The path is just going to be a little different."

Abbie's eyes rounded, filling with warmth. "If it will help cheer you up, I can stay here the rest of the afternoon, and you can go take pictures."

Gabe said, "There is a bridge I've been wanting to check out. I can be back by six."

The Art on Traction gallery owner, her red hair blazing in the bright sunshine, stopped to peruse the photographs on the table. Gabe stepped over next to her. "Special today is one for ten or three for twenty on the smaller prints. Any of the photographs can be framed in the size of your choice."

Her pale, freckled fingers flipped through the stacks. "These are very good. Are you the photographer?"

"Yes, ma'am. Took everything you see here myself."

She stepped back from the table and turned toward Gabe. "Do you have an agent or showing in a gallery anywhere?"

"Not at the moment," Gabe said. "I'm currently shopping some things around to several galleries."

She removed a flyer from her purse and handed it to him. "I'm opening a new gallery down on Traction in an old automotive repair shop next month."

"I know that spot. I was just over that way talking to the owner of The Box," Gabe interrupted nervously. "Unfortunately, she passed, though."

"I think what you have would fit well in the show that I want to open with. Are you free now to come look at the space and discuss this further."

Gabe reached over and grabbed the nylon portfolio he thought he had retired for the day. "Of course. We can go through the work and, if you're still interested, decide which ones to use. I'm also out shooting a few times a week so if there's anything specific you're looking for that I don't have, I'm happy to do some new stuff." He looked over at Abbie, who bounced her thin eyebrows in excitement and held up crossed fingers. He said, "I guess the bridge will have to wait. I'll be back shortly."

The gallery owner fanned her arm down the sidewalk. "Shall we?"

At the gallery, she picked out the twenty pieces that he would eventually premiere at the opening. Only a month had passed since then, but so much had already changed. His work is hanging in an actual gallery; he has sold his first full-sized pieces; and the money from the Levi and Emily photos put them ahead of their bills for the first time in a long while.

Sitting next to Abbie on the bed, Gabe brings over his other hand on top of Abbie's. "I wouldn't trade my life with you for anything. We're through the tough part. Things are finally starting to go our way. It might have taken longer than we planned, but it's happening. I'm sorry if I made you feel differently. I know you were only trying to help."

"I should've checked with you first though," Abbie says. "I didn't think the police would get involved. What did Mr. Ambrose want when he stopped by?"

Gabe sits down on the bed. "They want to press charges. Wanted to know if I had other pictures—which I don't, if anyone asks. He was also pressuring me to be a witness. I told him that I couldn't really add or provide anything else. Hopefully they'll handle it from here and leave us out."

Abbie jerks up, folding her legs underneath her. "What about Eva from last night?" She shakes his hands excitedly. "Don't be mad at her. She was just doing her job. You should give her a second chance."

"Shouldn't you be cleaning your room?" Gabe asks, standing from the bed and angling toward the door. "This place is a mess."

◆◆◆

LEVI TURNS OFF THE Avenue of the Stars onto the private drive leading to the tall, IM Pei–designed Century Tower, the first residential project in Century City back in 1964. Jack Benny, Diana Ross, Michael Douglas, and many other stars over the years have lived here, and now Emily James. Paparazzi flock around the travertine-flanked iron gates at the entranceway. With his mobile phone to his ear, Levi navigates through the muck of photographers. "Since you won't answer or return my messages, I'm coming over," he says, ending the call and dropping the phone between his legs on the seat.

Paparazzi swarm the vehicle escorting it to the valet. Questions come from all directions.

"Do you expect to win the Oscar?"

"Is it true your relationship with Emily James is more than professional?"

"Is Ms. James really pregnant?"

Ignoring the inquiries, Levi stares straight through the windshield and stops the Jeep next to the valet stand. He snags the phone from the seat and exits the vehicle, leaving the engine running for the approaching valet.

The doorman intercepts him under the glass-canopy porte-cochere entrance into the building. "I'm sorry, Mr. Combs. I can't let you pass. I'll have to call up first."

Levi steps up to him, standing nose-to-nose, trying to intimidate. "Tell her I'm not leaving until I speak to her."

The paparazzi snap pictures of the mild confrontation. Sensing the attention his aggressive stance is attracting, Levi slides back. "Can I at least wait inside while you call?"

The doorman nods and leads Levi into the grand lobby, which is adorned in limestone and sycamore wood paneling. Levi sits on a couch in a waiting area by the sweeping staircase. The doorman walks to the concierge stand and picks up the house phone. Levi watches the conversation but can't hear what is being said. The doorman hangs up the phone and returns. Levi stands to proceed upstairs.

The doorman says, "I'm sorry, sir. She said to wait here."

"She wants to meet in the lobby?" Levi turns toward the glass front, smeared with paparazzi. "In front of all of them?"

"Yes, sir. That's what she said." The doorman returns to the entrance but does not go back outside. He turns his body, so he can monitor the front and Levi at the same time.

Emily emerges from the elevator. Levi rises and meets her in the middle of the lobby. "Let's go upstairs."

Waving to the photographers, Emily smiles while speaking, her lips not moving. "Why? There's nothing more to say. We had fun. Now it's over."

Levi moves between her and the photographers. "Is this you or your business managers talking?"

"It's my decision," Emily says. "Don't make this any harder than it is."

"But I need you right now." Levi attempts eye contact by moving into her line of sight, but each time he does, she turns her head the opposite way. "Everyone else is turning on me now."

She turns her eyes on him for a moment. "I'm sure you'll be fine."

Levi takes her hands in his. "I won't be though. Can we just go somewhere and talk? Everything changed after we were together."

Emily tries to casually lower her hands, but Levi won't let go. She glares at him. "Are you fucking nuts? Don't do this. Are you seriously making me be the mature one? You wanted to see me and now you have. It's time to go."

Levi's tone and words sharpen. "You're the one who wanted this. Don't pull away from me now. Let's fight this together."

Emily motions for the doorman to come over. "Bryan, can you show Mr. Combs out?"

Levi steps toward the approaching doorman and extends his arm. "I'm leaving." He looks back at Emily. "I can't believe you caused all this and now you're turning your back on me. How can you be so cold?" The doorman grabs Levi's arm to lead him out. Levi rips away. "Keep your fucking hands off me."

The doorman steps between Levi and Emily. The murmur and excitement of the paparazzi penetrate through the glass. Levi backs away. The doorman corrals Levi toward the entrance. Levi flings his hands in frustration toward Emily and heads out through the front glass double doors.

The paparazzi swarm around Levi. "What's going on between you and Ms. James?" one of them says. Levi shoves past him.

Another photographer blocks Levi's path. "Were you really fired from your next film?" Levi attempts to sidestep him. "What's it like to be dismissed by a seventeen-year-old?"

This time Levi doesn't avoid the question. He counters with a punch, knocking the photographer to the ground. Levi descends on top of him and releases a flurry of blows. Only a few of the other photographers attempt to pull Levi away. The rest are too busy taking pictures. Levi brakes free and runs toward his waiting Jeep. The paparazzi trail, snapping pictures and recording as Levi drives away.

CHAPTER 11

GABE WAITS IN HIS Suburban parked in front of Century City Mall across the street from Eva's office at Constellation Place. He hardly slept the night before. He never really wanted the photos in the first place. He would've given them to her if she had just asked. He was more upset because he thought what they shared was real and believed it could lead to more.

Gabe had never really dated anyone seriously, so he didn't have much experience handling romantic situations. In high school he was the awkward art student, more comfortable with his own ideas than other people. He had convinced himself that college would be his time. When that didn't come, he told himself once things were more stable with Abbie, opportunities for other relationships would surface. He thought Eva showing up at his opening was one of those opportunities. All of the other misfortune that happened to him over the years, he had to take. There really wasn't much he could've done about it. But this was different.

Gabe opens the Suburban door and steps into the street, still not sure what he is going to say or do once he sees her. A white Bugatti Veyron pulls up to the curb in front of Constellation Place, the glare from the noon sun shining down on the windshield, concealing the driver. Gabe reopens his driver side door to conceal himself, watching the car through his window. Eva bounds from the office down the walkway toward the idling French-made sports car. Gabe leans into the cab to further hide as she gets in the passenger side. The Bugatti's twenty wheels angle in his direction, and the car zips away from the curb. Glancing over his shoulder as the car passes, he catches a glimpse of Levi behind the wheel. Gabe climbs into the Suburban and reverses it around to follow. Weaving in and out, Levi makes quick, aggressive moves to advance one spot at a time. Unconcerned as long as he can see him, Gabe stays a safe but short distance behind.

At Olympic Boulevard, Levi turns left, accelerating and showing off the Bugatti's zero-to-sixty in two and a half seconds. Another car a few lengths ahead forces Levi to pump the carbon ceramic brakes and switch lanes. Lowering the car into the handling ride height, he opens the front diffuser flaps and darts around another car. "Anything new with the photographer?" he asks, raising his voice above the deep, vibrating growl of the turbocharged engine.

Eva squeezes her fingers around the leather door handle. "It won't matter if you kill us first. Just because this car will go this fast doesn't mean it has to."

Levi downshifts using the paddles on the steering wheel and settles in behind the SUV in front of them. "My bad. I'm just excited, and frustrated, I guess, if I'm being honest. We're so close to getting everything we've been working for. I just can't believe this shit is happening now."

"Even more reason why you need to chill the fuck out and stay out of the news. The Oscar stuff is probably already decided. People either voted for you, or they didn't. Just getting nominated is a huge boost. I'm more worried about your next movie. You're leveraged to the hilt in that. I told you, you should've let me bring in outside investors. Now with all this shit going on, no one is going to touch anything to do with you until they see how the public is going to react."

Levi speeds through the changing yellow light onto Peck into more congestion behind a moving truck unloading in front of one of the houses in the residential neighborhood. He bangs his hands against the steering wheel, leaning his head out the window to check for oncoming traffic. "We'll be fine. Those investors wanted too much back anyway. I'm tired of having to share the profits."

"It's more about sharing the risk," Eva says. "If this movie fails to earn back, you could be in some serious trouble."

"Fuck it. I'll just do another movie." He eases the nose of the car into the opposite lane and still seeing no oncoming traffic, curves around the truck. The double wishbone suspension absorbs each bump and depression of the uneven side street. "Or I'll just sell stuff. I came from nothing, so if I lose it all, I'm out nothing. I'm back to where I started."

"I don't think you realize how difficult it is to leave the lap of luxury once you've lived in it." She rubs her hand along the quilted leather seats. "But let's hope it never comes to that."

"That's why we need to get those pictures before this thing gets worse." He rolls through the stop sign onto Wilshire then cuts across traffic illegally onto Dayton Way and parks in a reserved spot in front of SJK Style, an appointment-only designer shop just off Rodeo. Levi and Eva exit the car and enter the store. A few seconds later, Gabe drives by and turns into a public parking structure across the street.

The inside of the store resembles a lounge more than a retail outlet. A bar runs along one wall with six stools and three high-top tables on the opposite wall. Artwork adorns the exposed brick walls. Male and female mannequins in designer outfits pose in casual interactions throughout. Two antique gold-painted wood and metal chandeliers hang from the stamped-beaded tin ceilings. A U-shape brown leather couch faces the back wall, which has a three-panel mirror on a raised floor partition in the middle and doors on each side leading to the men's and women's fitting rooms and restrooms. Five different suits hang from hooks on the right and the same number of dresses dangle on the wall to the left.

The proprietor, SJK—the S stands for Steve even though only his family calls him that since the boutique opened—descends the brass spiral staircase in the right corner from the office up above. "Welcome." Dressed in black from head to toe, he is long and thin with slick-backed raven hair and three days of stubble covering his sunken cheeks and chin. Immediately walking behind the bar, he says, "Some wine or maybe something stronger?"

Levi hops up on one of the stools. "You know what I want." Shuffling a handful of candied peanuts into his mouth, he turns to Eva. "Come on, we're here to celebrate. Best bloody martini in Beverly Hills. You got to have at least one."

Eva says, "I'll just have sparkling water if you've got it. I need to get back to work shortly." Eva is skeptical of Levi wanting to use SJK for the Oscars. She preferred that they to go to one of the bigger name designers, who had been pitching her since the nomination announcement, but Levi would not waver.

SJK pulls a bottle of wine from the cooler underneath. "How about a touch of white? Got a nice Pinot Grigio here."

"Just make her a martini," Levi says. "We're not going anywhere. Lakers tip off at four in New York. Might stay for that as well. SJK, how long have I been coming here?"

"Going on ten years," he says with a puff of the chest.

"How on Earth did you two even meet?" Eva asks. "I thought I introduced Levi to everyone out here."

SJK fills a shaker with ice and pours Ketel One on top. "We met out at Santa Anita on a random Sunday afternoon."

"Both were losing our ass," Levi chimes in. "I was down about five grand."

"Two for me," SJK says, adding his homemade Bloody Mary mix to the shaker. "We got down to the last race. It was some shitty seven-furlong maiden-claiming race." He puts the lid on the top and shakes the canister.

From the sidewalk, Gabe looks in through the window, keeping to the side to stay hidden. Seeing them laughing and having fun intensifies his pain and confusion about what he's even doing there. It's like the pictures all over again. He knows he shouldn't, but he can't stop himself. He realizes, no matter what happens, he comes out looking like the crazy one. If they see him, he's a stalker. If he goes in and confronts them, he is a naïve, moony fool. He knows that he's got no one to blame but himself. If he hadn't gone to the waterfall and taken the pictures, he would still not know who either of them are. Even if he didn't intend for the pictures to get out, they did, and he is responsible. Watching through the window, he knows he just needs to accept that and deal with it. But he's learning that knowing something rationally and being able to accept it emotionally are two different things entirely. Anytime over the past few days that he's felt any bit of space and detachment from any of it, the intensity he experienced with Eva that night sucks him back in. Standing there, watching her through the window, he doesn't want to leave. He wants to stay and confront her, to tell her how he really feels. But not in front of Levi. He knows there's no way she would choose him over Levi. "Fuck it," he mumbles.

"It's not worth it." Forcing himself away, he heads down the sidewalk toward the garage.

Inside, Levi continues the story about how he and SJK met. "All the horses were sprinters except for one. He hadn't run anything under a mile and an eighth and had been leading early in all those races but faded at the end. His four-furlong workout had been the best of the day earlier in the week too."

SJK removes two chilled martini glasses from the freezer. Frost forms on the inside and out. He sets them on the bar. "The kicker was the horse's name. Do you remember it?" Pouring from the shaker, he fills the glasses to just below the rim with the Bloody Mary mixture.

"How could I forget?" Levi says. "Eternal Damnation. I put my last four hundred fifty bucks on it."

SJK garnishes the fresh drinks with two dill pickles and slides them across the bar. "I remember I had only two hundred and four dollars left. The last dollar was all change. The teller looked at me like I was a total degenerate."

Levi removes the spear and bites the end. "We figured if we were busting, it might as well be on a horse named Eternal Damnation." He plops the pickle back into the martini and lifts the glass. "You're not having one, SJK?"

"I'll have a splash of the white now and one of those when we finish." Standing up a wine glass, he pours two ounces of Pinot Grigio and lifts it toward Eva and Levi. "What are we drinking to?"

"What else?" Levi says. "Eternal Damnation. May we all be so lucky to end up in the hell of our choosing."

"Chin chin," SJK says as they all touch glasses.

"Cheers." Eva says, sipping from her drink. "I assume the horse won?"

Levi gulps half his in a single swallow. "A fucking twenty-to-one long shot. I won nine grand."

SJK tops off Levi's drink with the last of the shaker and empties the ice, beginning the process again. "I took home four thousand eighty. Tipped the teller the eighty. Said, 'Aren't you glad I scraped together that last four?'"

"SJK invited me down the next day to have a drink at the store," Levi says. "Ten thousand dollars later, it was the most expensive free glass of wine I ever had. Haven't shopped anywhere else since though."

"I wondered why you always blew off meetings I tried to set with designers," Eva says, relaxing by the second.

Levi slugs more of the martini. "I told you I got a guy."

"Wait until you see what I have for you today." SJK walks out from behind the bar with another full shaker of bloody martinis and heads toward the back. "Shall we?"

Eva and Levi follow and sit on the leather couch. SJK fills their martini glasses again and sets the shaker on the rectangular teak coffee table. "You can see from what is hanging on the sides, I'm thinking blue. Most will go with black or white. Let's add some color and set you apart. Just because it's formal doesn't mean it can't be fun." He walks over to the dresses. "I'll show you my first choice, and we can work back from there."

Eva stands and walks along the dresses, touching the fabric of each one as she passes. "They all look lovely."

SJK takes the first one off the hook and walks toward Eva. "Based on your pictures, I estimated you at about a size four to six."

"With these hips, closer to an eight," Eva says, slapping her side.

SJK drapes the dress across his arms, presenting it to her. "I just love this strapless midnight blue Gucci Premiere gown.

The sapphire silk crepe fabric and fitted bodice will showcase your amazing figure."

She runs her hand along the dress. A calm, astral gaze floats from her eyes. "This looks perfect."

"I thought you'd love it," SJK says. "I'm going to have you slip it on and call up the tailor to get all the measurements. Don't worry if it's a little loose or tight anywhere. We can take care of all that."

On the couch Levi drains the rest of his martini and fills his glass from the shaker. He takes a glass vile of cocaine from his pocket and cups it in his palm. "SJK, okay for me to hit the head quick?"

"Of course. Take your time." He nods his head back toward the door to the men's salon. "I'll call up the tailor and get Eva taken care of, then we'll get you going."

Levi rises and pads toward the men's salon. "I'm well on my way already, so no rush there." Glancing out the front window to check on his car before he goes in the back, he sees Gabe's brown Suburban on the other side of his car waiting for traffic to move. "What the fuck?" he says, recognizing the older model truck is out of place in this part of town. He pivots toward the front. The Suburban rolls forward with the traffic. Levi quickens to the door and out onto the sidewalk. The Suburban approaches the intersection and turns right onto Rodeo. Levi jogs to the corner, but the Suburban is too far ahead to chase. He can make out only the first three letters of the license plate: 3AP. Repeating the sequence to himself, he treads back to the store.

Eva and SJK stand in the middle by the bar. SJK says, "Did something happen to your car? Never had any issues with vehicles out there before."

Levi pants, slightly out of breath. "Eva, do you still have the license plate numbers I gave you of that photographer? Was it three-AP something?"

"Yeah, it's in the email from my police contact." She angles to the bar and gets her phone from her purse. Locating the exchange, she says, "It was three-APR-one-four-four. Why?"

"That motherfucker was just outside. Thought you said he wasn't a pap. Sure seems like one. Pretty big coincidence that he would be in the same part of town as us at the exact same time. That's it. I'm calling Mick. I'm sure he knows someone who can take care of this guy."

"Levi, you've already done enough to jeopardize things. For once just let me do my job and stay out of it." She walks back toward the women's salon to try on the dress.

Levi trails behind, veering to the men's salon on the right. "I guess we'll see who handles it first."

Moments later, they both emerge from opposite doors, one barely able to move because of the tightness of the dress and the other unable to stand still. Firat, the Turkish house tailor, has also joined from his workshop in the basement. He has a tape measure draped around his neck and a cushion riddled with pins attached to his belt. His bright azure eyes soften the sadness in his sagging cheeks. Holding out his hand, he guides Eva up on the raised partition in front of the three-panel mirror. "Step up, please. Ah, yes. Very beautiful," he says seeing her from all angles in the mirror panels.

SJK steps up on the partition and stands behind Eva, straightening the subtle train. He reaches around and puts his hand under her chin. "Keep your head up, please." He pinches some of the fabric in the back of the dress. "Take it in a bit here, don't you think, Firat?"

"No, Steve. No," he says, obviously never buying that the initialed branding of the store applys to Steve as well. "Too tight below. She need to breathe."

"But it stretch," SJK says, matching the cadence of Firat's broken English. "Just a touch?"

"No, Steve. No," he says again. He takes out a piece of chalk from his pocket and makes several marks on her back and hips. "We let out here and here. Will be perfect."

"If you say so," SJK says. "You're the expert." He steps away to the right, leaving Firat to finish with Eva and takes a suit off the first hook on the wall to the right.

Levi, who had migrated up by the bar to make another drink and watch the beginning of the Lakers game, walks to the back. "You ready for me?"

Steve carries the midnight blue suit toward him. "I'm telling you, you're going to want to sleep in this suit. I had Armani custom make it for you based on your measurements. Check this out. It's a one-button wool tuxedo with a cashmere peak lapel. Pair a crisp white shirt, navy blue necktie and some Brioni shoes, and you'll absolutely own the red carpet."

Levi runs his hand over the cashmere lapel. "Yeah, this is perfect. Just perfect."

◆◆◆

THE NEXT AFTERNOON, LEVI eases into one of the private booths on the back patio at Big Dean's on the Santa Monica Boardwalk. A hulking man in his forties with a buzzed head fills the opposite seat. His ears protrude, bending slightly forward, from the thin temples of the rimless mirrored sunglasses. He curls his thick fingers around a twenty-four-ounce PBR. "What's going on? Mick said it was important."

Levi looks around to see if anyone noticed him slip in. "It's a bit more than the usual security." He removes a folded paper from his pocket and spreads it on the table. A grainy shot of Gabe printed from the Art on Traction website is on the front. "I need you to pay this guy a visit. He has some pictures of me that can't get out."

"Of course. Whatever you need." He spins the paper around. "How do I find him?"

Levi says, "His address and the address of the gallery where he has an exhibition are on the back."

The guy tilts the oversized can toward his mouth and pours beer without the can touching his lips. "You know he's probably not going to just give me the pics. It could get messy."

Levi again scans the area. "I hope it does. Do what you have to. This guy has created a shit storm for me."

"Hmm, let's see." The man scratches the stubble under his chin with the back of his fingers. "Going to cost you triple the daily rate."

Levi slides the picture toward him and puts his hands under the table to count out the money from his wallet. He leans forward and extends his hand. "Here's fifteen hundred. That should more than cover it."

The man drops one hand under the table, keeping his other on the beer. He takes the money and just stuffs it in his pocket without counting. "What if someone is with him?"

"Like I said, do what you have to," Levi says. "Needs to happen right away. The sooner and rougher, the better."

The guy nods, jiggling his puffy cheeks. "Consider it handled. I'll call you when it's done."

CHAPTER 12

GABE CLOSES THE FRONT storm door of his house. Drops of dew collide and stream down the glass. The neighborhood still sleeps. White blossoms peek out of the dark green leaves of the Magnolia tree in the front. Fog coats the windows of the cars parked in the driveways and lining the street. A single chirping bird cuts through the crisp air. Swinging the camera bag over his shoulder, Gabe shuffles through the small patch of grass that constitutes their front yard. Water kicks up covering his shoes and the bottom of his pant legs.

Walking toward his Suburban parked on the street, he presses the fob on his key chain to unlock the doors. The lights flash sending waves of red through the mist. He curves around the vehicle and stops at the driver's side back door. Rapid steps scuff against the concrete street from behind. Before Gabe can turn around, tBig Dean's thick hand grabs his shoulder and throws him to the ground. Rolling over, Gabe peers up at the foreboding figure looming over him.

A deep voice emanates from the shadowy outline. "I need those pictures."

Gabe attempts to get up. "What pictures?"

A boot drives into Gabe's ribs. "Don't make me do this. You know which ones." The guy kicks Gabe again, then picks him up and lands several blows with his fist, one to the face and two more to the body.

"There aren't any more," Gabe says, spitting in between gasps. "Everything's been released." His attacker responds by slamming Gabe against the side of the Suburban. His face bruised and bleeding, Gabe slides the camera bag from his shoulder and pushes it toward his attacker. "They're on the disc in the camera. Take it."

The guy snatches the bag and flings Gabe back to the ground. He takes out the camera and removes the memory card. Gabe squirms on the pavement in pain. Having what he came for, the thug spikes the camera next to Gabe. "This ends here, or I'll come back and finish what I started." He hurries off, lumbering down the street.

Gabe twists himself upright, leaning against the back tire. He watches the man get into a later model pickup truck but can't see any details or the license plate due to the sparse light.

◆◆◆

LATER THAT MORNING, THE same pickup turns off the PCH into a parking lot at Topanga Beach. The sun hangs directly above in a cloudless sky. Trolling through the parking lot, the truck stops behind Levi's open Jeep tucked between a late-sixties red convertible Beetle and a rusted white conversion van. Leaving the truck running, the man gets out and walks to the driver's side of the Jeep. He roots around in his pocket and pulls out the camera memory card.

Levi says, "I was surprised to hear from you so soon."

The guy rests his wrist on the door frame, his knuckles and back of his fingers scraped and bruised, and drops the memory card in Levi's lap. "You said it needed to happen right away. How's that for speedy service?"

Levi picks up the memory card, holding it between his fingers. "You sure this is it?"

"That's what was in the camera. The dude put up a little bit of a fight, but he eventually cooperated. They usually do. If that's not the right one, I'll go back…no charge. Just let me know." He turns and shuffles back toward his truck.

Two girls in their late teens wearing bikini tops and cutoff jeans walk from the beach toward the red Beetle. One whispers to the other and motions toward Levi. He turns his head away, looking back over his shoulder waiting for the guy to pull away so he can leave before the girls confirm their suspicion and he has to do the whole autograph-selfie thing.

◆◆◆

IN HER OFFICE, EVA sits at her desk with a phone headset on. "I understand that," she says speaking into the microphone extending down in front of her mouth. "All I'm saying is that—" Levi barrels in. Eva, still talking into the mic, says, "I'm going to have to call you back." She removes the headset and tosses it on the desk.

Levi holds up the memory card between his fingers. "At least one of us has been working on our problem."

Eva rises from the desk. "Please tell me you didn't."

"Someone had to," Levi boasts.

Eva walks out from behind the desk. "Jesus Christ, Levi, I told you to let me handle it."

"I found an easier way."

"But how?" Eva asks, her quivering voice revealing she is questioning if she really wants to know the answer.

Levi hands her the memory card. "Let's just say I out-sourced the retrieval process."

Eva takes the memory card and walks back around the desk, inserting the small disk into her computer. "He's not hurt, is he?"

Levi strolls around next to her to view the monitor. "He'll heal."

Eva opens the digital folder containing the files. On the monitor, a picture of the Bixby Bridge with its distinctive open-spandrel arches connecting the Big Sur coastline just south of Carmel fills the screen.

Levi waves his hand toward the screen. "Click through this bullshit. Must be toward the end."

Eva advances through more pictures of the Central Coast with the Santa Lucia Mountains rising abruptly from the Pacific. None of which are of Levi or Emily.

Eva says, "These are definitely his pics, but they're not from the waterfall. Are you sure they're here?"

Levi takes the mouse from her and clicks frantically through the images. "They've got to be. My guy took the disk right from the camera."

Eva steams from behind the desk, pushing her hands through her hair. "Why couldn't you just let me handle it?"

After several times backward and forward through the pictures, Levi flings the mouse across the desk. "I don't understand. They're supposed to be here."

Eva says, "Obviously your brilliant associate got the wrong memory card."

"I'm telling you, you better fix this," Levi says. "Because if my guy has to go back, he's not going to be very happy about being lied to."

Eva pads to the desk and removes her mobile phone from her purse. "Hopefully Gabe hasn't already gone to the police." She locates the number, then signals for Levi to be quiet while dialing. Swinging around to the other side of the desk, she stares out the window as she waits for Gabe to answer. After a brief pause, she speaks into the phone. Her voice changes into a sweet, lilting cadence. "Hey, babe. Been thinking about you."

Eva quiets, listening to the response. "My god. When?… Are you okay? Did you call the police?… Okay, I'm coming over… No, it's no trouble. Can I pick up anything for you on the way?… Sure. See you in a little bit." Eva ends the call and faces Levi. Her words regain a sharp and direct tone. "The good news is he doesn't know whether it was you or Emily who sent the guy. He sounds pretty bad. Could barely understand him. Your guy must've really done a number on him. The neighbors found him lying in the street."

"You expect me to feel bad?" Levi asks. "He brought this on himself. You better get the rest of those pictures or it's only going to get worse."

Eva snatches her purse off the desk and walks with Levi toward the door. "Just please go home and don't talk to anyone or do anything else until you hear from me."

"I'll give you until the end of the day, or I'm sending my guy back." Levi says. "Call me as soon as you have anything."

◆◆◆

GABE RECLINES IN BED, propped up with pillows against the curved sleigh headboard. His eyes are closed, his face bruised and swollen. A knock raps against the ajar door, pushing it open.

Eva slides through, stopping abruptly when she sees him. "You said it wasn't bad."

Gabe opens one eye, the other tremoring, struggling against the swelling. "You should see his boots. They're going to need a professional shine after what my face did to them."

Eva sits on the side of the bed. "Come on, I'll take you to the hospital. You really need to see a doctor."

"Bruises heal," Gabe says, placing his hand on her thigh. "I'm more upset about my smashed camera and the memory card."

Eva strokes his forearm with her nails. "All he wanted was the memory card?"

Gabe says, "Unfortunately for him, the wrong one."

"I don't understand," Eva says. "Why would anyone want to steal your pictures? Don't get me wrong, they're beautiful, but it seems like such an extreme move."

Gabe sits up, wincing in pain. "There's a bit more to the story. That day of the show when we met, I inadvertently took some photos of a certain celebrity with another much younger actress. You may have seen them in the news."

Eva continues the ruse, not knowing it is her that is being played since he knows exactly who she is and why she was at the gallery opening and is here now. "Wait, you mean? Noooo way. That was you? The ones of Levi Combs and Emily James on Forbidden Fotos? Those had to fetch a pretty penny."

"Yep, that was me." Gabe pats next to him on the bed, inviting Eva to stretch out beside him. "But I didn't sell them. I wasn't going to do anything with them. Abbie, thinking she was helping her dorky older brother get ahead, went behind my back."

Eva slides up next to him and kisses him, careful to avoid the bruises. "You mean cool and hip older brother."

Gabe laughs, grimacing from the shooting pain in his ribcage. "I'm pretty sure she's never thought of me that way. I just wish I could get the pictures from today back. I had some great shots on that card."

Eva continues kissing him, touching her lips to each of the swollen and colored contusions on his face. Gabe relaxes back into the pillows. Eva says, "Did you go to the police? They could find out whether it was Levi or Emily or whomever."

Not lifting from the pillow, Gabe shakes his head. "The DA came yesterday, but I told him I didn't have any other pictures and couldn't really add anything to what was in the ones that are out there."

"But there are more?" Eva asks. "Why didn't you just give the DA what you had? Aren't you worried that the person who did this might come back?"

Gabe says, "I just really don't want to get involved in any of it. I knew the DA would want me to testify. The attention will never stop, and I don't want anything to blow back on Abbie since she was the one who sold the photos."

Eva leans her head on his shoulder. "At least you're all right. That's most important. Is there anything I can do to make you feel better?" She rubs the inside of his thigh.

"As much as I'd like to take you up on that, I really don't think I physically can." He slides down in the covers. "I probably need to just get some rest. Rain check?"

"Of course," Eva says, swinging her legs onto the floor. "Can I get you anything before I go? Some aspirin, an ice bag, or maybe food? I can run out and bring something back."

"Only if I can drink it through a straw." His laugh leads to another groan. "Hurts too much to chew."

"I understand. Just rest then." Eva strokes his hair. "Call me later. I'll come back when you wake up."

Gabe closes his eyes and turns on his side. Eva bends down and kisses him again, staring for a moment before quietly closing the door on her way out.

In the hallway she checks the other rooms to see if Abbie is home. Not seeing anyone, she follows the hallway to the kitchen. "Abbie? Are you home?" She continues toward the studio and stops at the back door, listening one final time for any activity in the house. She hears only the hum of the refrigerator and faint screams of the kids playing outside in a neighboring yard. Satisfied she is alone, she hurries toward the desk and opens the laptop.

On the screen the dialog box appears again. This time she knows the password. Looking over at Milton lounging on the worktable, she types in his name. He stands up and jumps over onto the desk. She pushes him to the floor. The desktop appears on the screen. She searches through the directory and locates the files of Levi and Emily. Milton hops back up on the table. She reaches to push him away again. He arches his back and hisses at her. She takes her phone and a cord out of her purse and connects to the computer through the USB port. One by one, she transfers the pictures to her phone.

Gabe appears in the doorway watching her. "Find what you're looking for?"

Eva recoils. "God, you scared me. Why do you keep doing that?" She rises and angles toward him, snagging her phone and the cord and tucking them both in her purse. "What are you doing out of bed?"

He eases down the steps, letting one foot lead then the other follow and settle next to it before taking another step. He limps past her toward the computer. "Why didn't you just ask?"

Eva stops but doesn't follow him. "It's not what you think."

Gabe steps behind the computer, looking at the screen. "That's exactly what it is, Ms. Florez."

Eva grimaces at the sound of her real last name. "I'm so sorry. I didn't want to lie. You have to know, I didn't have anything to do with the attack this morning. I would never do that."

"So that's why you were at the gallery the other night. You wanted the pictures?" Gabe scans the screen, noticing all the files are gone. "You know what? It doesn't matter. I'm glad these fucking pics are gone. They've been nothing but trouble since I got them. Just take them and go. I hope they're worth it."

Eva watches him for a moment then turns and walks toward the door, stopping in the archway. "If you already knew who I was, why didn't you say anything before?"

"I don't know." Gabe limps toward her. "I think at first I just didn't want to believe it. Hoped you would change your mind and come clean. Wanted what we had to be real. Who knows? I guess I'm just an idiot."

Eva reaches for him, rubbing the side of his arm. "No, you're not. It was real. I mean, it is. The pictures are my job but what happened between us was all me. You have to believe that."

"Would you believe you?" Gabe asks. "Imagine how I felt when I pulled up the Forbidden Fotos article and saw references to Eva Florez and pictures of you with Levi in other articles." He shifts and stretches, uncomfortable standing in one place. "I think I need to lie down."

"Of course," Eva says, her hand running down his arm to his hand. "Let me help you back to bed."

Gabe pulls away toward the door. "I can manage. Please just see yourself out. I hope everything works out for you with the pictures. You earned them."

◆◆◆

ABBIE PEEKS INTO GABE'S room and creeps over to the side of the bed watching him sleep. His breathing is heavy and inconsistent. She touches the side of his bruised face whispering, "Who did this to you?"

Gabe murmurs incoherently and roles on his side, immediately groaning and returning to his back.

Abbie steps away from the bed and slinks out of the room. She heads down the hall, through the kitchen, and out into the dark studio. Flipping on the light, she angles to the worktable and searches through a stack of papers. Not finding what she's looking for, she goes to the desk and scours the top. Her quest still unfilled, she grabs his camera bag hanging on the back of the chair and ferrets through the pockets. In the bottom of the back pouch she finally locates Marcus' card. "Please don't be mad at me." She removes her phone from her back pocket and dials the number on the card.

Marcus answers on the first ring. "This is Marcus."

"Deputy Ambrose?" Abbie squeaks.

"Yes. Who's this?"

"It's Abbie Adams. We met at our house. You came to see my brother."

"Of course. Ms. Adams, how are you this evening?"

"I'm sorry for calling you so late," Abbie says, pacing in the garage. "My brother will be so mad if he knows I called you. I just don't know what else to do."

"Did something happen, Ms. Adams? Are you all right?"

"Yes, I'm fine. But I'm worried about Gabe. Someone attacked him this morning in front of our house and beat him up really bad."

"Oh no, that's terrible. Is he hurt? Did he file a report with the police?"

"He says he's fine, but I'm worried. He won't go to the hospital or call the police. Said he didn't know the guy. All that was taken was the memory card from his camera. It had to be related to those pictures of Emily James and Levi Combs, don't you think?"

"It sure seems that way. I was worried something like this would happen. Those pictures are extremely valuable and dangerous. I thought he said that there weren't any other pictures." Abbie is silent. Marcus says, "Ms. Adams? Are there other pictures? If you want me to help, you're going to have to trust me."

"I do. But you have to promise that you won't tell him I called you. He's already mad at me for selling them in the first place. I told him I wouldn't meddle anymore."

"It was you that sold the original ones?"

"Yes, I did it. But you have to believe me. I was only trying to help. This is all my fault. I thought he could make some money and get publicity for his new show. I never thought he would get beat up for it."

"Calm down. It's not your fault. You did the right thing calling me. Do you know how many other pictures there are?"

"I think there are twenty or so. Let me check. I can look on his computer." She scurries to the desk and types in the password. She opens the folder where the pictures were, but it's empty. "No way. Where'd they go? They were right here." She checks the trash folder, which is also empty. "They're gone."

It's now Marcus who is quiet on the phone. He had been calm and soothing, hiding his excitement. Now he struggles for words, sifting through his disappointment.

Abbie finds the words for him. "I bet he gave them to Eva. He said he would've if she had asked."

"You mean Levi's agent, Eva Florez? Your brother knows her?"

"It's a long story, but yes, he knows her. She pretended to be someone else to come over here and steal the pictures. When he found out, he said he would've just given them to her. He really didn't want anything to do with any of this. He won't get in any trouble, will he?"

"No, Ms. Adams. I'll make sure he doesn't, and I won't tell him you called me. You sure you two are safe?"

"I think we're fine. He already gave them the pictures it seems. What are you going to do?"

"I think it's time I paid Ms. Florez a visit at her office."

CHAPTER 13

SPOTLIGHTS CRISSCROSS AND DANCE across the golden facade of the Hollywood and Highland Center. The Dolby Laboratories emblem and letters glow in soft teal light above the rectangular entranceway to the eponymous theater. A gold curtain, pulled and tied off to the right, hangs across the opening. The red carpeting stretches from inside the theater through the entranceway, bending right in front of the bleachers and running through the tent to the drop-off area. A line of limos extends all the way down Highland Avenue. One by one they pull forward, waiting just long enough to allow the passengers to exit before being waved away by a team of frantic wranglers tasked with expediting the flow.

A silver frost and Moroccan blue Duotone Bentley Mulsanne Grand Limousine pulls up. Cameras flash and the crowd swoons in fervid anticipation. A white-gloved, tuxedo-clad valet opens the rear door, extending an arm inside to help out the guest. Eva emerges in the strapless midnight blue Gucci Premiere gown from SJK. She waves and smiles despite the obvious disappointment from the spectators who have no idea who she is. Despite being well-known around town with the industry crowd, her face is unfamiliar to the fans who camped out and assembled to get a glimpse at the arriving stars.

Stepping to the side, she sweeps her subtle train behind her to make room for Levi. Just the sight of his Brioni patent leather loafer leading from the back seat stokes the smoldering excitement of the crowd. The rest of him emerging in the custom Armani suit sends them into a frenzy. Standing next to Eva, he waves and smiles to the effusive congregation.

Levi offers his arm to Eva to begin the journey down the red carpet. Caustic questions from a cluster of cameras cut through the raucous reception.

"Where's Emily?"

"Were you her first?"

"Is it true she's carrying your baby?"

Levi steps toward the photographer who spewed the last one. Eva whisks him toward a familiar female entertainment reporter for an interview.

The reporter says, "If there was an award for the most frenzied welcome, you would definitely win it. How does all this make you feel?"

Levi regains his composure. "I was invited last year as a presenter, and that was amazing. To be here one year later as a nominee is really unbelievable. A dream come true."

The reporter swats away his clichéd response, going deeper to the topic viewers really want to hear about. "Does it take away from the experience that a lot of this hype is because of the pictures with Emily James?"

"She's a fine actress," Levi says, keeping his cool. "Working together on the film, we became good friends."

"Does that mean you will continue to see each other?" the reporter asks.

Eva intervenes. "Levi and Emily's relationship is not a matter of public discussion. We're here to celebrate the film and all the work by those who helped create it."

The reporter maintains her course of questioning. "Do you think the scandalous pictures will cost you the Oscar?"

Levi's jaw tightens as he leans forward toward the reporter in an aggressive stance. "Is this all you want to talk about? I mean, you only have me for a few minutes and this is it?"

Eva pulls Levi away leading him down the red carpet toward the next interview.

The reporter turns and speaks directly to the camera. "Well, as you can see, things are heating up on the red carpet. Should be an interesting night."

Eva guides Levi off to the side to straighten his tie before proceeding into the tent. "You have to hold it together. It's going to be a long night if you get riled up that easily."

Levi says, "Can you believe that bitch?"

Eva forces a smile for all the eyes she feels on them. "You know the game, they're trying to get a reaction from you."

Levi flutters his lips in frustration. "After all the hard work, all they want to ask about are those fucking pictures."

"You haven't made things easier with all your shenanigans lately." She brushes off each side of his shoulders. "The more you show it bothers you, the worse it will get." Looking up at him, she notices the white flakes coating the bottom of his nostrils. She takes a tissue from her purse. "Wipe your nose. That's all we need is for them to capture that shit on camera."

Levi takes the tissue and covers his nose, but instead of blowing, he inhales powerfully through each nostril to not lose any of the cocaine he had been doing in the limo on the way. "So help me, if I lose this because of those pictures, I'll—"

Eva adjusts his pocket square. "Try to relax and enjoy the night, okay? What's done is done."

The farther along the red carpet, the fluffier the interviews become. The queries devolve from journalistic obligation about Emily to the expected superficial trappings of the night, such as who they're wearing and where they're going to after. They finish their final interview in front of the bleachers and wave one final time before proceeding toward the towering portal entrance facing Hollywood Boulevard. For the first time in a while, they share the same intention and goal: to see how many drinks they can throw down at the lobby bar before the show starts.

They stroll through the Awards Walk, which features the backlit glass plaques for each Best Picture Oscar winner on a series of limestone portals. Eva says, "None of the bullshit will matter once your name is announced."

The theater lobby has five levels with a grand spiral staircase in the center. Eva takes each step slowly, gliding her hand along the cherry balustrade, partly to steady herself but also to make the moment last.

Levi, several steps ahead of her, turns around. "Come on, I need to get at least three martinis in me if I'm going to make it through this."

Eva stops, looking up at the silver oval dome above, no longer in a hurry. "You know what, go ahead. I'll meet you at the bar. I want to soak this in a bit."

"And face these backstabbing vultures by myself?" Levi holds his arm out, waiting for her. "Not a chance."

They ascend the remaining steps surrounded by images of past winners. Eva wonders if Levi even cares that in a few short hours he could be one of them, or if like most things he is just focusing on what he needs and wants in the moment. She had convinced herself that everything she had been doing since she had met him nine years ago was to get to this moment. She had really believed all along that what she was doing was for him, to help him. But finally, here, she realizes it was really for herself. She just needed him to get here.

At the bar, ordering two drinks at a time, Levi downs two martinis and cues up two more. When the lights flash to signal for everyone to move to their seats, he chugs the remaining one and a half so he has enough time to balance out the alcohol with one more visit to a restroom stall.

Inside the theater, the audience chamber is intimate, much more than the size of the stage would dictate. The overhead structure loops around like a tiara, supporting and disguising the grid required for the intricate lighting. Reflective ribs from the tiara extend down between the theatre's box seats, creating a continuous flow from wall to ceiling. A young attractive man and woman escort them to their seats, which are in the front row since Levi is a nominee, and at least when the tickets were dispersed, a favorite to win.

Eva sinks into her seat, her legs wobbly from the excitement and anticipation of the impending coronations. She rubs her hands on the deep plum upholstery appreciating the history of the ones who sat in the seats before her. The iridescent fabric and fine bronze mesh of the closed curtain shimmer before her.

Levi focuses more on those seated around and behind him, enjoying making eye contact and connecting, merely to let them know that he is in front of them. Turning back around, he smooths the back of his head, whispering to Eva. "How does my hair look? Hope these fuckers enjoy the view."

The lights in the theater dim, drawing attention to the stage. The curtain parts, and a popular male comedian host walks on stage for his opening monologue of culturally relevant but insignificant observations. For the following several hours, the stage fills with presenters, winners, musical acts, and other performances intended to honor the achievements in film from the past year. Levi repeatedly calls over his seat-filler so that he can escape to the lobby and the restroom for refreshment.

Eva sighs in relief when he returns right before the announcement of his award. She reaches over and grips his thigh, whispering, "I was worried you weren't going to make it back." She notices his dilated pupils and distant stare. "Are you okay?"

Levi widens his eyes and smiles. "Never better." His right cheek twitches from the recent stimulation.

The host walks on stage, stopping at the podium. "If you are one of the few people who has not seen the performance of our next candidate for Best Performance by an Actor in a Leading Role then you have to at least have heard the rumors about the source of the chemistry between the costars." Uncomfortable laughter and groans ripple through the audience. "Making us all reconsider the true meaning of the title, I direct your attention to the video screen with Levi Combs in *For Love.*"

Eva squeezes his thigh again, speaking through her smile. "Just let it go. He's only joking."

On the video screen, Levi in orange prison garb confers with his lawyer in a prison meeting room. The lawyer says, "Your daughter told me she was the one who killed your wife."

Shackled to the chair Levi thrusts back and forth reacting to the statement. "That's bullshit. She's just a scared little girl trying to protect her father."

"If the police get wind of this," the lawyer says, "they'll reopen the case and reexamine the evidence."

"You can't let that happen." Levi, unable to sit still but with no room to move, shifts in his seat. "We need to hurry this along before they find anything concrete."

The lawyer says, "You could change your plea."

"Do it." Levi bangs his shackled hands on the table. "Whatever it takes."

The lawyer leans forward, trying to lessen the weight of his words by whispering even though no one is listening. "But that could mean the death penalty."

"I don't care," Levi says. "I have to protect her. She can't be implicated."

The screen fades to black. In the audience, attendees, uncomfortable with Levi's alleged offscreen inappropriate relationship with Emily, quietly applaud the performance. Levi acknowledges the muted appreciation with several head-nods.

The winner for Best Actress in a Leading Role from the previous year walks to the podium. "And now the nominees for Best Actor in a Leading Role."

On the video screen, close-ups of the five nominees appear.

The presenter reads the nominees. "Brad Pitt in *Expiration Date*, Levi Combs in *For Love*, Leonardo DiCaprio in *Normal Like Us*, Jamie Foxx in *The Preacher*, and Joseph Gordon Levitt in *Outside In*." The presenter opens the envelope and removes the announcement. "And the Oscar goes to…Levi Combs in *For Love*."

The audience offers light applause mixed with murmurs of discomfort and reproach. Excited and triumphant Levi rockets out of the seat and bounds to the stage. At the podium his exuberance starkly contrasts the frosty response from the audience. "Based on your reaction, I'm not the only one surprised by this. Despite the negative press over the past week, I hope over time people will be able to appreciate this picture for the touching, humanistic story that it is."

Audience members squirm with contempt in their seats, shaking their heads and whispering to one another.

Levi continues his speech. "I'd like to thank the Academy for honoring me with this prestigious award among such other talented artists. I wish my mother were alive to enjoy this with me. She would be proud today and feel justified in encouraging me to drop out of college to pursue this dream. I'd like to thank everyone who worked on the film, especially the director, Frank Darabont. You are a true wu li master. And of course, I would not be here if it weren't for a very special and talented woman in my life. Someone who has taught me that to achieve anything great, we must put ourselves on the line and be willing to risk everything: my costar, Ms. Emily James. There is no doubt you will be in this position one day." Associating the word position with Emily among the swirling accusations deepens the malaise in the audience.

Music flows from the theater speakers, drowning out Levi and the collective groaning from the audience. Levi keeps talking but no one can hear him. A beautiful female stage assistant walks out to escort him from the stage. Reluctantly he leaves, upset by the reception of his acceptance speech.

In the audience Eva struggles to restrain the hurt from being snubbed in the speech, and that he gave all the credit to Emily. She didn't expect much. She had learned never to when it came to Levi. But to not even mention her after she was the one who discovered and nurtured him was outrageous. Others noticed it too. She can feel their eyes on her, but not in sympathy. This crowd didn't get to where they were by being compassionate and understanding. Uncurbed pity is the only kind of condolence they can muster. Forcing a smile, she stares straight ahead and claps.

Backstage in the press area, rising above the disappointment, Levi summons a smile to greet the press members waiting to interview him.

"How did it feel?" one of the reporters blurts.

Levi says, "Just amazing. As an actor you can't help but think about this moment throughout your career, but when it happens, you're still blown away. Very surreal."

The reporter clarifies the question. "No, I mean to get booed for winning."

Levi says, "Hadn't noticed. Guess not everyone is fan."

Another press member asks, "Are you still going to see Emily James romantically?"

Levi looks in the opposite direction. "No comment. Next question."

A reporter in the back speaks up. "Is it true that you two actually started seeing each other when she was fifteen and your relationship is why she got the role?"

Levi scans the back rows to identify the source of the question. "You people make me sick. Tonight is about recognizing achievements in the film industry and all you want to talk about are gossip and rumors. Get a fucking life." He blazes out of the room, his anger igniting further chatter among the press members.

On his way from the pressroom, Levi sees Emily on stage. He wallows in the wings waiting for her to finish.

At the podium she and Ira Bethel, another young actor and new client of Eva's, present another award. Emily says, "Getting started in this business is never easy."

Ira continues her sentence. "But after exhaustive effort and a little luck, you catch a break, only to realize..."

"That's when the work really starts," Emily says with perfect timing. "The following nominees for Best Original Screenplay have overcome the odds to not only make it, but also for their first work to be revered."

Ira says, "The nominees are Mikhael Gunderson for *Over the Influence*, Bella Stevens for *Wish List*, and Nathan Cranfield for *Nice To See Me*.

Emily opens the envelope. "And the Oscar goes to Nathan Cranfield for *Nice To See Me*."

Nathan comes on stage to accept the award. Emily hands him the Oscar and exits with her partner.

Emily notices Levi waiting, but, as she approaches, she looks away and walks by.

Levi, still holding his Oscar, says, "What? You're not even talking to me now? Did you hear me give you credit?" Emily keeps walking. Levi shouts at her back. "I don't understand why you're mad at me. This is all your fault." Chasing after her, he grabs her shoulder and spins her around. "And you're ignoring me?"

Emily looks around noticing all the people backstage watching. Reporters pour out of the press area to capture the confrontation. Faking a smile, Emily whispers, "What are you doing? Don't cause a scene."

Levi says, "Can we get together later? I really need to see you. We should celebrate this night together."

"I'm sorry. I have plans," Emily says, reaching down, pretending to admire his Oscar. "I'm sure with this, you will too."

He jerks the Oscar away from her like a petulant child. "Just like that, it's over? You don't have any time for me?"

Playing to those watching, Emily ignores his hostility. "Congratulations on your win." She turns and walks away.

His whole night falling apart, Levi storms off. The alcohol he had pounded before and during the show is overpowering the ample amount of cocaine he administered to stay level. He zips toward the restroom by the green room. He might not be able to control what is happening around him, but he isn't going to let himself be overrun by his buzz too. Unfortunately, the green room squatters and their concomitant sycophants overflow into the hallway and fill the restroom. Unsure where one line ends and the other begins, he reverses direction, ignoring the platitudes and insincere requests for him to join them.

Eva, wanting to escape the judgmental stares in the auditorium, flees backstage as well. As angry as she is at Levi, he's the only person she wants to be around. She intercepts him darting away from the green room. "Come on, let's go out the back through the loading dock." Levi stumbles. She latches onto his arm. "It looks like you could use some air."

Levi thrusts the Oscar at her. "Here take this. You deserve it more than I do anyway. You did all the work."

Eva's hands remain at her sides. "Would've been nice for you to say that out there in front of the sixty million people watching worldwide."

"So now you're pissed at me too? Boy, this night is turning to shit. Supposed to be the best night of our lives and here we are hiding in the back of the theater avoiding everyone. Suppose you have a bunch of parties you want me to go to?"

Eva slowly nods then stops. "You know what? Screw them. Don't give them the satisfaction. They'll be expecting you to go and they'll just be snickering and gossiping behind your back the whole time. But if you don't show, they'll think you're at another party and that will drive them crazy. Just avoid them all together. If you don't feel like going, don't. You don't owe them anything. Make them wonder where you are." She points toward the back of the theater. "Come on. We can duck out the back and not have to deal with this bullshit at all. I'll call the driver and have him pick us up."

They navigate through the empty crates and containers waiting to be refilled with the set equipment and decorations that will be shipped to some warehouse, inventoried, and probably never used again.

On the loading dock outside, a group of the stagehands are smoking. Eva lowers her phone and points away from the group. "Come on, we can wait over here. The driver will be here in ten minutes."

Levi angles toward them. "What's up, fellas? Can I bum one of those?"

A stagehand takes a pack from his breast pocket and extends it to Levi. "Help yourself." As Levi gets closer, the guy recognizes him and notices the statue in his hand. "Congrats on the win, Mr. Combs."

One of the other guys bumps the guy next to him, whispering, "Holy shit, you know who that is? That's Levi Combs. My wife's never going to believe this."

Levi offers the Oscar for the pack of smokes. "Can you hold this?"

The guy takes the statue with his free hand, immediately putting the other hand on it. One of the other stagehands comes over with a lighter. "Here, Mr. Combs. Let me light that for you." The others swarm around the guy with the Oscar.

Levi says, "Enough with that Mr. Combs shit. Levi is fine."

The guy who mentioned his wife said, "Do you think we could get a picture, mister, I mean, Levi?"

Eva strolls over. "It's kind of been a long night, guys. Hope you understand."

"It's fine," Levi says, stepping toward the huddle around the Oscar. "These guys are good people. Much better than those fucking assholes inside. Am I right, fellas?"

Laughter emanates from the group. One of the guys says, "Hell, yeah. Levi knows what time it is."

"Take one of their phones, Eva," Levi says and moves to the center of the group. "Any of you guys got any hooch?" The group quiets. "Come on. Someone has to have something. Don't worry. I won't say anything."

The guy who provided the smokes turns to one of his buddies. "Go ahead. Give it to him. It's cool."

The guy removes a pint bottle from his hip pocket. "Jack Daniels okay?"

"Damn straight it is," Levi says, his drawl coming back. "I might've left Tennessee but it ain't left me." Levi takes the bottle and downs a healthy swig. "Aahhh, that's what I needed. Grew up on this shit." He hands the bottle back. "All right, let's do this."

The guys circle around Levi. Eva gathers all the phones from the guys, but the first picture she takes is with her own. She's not going to let an opportunity for positive press pass. She knows that if something good happens, and it's not posted on social media, it never really happened.

CHAPTER 14

LEANING ON THE GLASS wall in the hallway outside Eva's dark office, Marcus sips coffee from a paper cup early the next morning. The elevator dings, and the number twenty-nine lights up on the display above the doors. He stands, smoothing the wrinkles on his tan suit jacket with his free hand.

Eva's receptionist steps off the elevator, her eyes down and arm buried to the elbow in her Marc Jacobs black leather tote searching for the keys. Her yellow sheath dress glows in the dim hallway lighting. Shuffling toward the door, she doesn't notice Marcus, who remains silent waiting for her to look up. Grumbling about the keys, she stops and digs more frantically. Marcus advances from the shadow cast from the dark office in her direction. She glances up, startled by the tall, imposing figure coming toward her. "I'm sorry," Marcus says, stepping back toward the glass wall. "I didn't mean to scare you." He removes the badge from his pocket. "I'm with the district attorney's office. I need to ask Ms. Florez a few questions."

"Hang on," she says, returning her focus to her purse and locating the keys. "Let me get inside and look at her calendar. She usually takes calls at home and has a breakfast meeting so she doesn't come in until after nine or so." The receptionist flips through the keys on the ring and opens the door. Marcus lingers in the hallway, not following. She holds the door open before going inside. "You don't have to wait out here, silly. Come inside."

Marcus trails after her, stopping just inside the door as she locates the switch and fills the room with light. He says, "I can come back later if this isn't convenient."

She plops her purse on the desk and flips on the computer, settling into the chair while the screen on the left goes from black to the Eva Florez Enterprises logo that also fills the wall behind her. "Under normal circumstances, after a big win like last night, I wouldn't expect to see her until later if at all. But with the way things went down, going to be a busy day and week. Levi's got another film opening soon. Did you see the awards show last night?"

"I did," Marcus says, concealing his delight. "It looked like things only got worse in the press conference backstage. I read this morning that he was MIA from all the parties too. Probably not how they envisioned the night would go."

"One thing I've learned working here: you never know what is going to happen when Levi Combs is involved." She turns her eyes to the screen, wiggling the mouse and tapping the button to open the email application. "Yep, look at this. I already have eleven emails from her." She switches to the calendar view. "She had a breakfast meeting with the LA Times entertainment editor at eight but has phone calls scheduled all morning starting at nine thirty, so she should be in shortly. Do you want me to call to let her know that you are here?"

"No, I don't want to bother her. I have enough to keep me busy while I wait," he says, holding up his phone. The truth is that he doesn't want Eva to know he's there at all. It's why he arrived so early, and after a night he expects she was up late. He wants to have the element of surprise and to catch her when she might not be at her best and possibly eager to vent. Several reporters had written about Levi's omission of Eva from his acceptance speech and the tense interactions between the two after the award presentation.

Twenty minutes later Eva glides in, pulling a black carbon fiber Lamborghini suitcase. Wheeling the piece of luggage next to the desk, she glances at Marcus through her black, round Chanel half-tinted sunglasses and turns her back to him, facing the desk. "Pick one or two of the items inside for yourself, except for the trips, and inventory the rest for gifts to clients."

The receptionist springs up, clapping her hands. "I saw online that the gift bags this year were valued at a hundred-and-fifty grand." She pulls the suitcase up on the desk, forgetting about Marcus.

"That's only one of two. Levi didn't even want his." Eva drops her keys on the desk. "It's down in my car. Once you're finished with this one, please go down and grab the other and do the same."

Marcus rises from the white leather contemporary sofa behind them. The receptionist is facing him, but her focus is on the bag as she unzips it and splits it open on the desk. She immediately grabs one of the boxes. "A year's supply of Healing Saint skin serum!" She snatches a white draw-string bag. "Look, at this. A complete beauty collection from Whoosh. This is better than Christmas!" She returns to rifling through the suitcase. Eva puts her hand on the receptionist's arm, drawing her eyes upward. With a subtle backward nod of her head, Eva reminds the receptionist of Marcus, dashing her dreamy daze. The receptionist says, "Geez. I'm sorry. This is Deputy DA…"

Extending his hand, Marcus maneuvers around the glass coffee table. "Marcus Ambrose. I'd just like to ask you a few questions."

"Is this something that can wait?" Eva plucks the card from his fingers, speaking before he can answer. "I'm fighting fires from every angle. Later in the week perhaps?"

"I'm afraid it can't," Marcus says. "I really think it's in everyone's best interest if we speak now. I promise it will be only ten to fifteen minutes tops."

Eva turns her wrist to see the time. "I'm supposed to have a call with *The Hollywood Reporter* in five minutes, but I can probably push that back a few. "Joelle, will you get a hold of Bobby and tell him I'll call at nine forty-five?" Joelle nods and works the mouse to locate his number. Eva waves her arm toward her office. "Please, after you." Marcus walks by following her lead. Eva's sunglasses remain on, but her eyes are visible through the half-tinted lenses, scanning him up and down. "Your card says sex crimes division. Not sure how I can help you." She trails behind him and shuts the door.

Marcus stands in the middle of the room looking at all the movie posters on the walls. He walks over to the one with Levi and Emily in *For Love*. "I don't know. With the way last night went, I think you can probably figure out why I'm here." He taps the glass-framed picture. "It seems congratulations are in order. Such chemistry between those two."

"It was a pretty amazing night," Eva says, settling in to her desk chair and unpacking her laptop bag. "The phone has been ringing nonstop, which is why I don't have much time this morning. Did you see the film?"

"No, unfortunately not." Marcus turns from the poster and pads back toward the desk. "I just can't seem to stay focused for two hours to enjoy a movie. I'm more into the television drama series. I did see the pictures of those two at the waterfall though." He points his thumb over his shoulder back toward the poster. "Those were something, huh? Definitely not your typical family photos."

"Mr. Ambrose, as I said, today is an extremely busy day. Is there something specific you want to ask me?"

Marcus curtails his words. "Did you know?"

The quick jab catches Eva off guard. She just repeats the words back to him. "Did I know what?"

"That they were more than costars"

"I don't think I like your insinuation." Eva picks up her phone. "Should I have my lawyer present for this?"

"I'm not insinuating anything," Marcus says, stepping closer to the desk. "I believe everyone last night made it pretty clear what people are thinking. My office is just trying to get to the truth."

"I'm sorry you wasted your time coming here this morning. I could've saved you the trip. Mr. Combs and Ms. James are nothing more than colleagues and friends. The pictures being circulated are from an afternoon hike and swim a few weeks ago. Any person or publication implying anything more will be served with a libel and defamation of character suit. Any further questions should be directed to our legal team." Eva removes her lawyer's card from her middle drawer and slides it across desk.

Marcus picks up the card and reads it. "In your next call with them, you may want to ask what happens to a person who knows a sex crime has been committed and does nothing, or worse, tries to cover it up." He slides the card in his breast pocket. "I do appreciate you taking the time to meet with me this morning. I'll let you get on with your phone calls. No need to see me out." Eva remains stoic, offering only silence and an impassive stare in response to his threats. Marcus nods, then streams out.

Joelle is hunched over her desk, still perusing the products from the Oscar windfall scattered across the top. Marcus strides by. "Happy shopping." But it's he who is the most content. He had rehearsed the encounter in his head most of the previous night, thinking through all the various scenarios of what she might say and what he would say back to her. For once no one went off script or flubbed a line. It was a performance any director would've loved to have. Clean and crisp. Nothing missing and nothing wasted.

Waiting for the elevator in the hallway, Marcus beams triumphantly. His adrenalin surges, causing his hand to shake as presses the down-button. But as the lights flash and bells ring returning the elevator to him, everything around him slows. He thinks of Levi, feeling closer to him than ever before. He finally knows what Levi must feel after nailing a performance. It's not for the applause or accolades. It's internal—the feeling of flawless execution.

◆◆◆

THE OWNER OF THE Art on Traction gallery works behind the counter. A middle-aged man and woman view the collection of Gabe's pictures hanging from one of the extended hydraulic lifts. A mid-twenties female circles the other lift that showcases another artist's work.

Levi shuffles in wearing a plain black crewneck T-shirt, jeans, and brown leather slide sandals. Tortoise-shell rectangular sunglasses conceal his eyes.

Despite Levi's casual appearance, the owner recognizes him and scurries over. "Welcome, Mr. Combs. Truly an honor to have you here," she says with excitement and nervousness, her red curls bouncing.

Levi leaves the sunglasses on underneath the bright gallery lights. "Are you showing the work of an artist named Gabe Adams?"

"Yes, we are," the owner says. Her arm waves across the gallery, the flowing long sleeves of her ombré-printed kaftan undulating from the movement. "He's a personal discovery of mine. One of LA's hottest emerging photographers." She leads Levi to Gabe's work hanging from the lift. The younger female patron has taken notice and snaps a photo of Levi with her phone. The owner says, "Most of his work has already sold, but we still have these eight, and he is bringing more today."

In silence Levi walks around the lift, pausing to examine each work.

Careful not to crowd him, the owner trails a few steps behind. "What do you think?"

Levi says, "Honestly, they're not really my taste—a little too pedestrian."

The owner shifts nervously. "Allow me to show you some of the other artists I'm featuring." She leads him over to the other lift with more city landscapes and industrial settings. "These have more of an urban feel."

"Ah, yes," Levi says. "These are much better."

"Outstanding." The owner relaxes, buoyed by the positive feedback. "Any particular ones stand out?"

Levi waves his hand at the lift and toward the back wall. "I think I'll take them all."

"Excuse me? You want all fifteen?" the owner says, excited but confused.

"Yeah, I want to buy all the work from these other artists." Levi takes off his sunglasses to emphasize his point. His eyes droop, streaked with red. "I'm redecorating an apartment building I own and think these will all work quite well."

He doesn't really own an apartment building any more than he has a real opinion on any of the pictures. Levi can't sit back and let Gabe thrive while Gabe's other pictures have wreaked so much havoc in his own life. Gabe ruined the Oscars for him, and Levi isn't about to allow Gabe to have success at his expense.

The owner doesn't respond, calculating the total sale in her head. Levi stares at her, waiting for an answer. The owner surrenders to the surprise and serendipity of the seeming sale. "I'm sorry. I just don't know what to say."

"There is one small stipulation," Levi counters.

"Of course." The owner encourages Levi toward the seating area with a wave of her arm. "Whatever you want. We can package and ship them anywhere. Just name it."

Levi slides the sunglasses back on. "You have to remove Mr. Adam's work from the gallery and agree not to show it again."

Confusion returns to the owner. "What? Why? Wait. I don't think I can do that," she says.

"Sure you can," Levi responds. "Remove the remaining pictures and don't accept the replacements, and you sell fifteen pieces today. "

Believing she is in a negotiation, the owner says, "But I already have a commitment with Mr. Adams."

Levi says, "I guess you'll have to break it. You also have obligations to these other artists—who, by the way, have much more talent. Not to mention, think of all the future traffic I can push your way." Levi takes out his credit card to close the deal. "Up to you. You can ring it up here or you can leave things the way they are, and I walk out."

The owner reluctantly takes the card and goes behind the counter. "I really wish you would reconsider this unusual request, Mr. Combs."

Through the open garage bay door in front of his work, Gabe walks in carrying two new pictures. He stops when he sees Levi.

Angling toward Gabe, Levi says, "Sorry, my friend. That work will not be needed after all."

"What do you mean?" Gabe looks at the owner. "What's going on?"

Frazzled by the tension, the owner tears the credit card slip from the machine and with shaking hands, extends it toward Levi. "Uh, Mr. Combs, that card has been declined. Do you have another one?"

Gabe moves to the counter in front of the owner, who will not even look at him. "You going to tell me what's going on?"

Levi strolls over next to Gabe and hands the owner another card. She swipes it and waits for the charge to go through, finally addressing Gabe. "Uh, yes. Bit of an awkward situation. You see, Mr. Combs has agreed to buy fifteen other pictures if I don't show your work."

"That's just ludicrous," Gabe says. "And you agreed to it?"

The owner taps her fingers nervously next to the machine. "I'm afraid it would be unfair to the other artists not to."

Gabe stands directly in front of her, not allowing her to hide from the decision. "You mean it would be unfair to the gallery not to."

"I really hope you understand. This is a new gallery. I can't afford to turn away a bulk sale like this and to have a client like Mr. Combs could be a tremendous benefit." The credit card machine buzzes from the printing and spits out the approved receipt. The owner rips it off and hands it to Levi with a pen. She turns back to Gabe. "If it affected only me, I would decline. I have to think about these other artists."

Levi signs and slides the receipt back to her and turns toward Gabe. "Don't fret. I'm sure you can find another gallery. Maybe that owner won't be so easily persuaded."

Gabe looks him up and down. "You're pathetic. You have everything, and I'm just scraping by raising my teenage sister. But none of that matters."

"At least you have your Forbidden Fotos money to fall back on. If all else fails, maybe you should consider working as a paparazzo. You really seem to have a knack for it."

Erupting with rage from all the emotion of the past weeks, Gabe drops the pictures he's carrying and shoves Levi, who after stumbling back a few steps, snickers at the feeble aggression. His derisive amusement further incites Gabe, and he charges and tackles Levi, knocking him out of his sandals. Gabe rolls on top of him. Continuing to laugh, Levi easily throws him off.

The owner chimes in from behind the desk. "Come on. Please stop. This isn't going to solve anything. I'm really sorry. I had no choice."

Gabe spins away and scrambles toward the door. "Whatever. This is fucking bullshit. I hope you can sleep at night, you sellout. You'll get what's coming to you. You're fucking pathetic."

Levi stands up, brushing off his jeans and stepping back into his sandals. He picks up one of the new pictures Gabe had brought with him from the floor. "Don't forget your art on your way out." Gabe shoots out the door, not turning back. Levi sets the picture on the counter. "These artist types are so sensitive, am I right? They just don't get the business side." He looks at the small refrigerator behind the counter. "You wouldn't happen to have any alcohol in there, would you? I think this calls for a celebration."

The owner stands motionless for a moment, then slowly nods. "Of course. Champagne, all right?"

Levi bangs his hand on the counter. "Now we're talking!" The owner doesn't reveal that the same champagne purchased for and served at Gabe's opening is about to be served at his closing. Levi turns to the young female who had been standing off to the side filming the entire encounter on her phone. "Care for some bubbles?"

The girl lowers her phone and stops filming. "Me?" She looks around and not seeing anyone else, flips her auburn hair nervously. "I mean, sure. Why not?"

"Going to need three glasses," Levi says to the owner.

She still puts only two on the bar. "I'm going to let you enjoy this bottle on your own if you don't mind. I have a lot of work to do getting your purchases ready and removing Mr. Adams' work. Also, I have to figure out what I'm going to use to fill the space. You sure I can't persuade you to reconsider your condition?"

"I'm afraid I can't. I'm sure you'll think of something," Levi says, placing his hand on the small of the young lady's back and guiding her to the bar. "What's your name, love?"

"Mara," she says, placing her trembling hands on the edge of the bar to steady herself. "Holy shit. My friends are never going to believe this. Do you care if we take a selfie?"

"Of course not." Levi's hand remains on her back, stroking up and down. The owner pops the champagne and fills the glasses. Levi says, "But here's the thing. I'm going to need you to delete that video and any other pictures from earlier. I'm sure you understand. With all the bad press I've had lately and a new movie coming up, I don't need another unflattering story out there."

"But it wasn't your fault. That guy totally started it," Mara says.

Levi picks up both glasses and hands one to her. "You know that and I know that, but most people will assume the worst. It's best if what they see is you and I having a nice afternoon drinking champagne. Wouldn't you prefer that?"

The owner slides the bottle across the bar. "I'll leave you folks to it. Please feel free to help yourself. I'll be right over here if you need anything else."

Levi keeps his gaze on Mara and just nods his head in response to the owner. Mara stands motionless and silent. His stare captivates her, stifling all movement and sound. "Now let me see your phone." He removes his hand from her back and holds his open palm in front of her. She types in the access code, her hands still shaking, and passes it to him. Levi pulls up the camera files and deletes them one by one. "There that should do it. Now about that selfie." He holds out the phone in front of them and crouches over next to her. "Hold up that champagne and say, 'I love bubbles'" He snaps the photo. "Let's do one more." He steadies the camera in front of them and before pushing the button, he turns and kisses her on the cheek. Her eyes widen with surprise and excitement. "That one should generate some clicks for you." Giving her back the phone, he picks up the bottle from the bar. "Now let's sit down and relax."

They walk over to the sitting area and settle into the small sofa. For the next hour they drink and talk, mostly about Levi, which is his favorite subject, so he's able to maintain interest quite easily. As the level of champagne nears the bottom of the bottle, the owner offers them another. Mara defers to Levi. He declines, dousing her with disappointment. Instantly lifting her back up, he says, "What are your plans this evening? Would you like to continue this party at my place?"

"Um, no. I mean, I have no plans," she stutters, the alcohol unable to quell her racing adrenalin and nerves. "I would love that. Do you want me to follow you? I drove here but I guess I can just leave my car and get it later."

Levi cups his hand over her tanned thigh. "Just ride with me. I'll have a car service bring you back later." They put their empty flutes on the glass table and stride toward the door. The owner wanders over, glistening from the work of removing Gabe's pictures and carrying them one by one to the back. Levi says, "Thanks for the hospitality. Apologies for any drama, but I think you made the right decision."

"What about the delivery of your purchases?" she says.

Levi doesn't falter, talking over his shoulder as they walk out. "I'll be in touch. Just hold them until you hear from me."

Strolling down the sidewalk toward Levi's Bugatti, Mara says, "Holy shit, is that yours? I mean, of course it is. Who else is driving that around here." She yanks her phone out of her back pocket and skips toward the car. "Do you mind?"

Levi reaches in his pocket and unlocks the car with the fob. "Here, give it to me and get behind the wheel." She hurries back, handing him the phone then running to the car, sliding into the driver's seat like easing naked into fifteen-hundred thread-count sheets. He snaps several photos. She lingers in the seat, hoping he might let her drive. Levi says, "Sorry, love. I'm going to have to take it from here. My insurance company would skewer me if I let someone else drive this beast."

CHAPTER 15

Levi completes the hour and a quarter drive with Mara to his house in Malibu in forty minutes. Pulling up to the gate flooded with paparazzi, Mara says, "Do you want me to duck down or cover my face or anything?"

"Not unless you're embarrassed to be seen with me," Levi says, activating the code to open the gate. He navigates through the hyped-up horde, periodically slipping the car into neutral and revving the engine to keep them at bay. But that still doesn't deter the questions.

"How old is this one?"

"Did you check her ID?"

"Do you make her call you daddy?"

Levi clears the gate and watches in his mirror to make sure no one sneaks through. He reaches over and cups her thigh again. Her skin dimples with excitement. He shakes his head, eyes still fixed on the reflection of the closing gate. "Sorry about that. Welcome to my world."

She puts her hand on his. "I don't mind. I'm the one next to you."

Levi opens the garage and parks in the open space next to the Jeep. A BMW 3 series, and an older model Pontiac GTO fill the other two spots. He lifts his hand from her leg and turns his palm up. "I want to keep it that way so I'm going to need your phone from this point on. I'll give it back to you on the way out. I hope you understand."

She picks up the phone from between her legs. "Just let me send a message to the friends I was supposed to meet, so they know where I am." She fires off a short message with the selfie from the gallery and deposits the phone in his hand. "There you go. All yours."

Levi's eyes flip between her and the phone. "Are you talking about you or the phone?"

"Considering the circumstances, I'd say both," Mara says, suddenly calmer and more confident after surrendering all the power to Levi. She no longer has to think about what might transpire, only react to what is happening. Before, he could've ended things at any time. Now he is stuck with her. She accepts whatever consequences come with that because she is on the inside, and the rest of the world is on the outside.

Levi leads her through the garage into the foyer area that immediately opens up into an expansive great room, offering a view of the ocean through the back glass wall across the lawn and over the trees. Levi plucks a remote from a holder on the wall. The glass wall disappears. Sammy Davis Jr. singing "Mr. Bojangles" flows from all directions. A panel slides in the wall revealing a stocked bar. Mara stops in the middle of the room mesmerized by the view. Levi proceeds to the bar. "You want to stay with champagne or switch to something else?"

"I'm going to need something stronger," Mara says. "You got any bourbon?"

"I'm more of a Tennessee-whiskey guy, but let's see what they stock back here." He goes behind the bar. "There's some Jim Beam, Knob Creek, or Makers Mark. No, I know what we'll have. I got this nice bottle of aged single barrel Blanton's that Leo owed me for a bet. If we're going to drink Kentucky urine, we might as well drink the top-notch piss."

While they talk, Sammy belts out, "*I met him in a cell in New Orleans, I was down and out. He looked to me to be the eyes of age as he spoke right out.*"

Mara drifts toward the back of the room, standing on the threshold between inside and out. Closing her eyes, she tries not to react to the casual way he referred to Leo, who will always be the mythic Leonardo DiCaprio to her. "Whatever you think is best."

Levi strolls over with two rocks glasses and the bottle. "You want to sit out—" She doesn't even let him finish the sentence and launches herself at him, suddenly not so comfortable with him having all the power after all. Her arms fly around his neck and her mouth devours his. The two glasses smash on the bamboo floor. He hooks his arms around her back, the bottle of Blanton's still clutched in his right fist. In between slobbering, frantic kisses, he says, "Whoa, whoa, whoa. Slow down. There's no rush. We got all night."

Sammy gives way to Frank Sinatra singing "Something Stupid."

"I'm sorry." She kisses his neck, rubbing her hands through his hair. "I just couldn't wait any longer. It's all just too much. Let's go to your room."

His right arm sweeps under her legs and his left hooks behind her back to scoop her up. Walking up the sweeping staircase to the second level, he says, "You're not afraid of snakes are you?"

"Literal or figurative?" The question is answered for her as he carries her into the room and tosses her on the bed. She scans the vivarium that covers the entire wall, looking for the inhabitant.

Frank croons, "*And then I go and spoil it all by saying something stupid like 'I love you'.*"

"You always listen to jazz? I read somewhere that people with high intelligence like jazz," she rambles nervously.

Levi laughs. "I don't think that applies to me. I'm just researching a role for a Rat Pack movie. Trying to get in character. All jazz, all day. Mostly cocktail and the standards."

She turns toward him, her face aglow. "Wow. The Rat Pack? That's amazing. Which character?"

Walking over to the vivarium, Levi pulls the stopper from the bottle and swigs several mouthfuls of bourbon. "I can tell you it's not Sammy."

Frank continues his serenade. "*I practice every day to find some clever lines to say...*"

She pushes Levi against the chest. "I figured that much, silly. It's probably Dean, isn't it? You're too tall to be Frank."

Levi still doesn't answer her question. "Did you know they didn't refer to themselves as the Rat Pack at all? They called themselves 'the summit' or 'the clan.'"

"It must be one of the guys no one knows," she says. "That's why you won't tell me."

The final lines of the song come through. "*And then I go and spoil it all by saying something stupid like 'I love you'.*"

"Peter Lawford was hardly a nobody," Levi says defensively. "I bet you didn't know he was JFK's brother-in-law. Had four kids with Jack's sister Pat. He was also the one who brought *Ocean's Eleven* to Sinatra, and he was quite the partier too. While at Betty Ford in the eighties, he had a helicopter air-drop cocaine to him. He would go for a walk in the desert, get his package, and come back ready for more therapy. They never even knew. You know how he got busted? His wife saw the helicopter charges on his credit card bill. Now that's a player."

"Geez. So sensitive," Mara says, pushing him again playfully. "I was only joking. I'm sure you'll be great."

"Mink Schmink" by Eartha Kitt plays next.

Levi turns toward the vivarium and taps on the glass. "My girl sleeps most of the day inside that log but she'll probably come out at some point."

Mara crouches down to look for her. "Is she dangerous?"

"Aren't all females?" Levi drinks again from the bottle and passes it to her, winking. "Nah, she's really a pussycat. I let her out all the time."

Eartha sings, "*Mink, schmink, money, schmoney. Think your hot now don't ya honey...*"

"That's so cool." Mara gulps some of the bourbon, studying the markings on the snake's back visible through one of the holes in the hollowed-out log. "It's a girl? She's beautiful. What's her name?"

"Hannah." He taps again on the glass. "Wake up, sleepy head. Come out and say 'hi.'" Hannah sticks her iridescent blackish-brown head and neck out of the log and slithers toward them. "That's my girl." She rolls on her back, revealing the smooth underside of her cream-colored throat.

"*Silk, schmilk, satin, schmatin. A penthouse high in old Manhattan. That's not enough if haven't got love.*"

"God, she's fucking amazing." Mara turns to Levi, pushing him back onto the bed. She sets the bottle on the nightstand and kicks off her sandals, climbing up and straddling him. She unbuttons his pants. Her nervousness forces out unnecessary and brusque words. "I'm warning you though. I'm so wet right now. It's a hurricane down there. Just being here. Watching Hannah. I always wanted a pet snake." She lifts her shirt, revealing the tattoo of a snake twisted and coiled along her right side. "I had to settle for this one."

Levi pulls her shirt the rest of the way off, tracing his finger along the body of the snake. "I like yours too." He drops down and drags his lips over the tattoo, stopping where it disappears into her shorts. She unfastens her embroidered turquoise bra and tosses it on the floor next to her shirt. Levi rolls her off him onto her back. "Do you trust me?"

"At this point, I don't have much choice, do I?" She unbuttons her shorts and wiggles out of them, leaving on her matching sheer thong.

"*Pearls, schmearls, ermine, shmermen. From Jim or Jack or Joe or Herman. That's not enough if you haven't got love.*"

Levi stands and peels off his shirt and drops his pants, which are his final layer. She sits up crawling toward him. He pushes her back. "Not yet. I want to try something. Lie on your back in the middle of the bed." He opens the drawer to his nightstand and pulls out four ropes with slipknots in both ends.

"Seems like you try this quite often," Mara says, remaining in the middle of the bed.

"*Ring, schming, jewelry, schmellery. Don't you know that's just Tom Foolery? What have you got if you haven't got love?*"

"This isn't the new part." He loops one of the ends around her right wrist then runs the rope around the corner of the bed frame and tightens the other end around her wrist again. "If this gets to be too much at any time, just say something, and I'll stop." He moves down and anchors her right leg the same way then her left ankle and other wrist.

Mara stretches her arms and legs testing the ropes. "What should I say? You mean like a safe word, right?"

He holds the end of the bottle over her mouth. "You want a drink?" She nods, her eyes wide with excitement. He pours a few drops on her lips. She cranes her neck forward wanting more. He tilts the bottle, filling her mouth.

She gulps it down. "More, please."

"*Cars, schmars and princes, schminces. With caviar and chicken blintzes. Don't mean a thing if you haven't got love.*"

"Say whatever you want. I don't think it matters as long as it's not 'harder' or 'tighter.'" He dumps more bourbon on her, missing her mouth onto her chin and neck and down her chest to her stomach. He licks it off working his way down to her waist.

She sucks in a full breath, expanding her chest. "Yeah, baby. Right there." Her stomach quivers as she slowly exhales. "How about 'pelican'? If I say 'pelican' you have to stop immediately."

"Pelican it is." He runs his finger under the waistband of her panties. Unable to slide them off with her legs anchored, he says, "I guess I didn't think this through." He sets the bottle on the nightstand and kneels between her spread legs. She adducts her thighs as far as the ropes will allow trying to wrap around him. He hooks his fingers under the waistband on the side of her hips, and with a single, quick tug, he rips them off.

She shrieks, writhing and grinding her hips into the bed. "Come on, come on, come on. I can't take this. I need you inside me."

"*Love is just a simple thing that you can't buy. You can't get it wholesale, darlin', why try?*"

Levi crawls over top of her on all fours, careful not to touch her anywhere. She wiggles her body side-to-side yearning for contact. He shakes his head. "Not yet. You're going to have to wait." He rolls over off the bed.

"*Tips, schmips, angle, schmangle. Play around and get entangled. What have you got, if you haven't got love?*"

She kicks and pulls trying to grab at him. "Where are you going? Don't leave me here. Not like this."

"I'm not going anywhere." He walks over to the vivarium and opens the door. "I think Hannah wants to join us." He reaches his right arm inside. Hannah slithers toward him and climbs up his arm, over his shoulders, and down his left side. "That's a good baby. Such a pretty girl." He strokes his hand along her dorsal scales. "I have someone I want you to meet." He crawls up on the bed. "Hannah, this is Mara. She wants to play with us."

Mara squirms away as far as she can go. "Levi, are you sure about this? Have you ever done this?"

He guides Hannah onto the bed. "I let her out all the time. She loves coming up on the bed with me." Hannah crawls along the side of Mara toward her head.

"No, I mean during sex." She tugs at the ropes trying to move away. "I don't think this is a good idea. Do snakes get jealous? What if she sees me as a threat?"

Hannah's tongue flits in and out as she approaches Mara's arm. Levi says, "Nothing to worry about. She's a total lover. Just don't act afraid. It might spook her." He climbs on top of Mara, kissing her, rubbing his hands along her arms up to her hands. "Forget she's even here." Hannah crawls over their arms and circles around their heads. "Just close your eyes." He reaches down and pushes inside her. "Just remember, 'pelican,' if it's too much."

Mara whimpers, her body shuddering, then tensing. She responds with a passionate kiss. "Deeper. I want to feel all of you." She thrusts her hips off the bed into him.

Hannah curls around their heads and glides over Levi's right shoulder onto his back and down his body. He arches his back, bracing himself up with his arms. Mara's eyes remain closed. Levi groans in pleasure as Hannah slithers across his ass onto the bed between his legs. He drives his hips harder, faster.

A restrained yelp escapes from Mara. She bites her lip and growls. "Oh God. I want to scream, but I'm afraid. Where is she? What is she doing?"

Levi looks over his shoulder down his back. "She's between our legs by your right foot. Wait for it. She's almost there." Hannah crawls across Mara's ankle and up along her leg. "Feel her?" Hannah continues along Mara's body rubbing against the tattoo up to her armpit." Levi slams into Mara harder. She cries out. "I can't hold it." Mara opens her eyes and sees Hannah only inches away. "Stop! I can't take it anymore. Pelican! Pelican! Stop!"

Levi doesn't stop. He follows through with three more long, deep strokes, his body tensing, tightening, holding, then relaxing. He crumbles in a heap on top of her, both of them gasping and writhing. Hannah stays pressed tightly against them. Levi laughs. "Best threesome ever. I think she likes you."

"That was so amazing. I can't believe we did that. Get up. Untie me. I need to move around. I can't lie here anymore."

Levi rolls off Mara away from Hannah, who takes it as an invitation to replace him and crawls across Mara's chest. He says, "Yep. She definitely likes you."

Mara pulls at the ropes. "Just hurry up and untie me."

Levi scoops up Hannah and carries her back to the vivarium. "Was that fun, baby? You like that huh?" He lowers her inside. She immediately crawls to the small pond. Levi goes back to the bed. "Hannah's got the right idea. Let's go for a swim." He unties Mara's right arm then moves down to her right ankle.

Mara uses her free hand to undo the rope from her left wrist. "That sounds perfect. My whole body's tingling." She frees her left ankle and slides off the bed, shaking her arms and legs.

Levi walks over and kisses her. "You know what they say, once you go snake, the rest is all fake."

CHAPTER 16

MARCUS DRIVES NORTH ON the PCH toward Malibu. His phone buzzes on the seat next to him. He picks it up and swipes his thumb across the screen to read the new alert. Another ocean-view picture at Nobu Malibu pops up from Emily James's social media account. The alerts had been coming for the past hour, prompting him to drive there for an unofficial visit without her agent or lawyer present. Based on the stream of photos and videos, she and two girlfriends are enjoying a late breakfast on the deck. He hadn't seen any pictures of the food yet, which are always part of the ritual that seems to happen at least once a day since he has started following her account. If it wasn't her posting, it was one of her friends or a fan tagging her in a picture. Marcus pretty much knew exactly what Emily was doing and where from morning to night. Today, no food yet means he still has time to catch her.

At the restaurant, Marcus avoids the valet lane and parks in a spot far from the front just in case he needs to leave in a hurry. As he walks through the parking lot, he reaches in his pocket and cups his hand around his badge to have it ready if he needs to get by a staunch maître d' or manager. He's dealt with them before. They'll do anything to protect their celebrity business. They know if the celebs come, the tourist dollars will follow.

Marcus breathes a sigh of relief, seeing a young girl alone at the hostess stand. He flashes the badge and breezes by, not even letting her ask whether he has a reservation. He slides the badge back in his pocket and pulls up the last picture from Emily on his phone, an open-air shot on the deck. He weaves through the restaurant, matching the picture on his phone to the view into front of him to locate the table. The retractable doors surrounding the bar are open on this temperate sun-soaked morning. He angles to the patio and spots Emily and her friends in the left corner.

A mother and teenage daughter crouch behind the cushioned wicker loveseat Emily is sitting on. Emily holds up a phone and snaps a selfie of the three of them and hands it to the mother, who shows it to the daughter as they bounce back to their table. Emily's friends sit on a similar two-person couch across from her. A waiter places the last dish from his tray onto the two teak square tables pushed together between them. Her friends, one with a black, braided ponytail swept around to the front, and the other with a side down-do with long, wispy auburn curls snap pictures of the colored assortment of fresh fish on the table.

Marcus walks to the table. The girls look up at him. Wispy Curls rolls her eyes at Emily. "Another one? Seriously, Em, you have to really think about getting security."

Emily, chopsticks balanced between her fingers, points at Marcus. "Let me guess. For your daughter? No, you're not married. Must be your niece." She holds out her other hand, not even listening for the response. "Just let me know who to make it out to." She looks back at her friends. "Last one, girls. I promise."

Braided Ponytail says, "A star's work is never done. I don't know how you live like this."

Marcus pulls his badge out, extending it toward Emily's lingering hand. "I've got a tip for you: Don't post to social media every two minutes and you might have some privacy."

Seeing the badge, Emily recoils her arm and focuses back on the food. "How can I help you, detective?" She snares a piece of salmon and pops it into her mouth.

"I'm not with the police," Marcus says, watching the other girls squirm while Emily remains calm and resolute. "I'm with the attorney's office. Sex Crimes Division."

"God, please tell me you caught that perv who sent me the jar of his pubic hair," Emily says.

Wispy Curls drops the piece of fatty tuna she was about to eat back on her plate and feigns gagging. "Please, Em, tell me you're joking."

Emily shakes her head. "A whole mayonnaise jar full."

"Ew, he really used a mayonnaise jar?" Braided Ponytail says. "Hopefully there wasn't any of his mayo in there." All three girls break out laughing.

Wispy Curls says, "What an idiot. Couldn't they just look him up based on his DNA?"

"Actually, no," Emily says, completely forgetting about Marcus and rambling on. "The police said that there wasn't a match in the computer. If they catch him, they could use it to prove it was him once they have a sample of his DNA, but until someone is in the system, there's nothing they can match it to."

The waiter comes to the table and stands next to Marcus, reminding the girls that Marcus is even there. The waiter says, "How is everything? Anything else I can get for you?"

"Sooo good," Emily says. She looks to her friends. "Ladies?"

Wispy Curls drains the rest of her drink. "I'd love another one of these acai punches."

"Coconut water for me," Braided Ponytail says and plucks a piece of unagi from a plate.

The waiter acknowledges the requests and departs. Emily slurps miso soup directly from the bowl. Marcus uses the temporary engagement of her lips to finally use his own. "The real reason I'm here is about the pictures that have surfaced of you with Levi Combs." Emily slurps louder from the bowl. Marcus elevates his tone. "The district attorney is contemplating pressing charges against Mr. Combs for his predatory actions. We're wondering if you will be part of our case."

The previous incessant activity at the table ceases. The other girls stare at Emily waiting for a response. The sudden awkward moment does not affect Emily. She remains placid, slowly lowering the bowl to the table. She picks up the white linen napkin and pats the residual broth from her upper lip. Finally looking at Marcus for the first time since he walked up, she says, "I'm sorry. What was your name again? You don't happen to have a card, do you? I'm sure you understand. I get approached by a lot of people."

"Of course." Marcus pops two fingers in his breast pocket and pulls one out, offering it to Emily. "Feel free to look me up online."

Emily glances at the card and passes it over to Wispy Curls. "Check him out for me, will ya?" Wispy Curls sets the card on the table and picks up her phone, reading the text while furiously typing with her thumbs. Emily sinks back into the cushions, peering up at Marcus. "Since I doubt you just happen to be here at Nobu having brunch, I'm going to assume you did some homework to know I was here."

Wispy Curls holds up her phone toward Marcus. Braided Ponytail leans over, and they both examine the screen and Marcus. Wispy Curls says, "It's him." She lowers her voice and speaks in a slow, serious tone. "Deputy District Attorney Marcus Ambrose." The girls giggle, pausing to exchange looks of feigned fear. Each impression elicits greater amusement, which causes a more histrionic expression than the one before, eventually resulting in rolling laughter from all three.

Marcus rubs his head from forward to back, realizing he made a mistake. While Emily has years of more work experience than him, around her girlfriends, she regresses back to the adolescent she is. Marcus elevates his voice to be heard over the laughter, which is finally waning. "I'm sorry for interrupting your meal. You have my card if you think of anything that might be useful to our investigation."

Emily sits up and slides to the edge of the loveseat, leaning toward Marcus. The teenage girl who was here just seconds ago disappears as quickly as she had come. The flintiness of her face follows down to the rest of her body. Her girlfriends recognize the change in her and fall back into their seat. Emily says, "As I was saying, if you researched to know I was here, then you also know that I have nothing more to say about those pictures that hasn't already been said. Levi and I were out hiking and went for a swim." Her steely stare holds everyone in place. Even the waiter, who was approaching the table for another check-in, stops a safe distance away. Emily says, "I will keep your card though and be sure to pass it along to my lawyer. I'm sure she'll reach out to your boss. They do belong to the same country club. She can inquire why one of his deputies was out at Nobu in Malibu in the middle of the morning asking a teenage girl for a statement on a matter that is not even an open investigation." She turns back to her girlfriends, instantly changing back to the rollicking girl of moments ago. Her friends follow her lead and resume their roles in the farce. The waiter continues his course to the table.

Marcus steps away and slinks back through the dining room. As good as he felt after his visit to Eva's office, he knows he bombed this one. He leaves the restaurant and shuffles through the parking lot to his car. He expected it to be easier because she was young, that she would be intimidated by his position. But she was stoic and controlled during the exchange and not affected at all. Regardless, he had just learned directly why Emily James is a star and what so many people who have worked with her in the past have discovered: the feeling of being upstaged.

◆◆◆

A BLACK MERCEDES SEDAN with tinted windows slows, approaching the Million Dollar Theater on Broadway. The flashing and glowing marquis protrudes from the Spanish Colonial Revival façade. The bursts of Churrigueresque decoration, statues, and longhorn skulls loom above from the historic twelve-story movie theater built in 1918.

Black lettering on the marquis spells out *Wrongside Right Starring Levi Combs* in two lines against the backlit display. Levi slides over in the seat, looking at the sparse crowd milling around on the sidewalk. He had longed to have a premiere here because of its history. It was one of the first movie palaces in the country and the northernmost in this Broadway Theater District. He became obsessed with this area when he first moved to LA. The theater had once been the second run of the vaudeville Orpheum Circuit, a stage for acts like the Nat King Cole Trio and The Honey Drippers, and the mecca for Spanish language entertainment during another run. One of his earliest photo shoots was at the Bradbury Building, the oldest landmarked building in LA, across the street. It was a dystopian cologne ad, which really didn't make any sense at all to him. He thought if things got as bad as they were portrayed in the ad, no one would care how they smelled. Levi spots Eva fidgeting with her phone, talking to a reporter in front of the theater. A photographer stands close by repeatedly looking at his watch. Spectators sprinkle the barricade, not even two-deep at any point.

The driver angles the car toward the curb. Levi leans toward the front. "Don't stop. Let's go around the block and allow more people to arrive." The driver accelerates back into traffic, driving up Broadway. Levi just stares out the window. Coming back to where he started was supposed to show how far he had come. Instead he is looking like all the other fading lights that had passed through here trying to reclaim their former brilliance. The driver turns on Sixth and loops back up Main to Third passing by the Bradbury again. Levi bends toward the front seat, looking through the windshield at the crowd in front of the theater, which appears to have diminished even more in the ten minutes it took them to circle the block.

The driver slows at the intersection. "Want me to keep going or stop?"

Levi flops back in the seat. "Fuck it. Just drop me off."

The driver flips on the turn signal and guides the car to the curb. Eva takes notice of the vehicle, recognizing it from the first time around since she had arranged it. Levi pushes the door open and exits onto the red carpet amidst a few cheers drowned out by boos.

Eva approaches, speaking through a pained smile. "Nice to see you could make it."

"Where is everyone?" Levi asks, looking around and waving to the imaginary legion of fans expected to assemble but who never showed.

Eva takes his arm and leads him toward a reporter waiting by the box office window underneath the marquis. "A lot of cancellations and even more no-shows. But you would know that if you had returned my calls."

"Why, so you could nag me about the other shit? No thanks."

"I don't need to say anything. Look at the results of your work over the past few weeks." Eva steps to the side, opening her hand toward the reporter. "Go ahead. Your public, all one of them, awaits."

Levi walks up to the reporter, who nods at the cameraman. Bright light washes over her and Levi. The reporter says, "I'm downtown at the famous Million Dollar Theater with Levi Combs for the opening of his new movie *Wrongside Right*. Levi, what do you think about the turnout?"

Levi scans the surrounding area. "I think someone printed the wrong date on the invitation."

The reporter smiles at the attempted humor. "You're one of the producers and main financial backers on this film. Are you at all worried about your investment?"

Levi says, "I think over time the quality of the work will speak for itself and the financial return will come."

"That will require people to see it," the reporter jabs.

Levi glares at her but recovers, nodding and grinning in her direction. He knows he can't afford another confrontation. "Let's wait until the weekend is over to discuss the numbers."

The reporter asks, "Do you think your recent actions are the cause of the poor showing? I mean you did just win an Oscar. That alone should fill the seats."

Levi narrows his stare, growing impatient with the probing questions. "Is there anything you want to ask about the film? I mean, that is why we're here."

"Is it true you were behind the attack on the photographer who released the pictures of you and Emily James?"

Levi feigns surprise. "No idea what you're talking about. But I just want to say that I think people will really enjoy the positive message in this film. Thanks for coming. I think we're getting ready to start." He moves toward one of the other actors in the film laughing and chatting with another reporter by the door.

Eva remains off to the side, becoming more concerned watching Levi flounder. They have come so far and are falling so fast. She thinks about all of the time and money she has invested just to get to this point, and how he has wiped it away in just a few weeks. She remembers the opening weekend of his first leading role. So much has changed since then—professionally and personally. At that time, she thought their relationship could actually be more than business.

It was a Sunday evening. Their first big movie had been released that Friday. The numbers had been trickling in all weekend, teasing them with good news. Leading into Saturday, the movie had been slightly ahead of a Ryan Gosling and Emma Stone romantic comedy in the box office but had dropped to second heading into Sunday. At $52 million, the movie revenues had already exceeded the costs, so that meant Levi would be viewed as a bankable star and other opportunities would come. But winning the weekend would enable Eva to demand an even greater price the next time. The $250 thousand she had secured for Levi was his largest payday so far, but it was the two and a half percent on the backend she had been able to negotiate that would put them over the top. A $65–70 million opening weekend would mean $150 to $200 million was a realistic possibility in the coming year. Working together, they had done well to get by financially, never having to work other jobs like most starting out in the business, and they had been able to increase their earnings every year. Of course Levi never saved any of it. Like so many with a sudden influx of disposable income and a lot of free time on their hands, he had spent his increased income on clothes, jewelry, and cars. Eva poured most of her money back into the business and a nicer place to live. She still wasn't making enough money to justify a separate office location, but that would change with this payday.

Knowing they would both be sweating the outcome, Eva invited Levi over to her loft at the Roosevelt Building. The rent at thirty-five hundred per month was more than she could afford, but it was her office as well, so she could write off the festivities for the evening. She peeled off the foil and untwisted the wire that encased the top of their third bottle of Armand de Brignac champagne. The cork popped prematurely, startling them both. As much as they had already consumed, the only surprise should've been that they were feeling anything at all.

Champagne spilled from the top and ran down the side of the bottle, streaming onto the floor. The gold metallic bottle with the distinctive pewter ace of spades logo glistened in the track lighting shining down from the vaulted ceilings. She picked up a napkin next to the untouched cheese and charcuterie spread on the glass coffee table. She thought it would balance out the drinking, but the stress and uncertainty of the evening was more conducive to alcohol than soppressata and aged Gouda.

Seeing the spilling champagne, Levi rushed over. "Stop! Don't waste it." He took the bottle and licked up the side. "This stuff is too good."

Eva's phone vibrated on the table. She picked it up and read the message. Looking up at Levi, her eyes danced with excitement. She tossed the phone on the couch and snatched the bottle from Levi. "The day's numbers are coming in. We hit seventy-two million." She covered the mouth of the bottle with her thumb and shook, spraying the three-hundred-dollar champagne all over Levi. "Eight million ahead of Gosling." She shot more champagne on Levi. "We did it, Levi. We're going to win the weekend." He grabbed the bottle and turned it upside down over her head. The bubbles foamed in her thick, black hair and streamed down her face. She pushed his arms up. "What are you doing? Stop!" The champagne spilled over both of them and onto the table.

"Fuck it," Levi said. "We can afford it." He shook the last drops from the bottle. Her arms, slippery from the champagne, slid across his, and she fell against his chest. He dropped the bottle and wrapped his arms around her as the bottle bounced and clanked on the polished concrete floor and rolled underneath the coffee table. Their laughing and excitement faded to silence. She stayed pressed against him, securing her arms around his waist. He lifted his hand, stroking the back of her head. She stared up at him. Seconds passed, each of them waiting for the other to act. He bent down and kissed her forehead, tasting the drops of champagne beaded on her skin. She tilted her head back further and drew his lips down to hers.

In that first kiss, all the tension, fear, and struggling of the past five years ignited. Neither of them hesitated or resisted. They succumbed to the emotion and the consequences of their indulgence. The effort, the risk, and the faith in one another compounded into a solitary, all-encompassing passion that burned around them, and most of all, through them. Their mouths consumed one another. Levi reached down, pawing at her tight, black leather pencil skirt. She reached around and pulled down the zipper in the back. The skirt wilted to the floor, revealing only bare skin. Lifting one foot, she kicked the skirt off, leaving on her black, chunky-heeled ankle boots.

Levi placed his hand on the small of her back, pulling her close. She hooked one leg around him, hopped up, and interlocked her other leg to lift her up. His arms slid underneath her, supporting her full weight, maintaining their embrace. He walked over to the window and lifted her onto the granite sill. Her body shuddered from the smooth, cool surface. Levi pulled back and kicked off his loafers. She leaned back against the windows and admired the beauty she had discovered and was about to experience. He unbuckled his belt and frantically shed his pants, almost toppling himself in his haste.

Eva followed his lead and stripped off her sleeveless top and lace bra. She then removed Levi's shirt and swung her legs around him, driving the heels, which was all she was wearing at that point, into his backside as she yanked him toward her. Their hot skin melted together. He pulled her hair back, exposing her neck. His lips moved from one side to the other. Her head writhed, twisting her entire body. The cold window on her lower back and bottom contrasted the heat between them. She reached down and guided him toward her. He lowered his hand, feeling for the opening and plunged inside her, lifting her off the windowsill onto him.

She kicked the thick heels into his hamstrings wanting more. "Deeper," she moaned and closed her eyes.

Levi bent his legs, rotating his hips in quick, forceful thrusts.

"More," she said. "I want to feel all of you."

Levi pushed harder, growling with pleasure. "God, I've wanted to do this since I met you."

"Yeah?" she whispered. "Don't stop. Harder." She dropped her legs to the floor and spun around, reaching behind to find him. Once he was again inside her, she bent over and worked backward, using her hands on the window for leverage. Her sweaty palms fogged the area around her hands.

Levi planted his palm in the middle of her back and pushed her forward. She arched her spine, embracing the cool window on her sweaty chest and face. He grunted as he slammed into her. "You feel amazing."

She just kept repeating three words. "More. Harder. Deeper."

Levi attempted to accommodate, but it wasn't enough to sate her demonstrative mantra. He lifted his left leg up on the window ledge to open up his hips and deepen the stroke.

Eva moaned approvingly, bending down at the waist and pushing further back into him. She reached up and wrapped her hand around his ankle, now by her ear. Digging her nails in, she pushed and pulled, using his ankle to steady herself and synchronize with his movements, both encouraging each other with the same affirmative word over and over as their pace and breathing quickened until their bodies simultaneously tightened and shuddered, convulsing and dropping to the floor in a heap of exhaustion and satisfaction.

They lay on the cold concrete floor in silence. As their heart rates lowered and body temperatures decreased, they pressed closer to one another for warmth and comfort. Eva eventually climbed on top of him and started again. They would finish there and one more time in the bedroom before falling asleep, her shoulder nestled into his armpit with her head resting on his chest. No words or questions about what had happened or why were spoken as they drifted off.

When the light of day brought the exposure and responsibility of their actions, Levi slid out of bed, quietly got dressed, and slipped out the door. Eva was awake but pretended to sleep. She just lay quiet, listening to his movements, still able to smell him on her and feel him next to her, inside of her. In that moment, she no longer wanted more. She had finally had enough.

◆◆◆

AT HIS DESK, MARCUS reads the recap of Levi's failed premiere on his computer with satisfaction. Consumed by the article, he doesn't notice the head deputy's assistant walk up beside him. She clears her throat. "I don't know what you did, but it's not good."

Marcus rotates in his chair and slides back to create space between them. "Why, what happened?"

"Don't know the full story, but you need to come with me right now." She waves her hand and moves toward the head deputy's office. "The mayor called. Doesn't seem good."

Marcus rises and fetches his suit jacket from the chair next to his desk. "Hang on. Let me get my coat."

Not stopping, she says, "Unless it's bulletproof, I wouldn't worry about it."

Marcus picks up his pace, putting on the jacket and catching up alongside her at the same time. "That bad, huh?"

"The mayor barely even let him finish his sentences. Last thing the head deputy said was, 'Don't worry, sir, I'll take care of it.'"

They arrive at the office door. The assistant steps to the side, yielding for Marcus to proceed. "You're on your own. Good luck."

Marcus straightens his body and strides in. "You wanted to see me, head deputy?"

"Close the door behind you." He stands and walks out from behind the desk. All the years Marcus has been working for him, he's never been in a closed-door session. He knows others who have. Those visits usually followed with a few empty cardboard boxes and a security escort to the parking garage. The head deputy waits for the door to latch before continuing. "I thought I made myself clear." His voice escalates in sound and intensity. "You were not supposed to talk to any of the parties until you had something. I mean, what were you thinking? Ambushing a seventeen-year-old girl in a public place with no legal representation?"

"But, sir—"

The head deputy roils across the room, passing on the reprimand he had just received. "Do you know how bad this makes us look? Emily James' lawyer, who happens to be a close personal friend and major contributor to the mayor's reelection campaign, is threatening to sue for harassment." Marcus remains quiet, just nodding, waiting for the head deputy to run out of steam, which, based on his ire, could take awhile. "What part of, 'It's an election year. Make sure you have something' didn't you understand? And then you told her that you found her through her online posts? Our office now has nothing better to do than stalk celebrities through social media?" The head deputy pauses. Marcus doesn't respond, thinking the questions are rhetorical. "Well," the head deputy says, "Don't just stand there. Tell me why I shouldn't fire you like the mayor wants me to?"

"Sir, I did, I mean I do have something. The sister of the photographer called me. She confirmed there are more photos and that there was definitely sexual intercourse. With those pics, I thought if I could get Emily as a witness, it would be a slam dunk."

The head deputy relaxes hearing the new information. "You have these pictures?"

"Not yet, but—"

The momentary calm passes. The head deputy launches another assault. "You better get them. If we don't have enough to file charges in the next week, I have no choice but to—"

Marcus interrupts him this time, not needing to hear anymore to understand what is at stake. "Don't worry, sir. I understand. I just need to get a warrant for Levi Combs' agent's office. That's who has the pictures."

"If that's the case, use Judge Romans," the head deputy says. "She'll be most supportive and won't care about the political implications."

Marcus nods. "Yes, sir. I'll get right on it. Thank you, sir."

CHAPTER 17

G ABE WALKS UP THE driveway toward their house. Abbie's car occupies the middle, filling both spaces. The neighbor boy shoots baskets next door, combatting the waning daylight.

Emily approaches from the shadows. "Mr. Adams?"

Gabe, distracted watching the boy make a long shot, hadn't noticed her. He looks again, still not recognizing her. "I assume you're here to see Abbie." He motions toward the house.

Emily says, "Actually, I'm here to see you."

Their approach activates the floodlight. Gabe recognizes Emily in the added light. "Oh, Ms. James. I'm sorry. I didn't know that was you. My sister is around the same age. Thought you were a friend of hers. Let's go around back to my studio." Gabe leads Emily around the side of the garage to the back door.

Emily says, "I was hoping to talk to you about the pictures you took."

Gabe unlocks the door and reaches in to turn on the light. The two rows of long fluorescent bulbs buzz above while warming. He says, "There's really not much to talk about."

Emily walks over to three framed pictures leaning against the wall. Gabe puts his camera bag on the desk. Facing away from him, Emily studies the pictures. "I think you have the wrong idea about what was going on between Levi and me."

Gabe talks to her back as she examines the pictures. "No, it was pretty clear."

Emily turns and faces him. "I mean why it was happening."

"I don't really care about why or any of it really," Gabe says. "It's not like I'm doing anything about it. It's really out of my hands. I just know that any action taken will be for your own good."

Emily walks toward Gabe. "How is hurting my career and his for my own good?"

Gabe moves to keep the large rectangular worktable between them. "It's really not up to me. The DA has taken up the matter. You're best to direct your questions to his office."

"I don't know about that. I think you have more influence than you realize," Emily says, moving around the edge of the table toward him. "Just say the pictures are misleading and that Levi and I were just swimming from what you could tell."

Gabe slides to his left mirroring her movement to keep distance between them. "But that's not true. You and I both know it."

"Are you listening to yourself?" Emily asks, elevating her tone. "Stop living in fantasyland. Reality is the story we tell."

"Why should I lie and have this blowing back on me? Nothing will happen to you. You're a minor. They'll go after Levi."

"But they shouldn't. I knew exactly what I was doing." Emily leans on the table, pushing her breasts toward Gabe. "I'm not a little girl. You grow up fast in this business. It's not like it was my first time."

For once, Emily was telling the truth. She was barely a teenager her first time, and it was all by her own doing. She had determined when it would happen and had carefully chosen with whom. *Funwalla* had been on air for two years and was an instant success, which pretty much allowed her to do anything she wanted. The show was making so much money, the studio didn't care, and her parents surely didn't either. It had already gotten them a new house and new cars and new jobs as her managers, which as parents, they should've been fulfilling already, but this paid way better than their obligatory domestic roles, and it wasn't that difficult either. All they had to say was yes or no to opportunities. Almost always the answer was yes. Work always came first, and Emily was happy to oblige. She dropped out of school and instead had a tutor come in five days a week in the mornings. She had tried to stay in school at first, but it became too much of a disruption for her. Everyone was better off if she stayed as close to the set as possible.

The day she had chosen for her big day was the final day of shooting for the holiday special. They were wrapping midday on the Wednesday before Thanksgiving and shutting down production for the holidays until the second week of January. With the planned party, she knew HE would be there, and it would be chaotic. No one would notice if the two of them slipped away. Even though she had her own dressing room, she was rarely alone in it. It was either hair and makeup, running lines with castmates, schooling with her tutor, or her parents pestering about some appearance or opportunity to further her career. The latter she had taken care of by getting them tickets to the Jolie-Pitt Foundation holiday charity luncheon to raise money. She knew her parents would never miss a chance to network with the elite powerbrokers that would surely be in attendance.

The he in the plan was Caleb, the cable wrangler on *Funwalla*. He was the assistant to the boom operator responsible for moving and preparing sound equipment on the set. Only twenty-five, he had graduated from UCLA film school three years prior and was working his way up, finally starting to see some progress after nothing but gopher jobs the first few years. Emily wasn't totally sure he would go for her, but she did always catch him staring. She was the star, so people were always watching her, but with him it was different. It was how he looked at her, and that when she caught him, his eyes didn't divert. Most people, the second her eyes met theirs, they looked away. His lingering stare tickled something inside her. She knew it was more than a crush. She had gotten over those years ago. Crushes were for little girls. It was time for her to become a woman.

Like most things with Emily, it was more of a conquest, a mission to complete. When she got something in her head, it was going to happen, one way or the other. No was not an answer she heard very often, and when she did, she didn't accept it. Another advantage of making her move on the last day of shooting was that if it didn't work out, she wouldn't have to see him for almost six weeks, plenty of time for both of them to forget, or for her to have him fired.

Although it was supposed to be a dry set since so many of the cast were under twenty-one, the majority of the staff were not, so there was always alcohol around at the parties. It was just concealed, furtively poured in white paper cups with whatever liquid was supposedly being consumed.

Emily waited until Caleb's third trip back to the prop closet, which was where all the liquor was hidden. She intercepted him before he made it to the group of grips and gaffers regaling tales from previous jobs. "Hey, Caleb. You got a second?"

Even though she said his name, he looked around to see if there was someone else she was talking to. "Me?"

She sauntered up, stopping in front of him. "Of course, silly. Do you see another Caleb?"

The rosiness in his cheeks from the alcohol spread to the rest of his face. "I guess I'm just surprised. I didn't realize you even knew my name."

She touched his forearm, caressing gently. "Of course I do. Like your boss says, it takes teamwork to make the dream work."

He flopped his head forward, shaking it back and forth. "Ugh, don't quote him. I hear his damn sayings in my sleep."

"So, like, I know you're technically off-duty and stuff." She rocked back and forth on her heels nervously. "But I was hoping you could come into my dressing room and have a look at my sound system. It seems like one of my speakers is not working. I mean, it can probably wait until after break, but I was hoping to get it fixed before, just in case I'm here working over the holidays."

Caleb looked over at his collection of cronies to check if anyone noticed him chatting with the princess, which was what they referred to her as. From their preoccupation with one another, it didn't appear to him that any of them had even noticed he had stepped away. He said, "I guess I can take a quick look. That way if we need some new parts, we can order them, and they'll be here when we get back." He glanced again at the others then turned back to Emily. "Lead the way."

Walking back to her dressing room, Emily, for the first time since season one, which was almost sixty episodes ago, felt nervous. The flutter inside her in his presence warmed her skin, and she became self-conscious about her steps, forcing her to concentrate putting one foot in front of the other. She loved the excitement and uneasiness swelling inside her.

Entering her dressing room, she closed the door and subtly locked it behind her. She thought being alone with him, away from the others would make things better, but it didn't. The heat on her skin transformed to sweat. She angled to the thermostat. "Geez, it's hot in here. I hate when the cleaning crew turns up the heat."

Caleb went straight to the receiver on the cabinet next to her desk and checked the wires in the back. "Everything looks fine here. Might be one of the speaker connections. Why don't you play some music and show me what the problem is?"

Emily slid the cord into her phone and cued up Miley Cyrus' "We Can't Stop".

The low voice of the intro boomed. *"It's our party we can do what we want."*

Caleb put his hand on the subwoofer on the floor next to the cabinet. "Bass seems to be working." He walked around the room listening to each of the five cube speakers mounted on the wall.

"It's that one in the corner." Emily pointed across the room and turned up the volume. The speaker crackled as the sound cut in and out. "Hear that?"

Caleb drifted in that direction, navigating through the collection of electric blue beanbag chairs covered with stuffed animals filling the corner underneath the speaker. He tilted his ear toward the speaker. "Sounds like you got a short or maybe just a loose connection." He looked around for something to stand on.

Emily pulled over the bench from her makeup table. "Here. Use this." Creating a path, she kicked the beanbags against the wall, sending the stuffed animals tumbling in all directions. "I used to collect these stupid things, so people always got them for me as gifts. Still do. Kind of ridiculous, huh?"

The chorus bellowed from the surrounding speakers. *"We can kiss who we want. We can sing what we want."*

Caleb took the bench from Emily and angled it in the corner. "Nah, it's pretty cute, actually. My older sister collected stuffed animals. Kept them over the years and gave them all to her daughter." He stepped up on the bench and stretched toward the speaker. "You should do that."

"I'm never having kids." Emily held her hand on the side of his thigh to steady him on the bench. "Be careful. I don't want you to fall."

Caleb looked down at her and all the beanbags and stuffed animals scattered around on the floor. "Looks like a pretty soft landing if I do." Emily kept her hand on his leg anyway. He reached up behind the speaker and wiggled the input wire. The music drifted in and out. "I think I found it. Somehow the wire came loose." He stood on his toes, bracing himself on the wall with one hand and popping the cord back in with the other.

The music blasted smoothly through the speaker. *"Can't you see it's we who own the night? Can't you see it's we who 'bout that life?"*

Caleb stepped down from the bench. Emily stayed where she was, her hand running up his thigh, across his abdomen, and up to his chest. He hesitated, unsure what to do. Emily just stared up at him. Her hand climbed to his cheek. He leaned to step around her. She corralled him around the waist with her other arm and pulled him toward her. "Don't go." She extended and kissed him on the lips.

The music resounded from all directions. *"And we can't stop. And we can't stop."*

Caleb kissed her back for a moment then pulled back. "Whoa, whoa, whoa. We can't. I'll get fired if someone finds out."

Emily dropped her hand to his inner thigh, stroking lightly. "No one will know. I locked the door. Besides, I'm the boss. If anyone says anything, I'll get them fired." She kissed him again, her hand climbing from his thigh to his waistline, unbuttoning his jeans.

Caleb tensed then relaxed, putting his arms around her and kissing her strongly.

Emily pulled him toward the beanbags pushed against the wall, lowering herself and him on top of the comfortable mounds. Although it was her first time, she was hardly an amateur and knew exactly what to do. She had researched this situation like she would have any other role. She peeled off his shirt first then hers, relishing the feeling of his bare, muscular chest against hers. Sensing his reluctance, she initiated every action. Her hands lowered to his waist. She pried down his zipper and yanked the jeans down to his knees. He laid on his back, staring at the ceiling like the helpless, willing victim he was. She rolled him over on top of the adjacent beanbag. The tail of a stuffed monkey and face of a penguin stuck out along the sides of his body. She stood over him and shed her black cotton leggings. Completely naked and confident, she lowered her lean, nubile body between his legs.

Caleb sat up, holding her wrists to stop her from pulling his boxers down. "I'm sorry. I just don't think this is a good idea. I could get in so much trouble."

Emily freed her wrist and pushed against his chest, forcing him back. "I told you. I'll take care of it. You're safe." She leaned over to a beanbag stuffed in the corner directly under the speaker. Reaching underneath, she pulled out a condom.

Caleb's forehead tightened as he looked up at the speaker and down at the beanbag, then at Emily. "I never had a chance, did I?"

She tore open the package and applied the condom, again demonstrating she had prepared in advance. "A girl has to take what she wants in this world."

Surrendering, Caleb placed his hands on her hips and guided her toward him. After several attempts, Emily found the spot and worked him inside her. She closed her eyes and rocked back and forth, feeling more pain than pleasure but relishing the satisfaction that another accomplishment had been made ahead of schedule, which was all anything ever was to her.

When they resumed filming after the holiday break, Emily ignored him, never even looking in his direction. Caleb tried talking to her once.

She looked at him impassively. "If you ever speak to me directly again, I'll have you fired." He ended up leaving the show on his own shortly after that. She never even noticed. He was just the first of the same relationship over and over. Emily would see someone she wanted, seduce him or even her a few times, and discard the person like he or she never existed.

In Gabe's garage, Emily says, "I don't see what the big deal is. I'm the one who came on to Levi. That was the first time we were together, and it was all me. I don't think anyone is really going to come after you because you stumbled upon me seducing someone."

Uncomfortable with her suggestive stance and speech, Gabe picks up a framed picture of an ocean sunset from the table and positions it with the ones propped against the wall to move away from her. "That's not for you or me to decide."

With his back turned, Emily moves around to the other side of the table, only a few feet from him. "Who knows what anyone will believe?"

Gabe turns back around, surprised to see her so close. Shuffling away, he says. "What do you mean by that?"

"Maybe it wasn't an accident you were there," Emily says, stepping toward him. "Maybe you've been following me." She unbuttons her blouse, her gaze locking with his. "Maybe you coerced me here to blackmail me with the pictures. Maybe we can work out another arrangement. The ending is really up to you."

Gabe stumbles back and knocks over one of the pictures. Changing direction, he darts toward his desk. "This is crazy. What—why are you doing this? Just stop."

Emily untucks her blouse from her tight skirt and unfastens the final buttons, revealing a pink lace demi-cup bra. She brushes the left collar of her shirt over her shoulder. "Guess it will be the word of a confused seventeen-year-old against yours."

Abbie's voice radiates from the kitchen. "Gabe? Are you home?"

Gabe looks at Emily. "Maybe not just my word."

Abbie appears in the doorway to the kitchen. "When did you get home?"

Keeping her back to the door, Emily buttons up her shirt.

Sensing she walked in on something, Abbie says, "I'm sorry. I didn't know you had company."

Gabe walks toward Abbie, motioning to the back door. "Not a problem. I think Ms. James was just leaving.

Abbie looks at Emily, who finally turns around. Abbie shuffles toward her, gushing. "As in…Oh my god…I am your biggest fan."

Emily's shirt is still untucked but buttoned except for the top two. Emily holds her hand out toward Abbie to shake and also keep some distance. She had learned the technique to prevent strangers from hugging her, which was their usual response when seeing her. Playing the girl next door on TV invites them to treat her as such. "Nice to meet you."

"I can't believe Emily James is actually in our house. Can I get a picture? Or even better, do you have time to sign your poster in my room? It'll take only a second. I promise. Or maybe later if you're busy or another time. Geez. I'm sorry. Listen to me. Just rambling like an idiot."

Emily breaks away, moving toward the door. "Like your brother said, I really should be going."

Abbie walks alongside her. "At least come say hi to my friends. Pleeeease. They will never believe you were here." She takes hold of her hand and leads her toward the house.

Gabe says, "Ab, I really don't think that's a good idea. Ms. James is really busy and needs to get going. We don't want to keep her."

Emily locks eyes with Gabe, seeing how badly he wants her to leave. "Quite all right. I'm happy to do it. I always have time for my fans." She follows Abbie into the house.

Gabe stands alone in the studio. He sags back against the door, emptying his lungs in frustration and relief while bumping his head against the glass.

CHAPTER 18

A BOX ELDER TREE midway between the house and the front gate stretches above the bushes and fence that encircle the property. Wedged between two of its branches twenty feet off the ground, Levi watches a mob of paparazzi lurking in front of the gate through a riflescope. A bottle of Jack Daniels pokes out of the hip pocket of his beige hunting vest. He lowers the rifle and lifts the bottle for a drink. Every day more and more of them gathered out front. If he left, they just followed or there were more waiting wherever he went.

Levi returns the scope to his eye and aligns the crosshairs on the back of an unsuspecting paparazzo. With rapid pulls of the trigger, he fires two shots. Red paint splashes across the back of the photographer in his sights. The other paparazzi scatter for cover. In the chaos, Levi lands three more paintball shots on the easy prey. Confused what is happening, they turn their cameras on each other.

Levi lowers the rifle and feeds the grin on his face with more whiskey.

One by one, the paparazzi emerge from hiding and look in every direction except up for the source of the attacker. Levi drops the empty bottle to the ground and slings the rifle around his shoulder to climb down.

Palo verde canopy trees and juniper bushes line the sides of the long, basalt paver driveway that connects the gate and the garage. Closely clipped grass fills the two inches of space between each of the arranged black igneous rocks. As he plods back to the house, the leaves to his right rustle and shake. He steps off the rectilinear path into the grass toward the stirring, but the only movement is the gentle shifting of branches from the light evening breeze. He steps closer, removing the rifle from his shoulder and poking into the bushes. Extending further into the bramble, the rifle is yanked from his hands. Levi jerks back, startled. Through the leaves, he sees the red jacket of the culprit retreating deeper into the thicket and lunges forward to chase.

Weaving along the matted path, the person scurries toward the white wooden fence twenty feet away. Levi lumbers after him, branches scratching at his legs and arms. Losing his short lead, the person slings the rifle over his shoulder. A camera swings over the other. He reaches the fence and leaps up. His fingers grasp the top lip, and using his momentum, he runs up the side. His right leg swings over, but his left still dangles down.

Levi springs toward the fence, jumping up and latching onto the trespasser's lagging limb. Falling back, Levi keeps his grip, pulling the person back on top of him. The guy scrambles to his feet, kicking Levi off and springing up to try the fence again. Levi easily wrangles him back down, delivering several blows to his midsection.

Dropping the rifle to the ground, the guy says, "Just take it, man. I don't want it that bad."

"What the fuck are you doing here?" Levi asks, driving the guy's head into the wooden fence. Blood oozes from the gash in his forehead. Levi bashes his head again into the fence. "Who sent you?"

The guy puts his hands over his head to shield further drubbing. "No one. I swear. I was just out front when the paintball attack happened. Somebody said there was a way over the fence, so I thought I would try it and see if I could maybe get a few photos of the shooter."

Levi drives his knee into the guy's midsection, causing the intruder to cough and wheeze. "And? Did you get any?"

"No. I swear." The guy falls to the ground and curls up into a ball. "I was about to, but that's when you found me."

"Bullshit! I don't believe you." Levi kicks him repeatedly, in the shins, thighs, and stomach. "I'm sick of you fucking parasites." The kicking becomes stomping. He drives his boot downward into the guy's shoulder.

The interloper rolls away, but the thick bushes keep him close. He gasps for air. "Please, just stop. You can check my camera."

Levi follows the last word with a boot to the guy's head. The pleas for mercy cease, and all movement stops. Levi looms over the body. Slow, steady breath seeps from the guy's lips. Levi nudges him with his foot. "Get up." The guy doesn't move. Levi picks up the rifle and slings it over his shoulder. Grunts and groans gurgle from below. Levi grabs the guy by the ankles and drags him back down the matted path toward the driveway.

Standing over the body in the grass, Levi looks back toward the solid wood gate to check for additional eyes or lenses on them. Not seeing any, he picks the guy up and slings the unconscious form over his shoulder. The camera falls from around the guy's neck. Levi loops it around the end of his rifle and follows the tree line toward the house. The sun dips behind the two-story structure, forming a halo along the roof. Levi lugs the lifeless lump through the house out into the backyard and drops him into one of the chaise lounge chairs by the long, rectangular lap pool. Still out cold, the guy lands with a thud, his head lolling over the side of the chair.

Levi retrieves a roll of duct tape from the house and secures his prisoner to the chair. Reviewing the pictures on the camera, Levi doesn't find any of himself, only a video of the other paparazzi being shot with paint outside the gate. Levi watches it several times, enjoying each viewing more than the one before.

Cupping his hands, Levi scoops water from the pool and throws it on his captive's face. Spitting and gagging, the guy lurches forward. Unable to move, he relaxes and settles into the chair. Flopping his head from side to side, he looks around assessing where he is and how he got here. Seeing Levi, the guy recoils, panicking. "Come on, man. I don't want any trouble. I'm just doing my job. I promise, I won't say anything. Just let me go."

Levi hovers over the guy, dropping the camera in his lap. "What if I wanted you to say something?"

Confusion twists his captive's face. "I don't understand. Now you want me to tell people what happened? You didn't have to beat the shit of me. You could've just let me go to begin with."

"You shouldn't have run," Levi says, picking back up the camera. "I didn't know what you had. But now I think this video is hilarious. I want you to sell it. Just don't mention our fight. You'll have to make something up about how you got the bruises. I don't need that biting me in the ass."

Despite being taped to the chair and in no position to negotiate, the guy asks, "What's it worth to you?"

Levi scoffs, shaking his head. "You don't really have much leverage, do you?" He pulls at the tape securing the guy's legs. "I mean, you were trespassing on private property. I can say I felt threatened and was protecting myself. Not to mention, a minute ago you were pleading for me to let you go. Now you're trying to capitalize on it? Probably want to rethink that approach."

"But that was before I knew you wanted something," the guy says. "With the way things have been lately, you can hardly afford any more bad publicity. I think five thousand should cover it for me." He waits for a reaction, but one doesn't come. "And I get to keep whatever I sell the video for."

Levi removes a folding hunter knife from his pocket and puts the tip of the blade underneath the guy's left earlobe. He presses the knife up to the bottom of the ear and flicks his wrist forward, slicing the soft, pendulous tissue. It dangles from the bottom of his ear, flapping as the guy writhes and screams. Levi says, "If you fuck me on this or ask for more, I'll find you and take the rest of your ear." He wipes the blood from the blade onto the guy's cheek. "And peel the skin off you." He drags the point of the knife along his captive's jawline, across the chin, and up the other side.

Fear floods the guy's face. "I promise. I promise. Just pay me and let me go. I swear you'll never hear from me again."

Levi withdrawals the knife, rotating it in his hand at his side. He watches the sun slip below the horizon. Streaks of light stream across the pool but do not reach him. Shadows creep in from all sides. Looking back at the photographer, he lowers the knife to his neck. Blood streams from the earlobe Levi already carved. Levi says, "Somehow I don't believe you. No matter what I do, you're going to want more. Everyone always wants more."

"That's not true. I don't even need the money." Tears stream from the guy's eyes back to his ears, mixing with the blood on the one side. "Delete the video. Whatever. I don't care. Just let me leave. I won't say anything."

"Everyone always wants more," Levi says, repeating himself. He presses the knife harder to the guy's neck. Blood oozes on each side of the blade. The guy begs for Levi to stop. In a single quick motion, Levi slides the knife across the guy's throat. The pleading changes to gasping then gurgling as the blood drains into his windpipe. Levi returns the knife to his side, watching the life leave his defenseless victim. "Everyone always wants more."

◆◆◆

EVA SITS AT THE desk in her office. Through the window, traffic crawls along the 405 with Santa Monica and Pacific Palisades coming to life. The financial returns from *Wrongside Right* listed by each box office populate a spreadsheet on her computer screen. Her face winces and contorts as she reviews the numbers line by line.

Levi breezes in and flops onto the L-shaped leather sofa wedged in the corner. Other than a bruise on his right hand, all signs of his altercation the night before with the photographer at his house are gone. He had lugged the body back into his house and stored it in an empty freezer in the garage. He burned his clothes in the fire pit while he bathed in the hot tub then sprayed down the concrete and scrubbed it with bleach. "You disappeared early the other night," he says, referring to the premiere.

Her eyes remain on the screen, searching for some sliver of positive news. "That's because you haven't been too interested in my help lately."

"Still would've been nice if my agent supported me." Levi lifts his legs onto the glass table.

The comment draws a glare from Eva. Her eyes return to the screen. "Don't even try to make this about me."

Levi sinks lower into the couch. "So how bad is it?"

"I've been on the phone since before six this morning with distributors. That should tell you something." Eva swivels in the chair toward Levi and pushes back from the desk. "Didn't make the top five and cleared only three point eight million dollars."

Levi says, "Looks like *Wrongside Right* was more wrong than right. But it'll pick up. Just needs some time."

"I don't know. It's not looking good. You're not helping matters with stunts like the paintball attack yesterday."

"Come on. That was just a joke," Levi says. "Did you see the video? All those paparazzi running around snapping pictures of each other. Fucking priceless. Already has over a million views."

"Too bad your movie hasn't."

"Aren't you just fucking hilarious this morning?" Levi says with an exaggerated smile, playing off her dig as humor. "We've had shaky openings before. We'll bounce back in the coming weeks. You said the early reviews were strong. Once they post and more people see the film, things will turn around."

"Doubtful. Most of those reviews are not being published or have been changed. There's more clicks in Levi-bashing than support, and it appears no one wants to sit through two hours of seeing your face. We're not even going to get a few weeks. Due to the poor performance, they're reducing the number of screens by fifty percent nationwide."

Levi drops his feet to the floor and springs up, marching toward Eva. "What? You can't let that happen. We'll have no chance to get my fucking money back."

"Not much I can do," Eva says, composed and measured. "It's a distribution decision. They want to put a product on screens that has the best chance of selling.

Levi pivots and paces in the middle of the room. "I can't believe this. We should never even be in this situation."

His panic has the opposite effect on Eva. She settles back into her chair. Seeing Levi unravel puts her back in control. She says, "Now you know why I was harping about the importance of the past few weeks."

Levi says, "So what's next? I want to get back to work. I need to be busy right now."

"You're going to have to lie low for a while," Eva says, "The whole strategy to drive up the asking price for your next role was built on winning the Oscar and a strong opening for the new film. Right now you are toxic. No one wants to put their money in anything to do with you. Fortunately for us, this town has a short memory. Eventually it'll blow over. We just have to find the right role...and you have to stop fucking up."

Levi stops in front of the desk, leaning forward, propped up by his arms. "But I'm going broke. I put most of my liquidity into the film and have lost pretty much all of my endorsement contracts."

"Levi, it's going to take time. We have to totally rebuild your image."

"What the fuck have you done to me?" Levi swipes his arm across the desk, knocking the outbox full of papers onto the floor.

Eva rises to confront him. "What have I done? I had everything set. All you had to do was show up. You were the one that had to have Emily James and to make it worse, retaliate with all your childish bullshit."

Eva's assistant Joelle appears in the doorway. "Sorry to interrupt."

"Not now," Eva says.

"But someone—"

Levi spins around. "What part of not now don't you understand, you stupid bitch?"

Marcus Ambrose steps around Joelle and into the office. "What I think your assistant is trying to tell you is that someone from the DA's office is here to see you."

Marcus walks up to the desk and presents a search warrant. "It's come to our attention that you're in possession of additional photos that were not published."

Eva reviews the warrant. "I think you received some bad information."

Marcus waves in two more people carrying empty boxes to begin the search. "Ms. Florez, I think you'll see that the warrant you hold entitles us to anything in this office that may contain those pictures including your computer. Do you really want to shut down your entire operation for something we'll eventually find anyway?"

Levi walks up to Marcus. "This is ridiculous. Talk to Emily James. She'll tell you nothing illegal happened." Levi studies Marcus' face. He looks familiar but Levi can't place why. Marcus has grown a full foot since the last time they saw each other and now looks down on Levi.

Straightening his body, Marcus says, "Mr. Combs, we're obligated by California law to investigate any alleged sexual misconduct with a minor regardless of if there is a complaint or not." Marcus, feeling Levi's scrutiny, turns away and addresses the evidence collectors. "Let's start here. Just pack everything up."

One of the evidence collectors moves to the other side of the desk next to Eva. She stands and drifts toward the windows.

Levi walks over to Marcus. "You're the DA on this case? Have we met before? Maybe at a charity function or some event?"

"Deputy Ambrose," Marcus says, purposefully avoiding using his first name. "No, we haven't. Only Ms. Florez and

I have met. I paid her a visit earlier in the week." He circles around Levi toward the desk. The evidence collector opens the desk drawers and dumps the contents into one of the boxes. The other collector sits in the desk chair and slides up to the laptop.

Eva steps forward from the windows. "Wait. This isn't necessary." She leans over the evidence collector at the computer and opens a folder on the screen. "All the pictures are in here." She highlights a list of twenty files.

Levi fires across the room at her. "What the fuck are you doing?"

Eva says, "If they take the computer, they'll have them anyway."

Marcus walks behind the desk. "You don't mind if we have a look just to be sure?"

Eva steps away. The evidence collector opens the files. Pictures of Levi and Emily cascade across the screen. One by one they review the images. Intermixed with the shots sold by Abbie to Forbidden Fotos are more revealing ones. There's the top of Emily's head rising out of the water directly in front of Levi standing in the creek with the waterline just below his pubic hair but concealing everything below. In another shot, she slides down his chest, her naked body visible from the mid-thigh up. Each picture is more compromising than the one before. The evidence collector inserts a memory card and copies the files.

"These seem to fill in the blanks from that afternoon." Marcus takes control of the mouse and ejects the flash card.

The evidence collector stops cleaning out the desk. "Leave everything else?"

Marcus nods, padding back toward the center of the room. "Yes. Our work is done here."

The evidence collector dumps the contents of the box he had been filling onto the floor and walks toward the door. The other collector seated at the computer rises and follows.

Marcus holds up the memory card. "Gotta love the digital age. All the info you need at the tips of your fingers. Makes these searches so much easier." He struts across the room, stopping in the doorway and turning back around. "Thanks so much for your cooperation. We'll be in touch."

Levi walks to the door, watching Marcus disappear into the reception area and out into the hallway. He spins back around, exploding toward Eva. "What in the fuck is wrong with you? He was here earlier in the week and you still have those pictures? Why didn't you get rid of them?"

Eva says, "No one other than you, me, and Emily and her people knew we were getting them."

Levi swipes his arm in disgust at her. "And that fucking photographer."

"Stop blaming everything on him," Eva says. "He wants this all to go away as much as we do."

"And you believe him?" Levi returns to pacing. "Maybe the DA put the squeeze on. Maybe that guy is playing you."

Eva sits back down in her chair. "Listen, you're lucky they left with just the flash drive. Who knows what they would've found in this office that I covered up for you over the years?"

Levi stops in front of the desk, pointing at Eva with the full force of his arm. "This—you—your incompetence is inexcusable."

Eva is unaffected by his emotion. She leans back in her chair, speaking from behind a cold stare. "Don't you think it's time you take some responsibility for your actions?"

Levi says, "I think you did this on purpose, didn't you?"

"Why would I want to sabotage your career?" Eva asks. "I've spent ten years of my life building it."

The words tumble out of Levi, one by one formulating his conspiracy theory. "You always did want our relationship to be more personal."

Eva shakes her head. "Have you lost your mind?"

"Why didn't I see this coming?" Levi says to himself. "You probably had that photographer follow me out to the waterfall. If you couldn't have me, you were going to destroy me."

"Will you just stop and listen to yourself?" Eva says. "All I've ever done is work my ass off to help you. Everything you have is because of me."

"And then this DA Anders—what was his name again?"

"Ambrose," Eva says. "Marcus Ambrose."

"God, that sounds familiar. Are you sure we haven't had any dealings with him before? I swear I know him."

"I haven't, other than the morning after the Oscars, when he showed up here. I told him to talk to our lawyers if he had any other questions."

The reminder that Marcus had already been here shifts Levi's attention back to Eva. "And you didn't think to tell me or get rid of the pictures or at least move them someplace safe?"

"What are you talking about? I know it's hard for you to see past yourself, but all I've been doing lately is cleaning up your messes."

Levi doesn't hear her response, falling further into his paranoia. "You wanted this to happen. You want me to lose everything so I need you again. Must've been hard watching me go for everyone else but you."

Her voice rises above his for the first time. "You are a complete fucking lunatic! You know that? The only thing that has been hard is watching your inflated ego destroy everything."

Levi takes a deep breath, nodding slowly on the exhale, finding calm in her choler. "You know, I think it's time for me to find someone who actually wants what's best for me."

Eva, still seated in her chair, just shakes her head. "So I'm to blame for all your problems, and your solution is to fire me? That's just brilliant."

"Effective immediately," Levi says.

"You know, that's fine with me." Eva rises and walks toward the door. "I'm tired of wasting my time on you."

Finally seeing some stress on Eva supplies the satisfaction he was seeking. "I should've done this years ago. You were nothing when I met you."

"And you're nothing now." Eva flings open the door. "Get the hell out."

Levi struts toward the door, stopping next to her. "Let's see how well you do when everyone learns how you sabotaged your biggest client." He turns and walks out. Eva slams the door behind him.

CHAPTER 19

G ABE TRUDGES UP THE Temple Street steps, craning his neck at the imposing Hall of Justice. The terra cotta cornice with ox skulls and acanthus leaves crown the matching granite sides. Bugsy Siegel, Robert Mitchum, Charles Manson, and Sirhan Sirhan were all housed here after their arrests. The autopsies of Marilyn Monroe and Robert Kennedy were also performed inside. And now Gabe plans to add to that history by becoming a witness against Levi Combs.

In the grand lobby, Gabe breezes past the ionic marble columns under the gilded, coffered ceiling to wait for the elevator up to the sex crimes division on the ninth floor. Stepping off the elevator, he approaches the young, red-haired, bespectacled male receptionist.

"May I help you?" the receptionist asks. His appearance and meek voice seem out of place in the ornate, intimidating setting.

"Is Marcus Ambrose in?" Gabe asks, looking around, trying to find comfort in the setting, and with what he is about to do. But after what Levi did to him at the gallery, he knows something must be done. He wanted to stay out of it, but Levi brought this on himself. Levi was the one who had sex with a seventeen-year-old, who hired someone to assault and rob him, and who took his gallery show from him. Levi deserves whatever happens to him.

The receptionist picks up the phone. "And your name?"

"Gabe Adams. It's about Levi Combs." Gabe drifts back toward the wall, examining a framed black and white photograph of the building's construction in 1924.

The receptionist dials, lifting his hand to conceal his words when someone answers. Lowering the phone, the receptionist speaks louder to Gabe. "He'll be right out."

Gabe turns around, nodding at the information, as he bounces nervously on his toes.

Moments later, Marcus emerges through the glass door behind the receptionist. "Gabe, what a nice surprise. You should've called. I would've come to you."

"Not a problem," Gabe says, curling around the reception desk. "Didn't want to wait. Is there somewhere we can talk?"

Marcus waves his arm back in the direction from which he came. "Absolutely. Let's grab a conference room." He leads Gabe back through the door into the office. They walk through the open floor plan area filled with workers paired in twos facing one another with their heads down at their desks. Marcus walks to a glass-enclosed conference room and opens the door, gesturing for Gabe to sit. He takes a yellow legal pad from a stack on the table and a pen from the breast pocket of his navy suit jacket and fills the seat on the opposite side of the table. "What brings you in?"

Gabe folds his hands in front of him and straightens his back, summoning the courage to follow through. He clears his throat, then speaks. "I've changed my mind about testifying."

Marcus scribbles down the date and time, drawing a line underneath. "Thought you didn't have much to offer other than the pictures?"

Gabe shifts in his seat. "I just really didn't want to get involved before. I was embarrassed for even having the pictures. And I was trying to keep my sister from getting tangled up in it all. But it's too late for that."

Marcus looks down, gliding the pen over the tablet, capturing the words. "Tell me what you saw."

Only a single word spills out of Gabe. "Everything."

Marcus stops writing. His eyes rise to Gabe. "I'm going to need you to be more specific."

Gabe pushes out his chest, arching his shoulders and releasing a breath. "The pictures show Emily James climb on top of him naked in the water, but there was a lot more that happened. Marcus busily writes down the details. Gabe continues, his right leg bouncing, shaking the conference table. "From there Levi lifted here up and they had sex standing in the water.

"Are you aware we have your other pictures? You sure you're willing to corroborate what they show?"

"Hundred percent," Gabe says. "I had a clear view... through my... my telephoto lens." Hearing the words aloud embarrasses Gabe even more. "You have to know, though. I wasn't there for that. I was there only for the waterfall."

Marcus punctuates the remark about the telephoto lens with an emphatic dot of the pen. "It was a closeup then? Anything else you can share?"

Gabe shakes his head. "Yes. After several minutes of heavy activity, Levi walked her out of the water to the shore. He lowered her to the ground and they continued."

Marcus jots down the new information. "Levi was definitely on top? I want you to think about this. It's very important. You're sure he climbed on top of her?"

"Yes, absolutely. No doubt about that."

Marcus underlines the last sentence twice. He looks up at Gabe. "In your estimation, how long were they engaged in intercourse?"

"That I'm not sure of," Gabe says shaking his head. "It seemed like several minutes, but I was pretty uncomfortable with the whole situation, so it could've been less. I mean, I had no idea who it was at the time."

Marcus cuts him off. "What happened next?"

"Some rocks tumbled down the ledge from where I was standing, and Levi looked up. He must've caught a glare or some reflection I think because he looked directly where I was. I panicked and took off."

"I want you to think back over it all," Marcus says. "At any time during the whole experience, did it appear like he was forcing himself in any way?"

Gabe hesitates, carefully considering his words. He wants to say yes and really complicate things for Levi, but he can't. The truth is as far as he is willing to go for his revenge. He says, "No, the whole thing seemed consensual. I thought they were a normal couple. If anything, it looked like she was the aggressor. He actually seemed to be resisting at first. As I said before, it wasn't until I showed my sister some of the pictures that I found out who they were and that she was only seventeen."

Marcus finishes writing, filling up almost the entire page. "I think that should do it. If you can wait about ten minutes, I'll have my assistant type up this statement for you to sign."

Gabe nods, leaning back in the chair. "What happens then?"

Marcus rises from the chair and walks around the table toward the door. "This, combined with the pics, will be enough to get an arrest warrant issued, and we can pick up and charge Mr. Combs."

Gabe rotates at the torso, following Marcus's movement around the room. "So, he'll be in custody?"

"Probably not for long," Marcus says, stopping in the doorway. "He'll lawyer up and be out in a few hours. Depending on the court schedule, it may be a month or two before this goes to trial."

Gabe sinks in the chair. "That's, disappointing. What kind of sentence are we looking at?"

Marcus says, "She's a minor more than three years younger so we'll ask for a year in prison and a civil penalty of ten thousand dollars."

"And the chances of that happening?" Gabe says, doubt creeping into his speech.

"The evidence is solid and with your testimony, it should be a pretty airtight case." Marcus moves out of the room but leans back through the doorway speaking to Gabe. "Be back in ten minutes. You sure I can't get you anything?"

"No, I'm fine," Gabe says, sinking back in the chair.

The door swings closed behind Marcus. He walks into the field of desks, firing commands across the office. Although everyone had been watching the conference room, trying to determine through the glass what was being said, all heads are down pretending to focus on other work as he speaks. One by one, heads pop up reacting to his instructions.

Gabe remains still in the chair with his back to the office. Relieved it's over, he stares straight at the wall with his hands folded in front of him on the table.

◆◆◆

AT HOME IN MALIBU, Levi reclines on his couch, watching an entertainment news show. The sixty-five-inch flat-screen TV mounted on the wall casts a flickering glow diminishing his disheveled demeanor. He hasn't showered in days nor shaved in many more. Whiskers push through into a full neck beard. His shiny hair from lack of washing is matted on one side and sticking up on the other. Black mesh shorts and a V-neck hang on his body for the third day in a row. Each night he discarded them by the side of the bed only to slip them back on the next morning. Crumbs mixed with dandruff cover the front of the shirt. Sweat and spots of urine and dried semen, which have absorbed into the shorts from repeated wear, evoke an acrid, musky scent that precede and follow him with every movement.

The days since he killed the photographer and fired Eva have been filled with mostly sleep, but deliveries—from food to drugs to sex, all the staples for a reclusive bender—parade through the gate from early evening to the late morning the rest of the time. All the negativity of the past weeks made it impossible to go anywhere and staying numb was the only way he could stay at home, so he burrowed in with no intention of leaving anytime soon. Since becoming famous, this is what he had learned to do both to celebrate and to sulk—or, in this case, to hide. Typically, one of these types of benders would last only two to three days, but once he had gone nine straight. The detox from that one almost killed him though. He had gotten used to having the night sweats, insomnia, anxiety, and some tremoring coming off one of the benders, but that time, severe vomiting, a racing heartbeat, and even some hallucinations were part of the withdrawal. After the fourth day and worsening symptoms, he thought about checking into a facility, but Eva didn't want the publicity, so she had a doctor make a house call. He hooked Levi up to an IV and fed him some benzos for the anxiety and a beta-blocker for the heart rate. Levi was back to normal in twenty-four hours, which was probably a bad thing in the long run. Without the painful recovery, there wasn't really anything to discourage the benders and incentivize him to find another coping mechanism. With everything that has happened this time, he knows the nine-day record is probably in jeopardy.

On the TV, the words of the female entertainment show host catch his attention. "Things just keep getting worse for Levi Combs. Take a look at this footage from outside the courthouse earlier."

The screen cuts to Marcus Ambrose addressing a group of reporters on the intermediate level of the steps of City Hall. American flags line the top of the five archways leading into the art deco building with the rectangular tower rising out of the shot. He says, "Due to additional evidence and a witness coming forward to testify, the DA's office has filed charges against Levi Combs."

A reporter in the crowd shouts a question. "What penalty will you be seeking?"

"In its ongoing effort of zero tolerance for child sex crimes, the State will be asking for the maximum penalty of a felony conviction and one year in a state prison facility."

Another reporter asks, "Is Emily James the witness?"

Marcus says, "The DA's office will not discuss any specifics of its prosecution at this time. Thank you." He turns from the group of reporters and walks up the courthouse steps.

The camera redirects from the podium to the reporter who had asked the last question. She says, "Levi Combs won an Oscar playing an inmate in *For Love*. Now it looks like he may play one in real life. Back to you in the studio."

The show switches back to the entertainment host in the studio. "Once again, another case of life imitating art. We'll be sure to keep you updated on the details as they unfold."

Levi sits up, picking up the half-empty bottle of vodka resting on the floor next to the couch. After chugging two mouthfuls, he puts the bottle on the glass table in front of him next to an open plastic sandwich bag of cocaine. A coated three-inch pink straw is immersed in the powder. He picks up the bag and fishes out the straw. Not even bothering to dump any on the table, he buries the straw in the bag and inhales once, then another time in the other nostril, tossing the bag and straw back on the table. He snags the bottle and paces in the dark room, gulping vodka with each trip back and forth. Drops of sweat form on his forehead, adding to the layer of oil already coating his face.

The buzzer for the front gate sounds. Assuming it's the female companionship he ordered, he opens the gate with the remote and doesn't bother to check the monitor. Putting the bottle down, he grabs five hundreds from a pile of bills scattered across the table and hurries to the door and out onto the front steps. A police car drives through the gate. Levi turns and scampers back into the house. Leaning against the door, he considers his options. He knows they saw him, so hiding in the house won't work. He fetches the bottle of vodka, lifting it to his lips and searching for the answer in the bottom. Hearing a car door slam, he rushes to the security monitor to the right of the door and watches the two police officers, a male in his forties and an upper-twenties female, exit the car and walk to the front. He hears their footsteps on the brick walk and opens the door before they ring the bell. "How can I help you, officers?"

The male officer notices Levi's rough appearance, scanning him up and down. "Levi Combs, we have a warrant for your arrest for violation of California Penal Code 261.5, unlawful sexual intercourse with a minor."

Levi shakes his head. "Are you fucking kidding me? This is ridiculous. I want to talk to my lawyer."

"You'll have your chance once we get to the station," the younger female officer says. "Will you please step outside and put your hands behind your back?"

Levi just stares back at her. "Is this really necessary?"

The male officer looks at Levi's casual attire and unkempt appearance. "Maybe you'd like us to come in while you change or at least get some shoes?"

Levi is not about to invite the officers in with a gun, cash, and drugs strewn across his coffee table, let alone what is in the freezer if they start poking around. Stepping outside, he puts his hands behind his back. "No, let's just get this over with.

The female officer handcuffs Levi and leads him to the car, reciting his rights. The officers get in the front seat and turn the flashers on but not the sirens. The car drives back through the gate through a swarm of paparazzi, all trying for a picture of Levi in the back seat. To avoid the coveted close-up, Levi topples over on his side and buries his face into the seat. No way he was going to make one of the photographers' years with a photo of this.

The officers take Levi to the Metro Detention Center Jail downtown since the DA filed the charges in Los Angeles. All the major news and entertainment media outlets have already assembled when they arrive. Additional officers form two lines to create a walkway from the street to the entranceway. When they pull the barefoot and sodden Levi from the back of the car, flashes and questions erupt, mixing with the one hundred and eight bronze bells chiming in the Sook Jin Jo art installation in front of the entrance. The tolls, intended to dispel defilements leading to suffering, are the only calming tones in the chaos. Tuning out the despoiling discord, Levi peers over at the bells as he walks by. Engraved in the metal clappers are words like integrity, dignity, reverence—all things he once had but lost.

Once Levi is safely inside, Marcus struts over. "Levi Combs, you have been read your rights and notified of the charges being brought against you—"

Levi doesn't allow Marcus to finish. "Lawyer."

"For violation of—"

"Lawyer."

"You will have an opportunity to contact your legal representation after you have been booked."

"This is such bullshit," Levi says, glaring at Marcus. "You'll be lucky to have a job when this is over. You'll spend the rest of your career in traffic court."

Marcus turns away, uncomfortable Levi might recognize him. He's so close to seeing all his work payoff. He can't risk being taken off the case and someone else coming and pleading it down to a fine and community service. He would've liked for more jail time to be on the table, but watching the Oscar debacle and movie flop had been unexpected bonuses, and the very public and embarrassing trial that would ensue and anything else that follows would be additional recompense. He turns to the female officer guiding Levi by his cuffed hands. "Run him through."

Before the officer can whisk him away, Levi responds again with a one-word answer, but it's different this time. "Ambrose!" The officer stops, assuming Levi had something to say to Marcus, but it was a realization not a request.

Hearing his name, Marcus instinctively stops and looks back at Levi expecting a question, but seeing the look on Levi's face, he knows Levi has finally made the connection. Wanting to avoid a confrontation, he turns to walk away. This is supposed to happen after, in the courtroom or at the prison,

He was supposed to be the one to tell Levi and watch the realization settle in. But instead, it's happening here and now, whether Marcus likes it or not. He steps back toward Levi, silent and stern.

"You're the little brother," Levi says, the memories tumbling back. "I knew I recognized you. You're Tamm—Tamara's little brother."

Marcus remains quiet, knowing his words could also be used to get him removed. He just stares back, smirking.

"Wait. This is about her? You blame me for what happened?" Levi lunges toward Marcus.

The officer yanks Levi back by the cuffs, dragging him toward the door to central booking. "That's enough, Combs. Let's go."

Levi fights back toward Marcus. "You have to believe me. I tried to help her, but she wouldn't stop." The other officer steps between them and helps corral Levi toward the door. Levi yells over top of him. "I hope it's worth it. You're done. I should thank you. Wait until I call my lawyers. They're going to chew you up. This case will be thrown out before you fall asleep tonight."

Marcus walks toward Levi as the officers force him through the door. Still under control and not wanting to provide any additional ammunition, he whispers to himself, "Nothing is ever your fault, is it Combs?"

On the other side of the door, Levi doesn't even have to call his lawyer. A contingency of representation shows up before the mugshot flashes dimmed. Once they speak to Levi, there are decrees of harassment, motions for dismissal, and petitions for release without bail. In the end, Levi is out in just under three hours, but not because the charges are dropped. It's due to the fifty-thousand-dollar bail that the law firm puts up for him.

CHAPTER 20

A T ART ON TRACTION, the gallery owner and a younger female employee hang a picture showing a mountain wild fire from the hydraulic lift on the right. An ombré of white to black smoke rises from the red and yellow streaks devouring the luscious green trees and shrubs blanketing a mountain slope. Eva walks through one of the open garage doors studying the new work. The younger female employee strolls over to greet her. Before any words are exchanged, Eva smiles and points at the gallery owner, who has her back to them, adjusting the wildfire picture. Eva walks up next to her, admiring the active flame ripping up the side of the mountain. Eva says, "How can something so beautiful be so destructive?"

The gallery owner, not realizing anyone was standing next to her, glances over, straightening in surprise. "These are all of Zaca. It absolutely gutted the San Rafael Mountains, northeast of the Santa Ynez Valley in Santa Barbara for months. Over two hundred and forty thousand acres destroyed. At the time, it was the second largest fire in recorded history. Now I think it's fourth or fifth. Just sad how these things are becoming so commonplace and getting worse." She looks again at Eva, her eyes traveling from top to bottom and back up. "Oh, it's you. I didn't recognize you at first. Eve, right?"

"Ev-a," she says, offering her hand. The gallery owner leans in, taking Eva by the shoulder, touching her cheek to Eva's and kissing. Eva says, "Wasn't sure you'd remember me."

"It's my business to know people." The gallery owner shuffles back a few steps analyzing the picture with the others hanging from the lift. "You know, this fire was started by someone repairing a water pipe? How ironic is that?"

Eva slides back next to her. "I remember watching it on the news as the firefighters worked on land and in the air to turn it away from that community."

"Paradise Road was the name of the community," the gallery owner says. "We have a great shot of that on the other side."

Eva scans the gallery, looking at the work on display, all of which is quite different from the last time she was there. "A new show already? Or did you sell all of Gabe's stuff?"

The gallery owner scrunches her nose as if smelling something foul. Motioning toward the sitting area, she says, "A bit of an unfortunate situation, I'm afraid." Eva follows, sitting next to her on the small sofa. The gallery owner says, "I had the most unusual request from a very well-known, wealthy client willing to buy a large collection of other works if I stopped showing Gabe's work." She fidgets in her seat, still uncomfortable with her decision. "Of course, I didn't want to do it, but I didn't really have much choice, you see. I am running a business here." The gallery owner perks up suddenly, tapping Eva on the knee excitedly. "You know what? I'm not sure what happened between you two that night, but if you're still interested, I can put you in touch with him. If nothing else, I'm sure he'd love to sell you a picture or two."

"Yes, I think I would like that." Eva leans over, whispering. "So who was the client? Anyone I might know?"

The gallery owner looks around to see if anyone is listening even though they are the only ones there. She lowers her voice to match Eva's. "You might. He just won an Oscar."

Eva feigns surprise. "Get out of here. No way." She slaps the gallery owner's knee. "Really? Levi Combs?"

"The one and only," the gallery owner reveals. Looking around again before speaking, she says, "Between you and me, he didn't look so good when he came in here. And now I just heard the DA is pursuing charges for those pictures with Emily James. How scandalous! To think he was just here in my little gallery. Only in LA."

"That's so crazy. Maybe you backed the wrong artist," Eva says. "All this publicity surely would've driven up the prices for Gabe's work."

"Believe me, I know. Been kicking myself ever since. To make things worse, Gabe also showed up while Levi was here, and there was a bit of a scuffle. Quite an ordeal to be honest." She stands and walks behind the counter. "I feel absolutely terrible for what happened. It would be so great if you reached out to him and could help in some way." She sets one of Gabe's cards on the counter and slides it toward the edge in Eva's direction.

"Of course," Eva says, rising and approaching the counter. "I'll even tell him you sent me." She picks up the card, cupping it in her hand.

"That's not necessary," the gallery owner says. "I just want everything to work out for him." She hands Eva a flyer. "Here's some info on the new show that kicks off here this week. Hope to see you at the opening."

Eva takes the flyer in the hand with Gabe's card, thanking her once again before leaving. On the way to the car, she tosses both in a trashcan. As she drives away, she knows she can't just show up at his place unannounced after what happened, but she doesn't want to leave things as they are either. She dials his number.

Gabe answers on the third ring. "Gabe Adams Photography." Eva is quiet. He says, "Hello? You've reached Gabe Adams."

"Hey, Gabe. It's Eva." She winces at how nonchalant she sounds. "I know you probably don't want to speak to me, but I was hoping we could talk." She pauses for a reaction. Hearing nothing, she barrels on. "I heard what happened at the gallery. I feel terrible about it. If it makes you feel any better, he fired me too, and it sounds like he's getting arrested." She waits again for him to speak. "Are you still there?"

"I'm here," Gabe says, not revealing he is the star witness in the case against Levi.

Eva, hoping Gabe will see her, drives down Mission to get on the Santa Ana Freeway to head toward West Covina. "I really wasn't sure if you'd answer."

"I didn't recognize the number. Probably wouldn't have answered if I did," Gabe says, his voice low and distant. "It's different than the one I saved in my phone…the one you gave me."

"I'm so sorry about that," Eva says. "I just feel sick about what happened."

"You already said that," Gabe points out. "Is there something you wanted?"

"I'd still like to buy some of the pictures if you have them." Eva angles the car onto the Ten, her navigation system showing his house is twenty-two minutes away. "I also have some other work, if you're interested."

Gabe quiets for a moment. He wants to tell her to get bent, but he knows he can't afford to. After losing the show and having so much invested in inventory, he needs every sale and opportunity he can get. No matter whom it's from. He closes his eyes, swallowing hard, before reluctantly spitting out the words. "I'll be in the studio all afternoon if you want to stop by."

Eva says, "That'll work. I'm not too far from you now. I can come by in twenty to thirty minutes if that's not too soon."

"Didn't realize you did much business out this way," Gabe says unable to stifle his skepticism. No one can ever be anywhere in LA in twenty minutes unless they're already en-route or in the neighborhood.

"I had a luncheon at the Rose Tea Garden at the Huntington in Pasadena, so I was right next door," Eva lies. "Thought I'd call before I headed back to the office. We can arrange another time if that's better."

"No, now is good," Gabe says. "No sense in you driving all the way back. I guess I'll see you soon then. Just come around back to the studio.

Thirty minutes later, Eva is knocking at the back door. Gabe stands at his twenty-four-inch inkjet printer, holding the edge of a poster-sized photo as it feeds out of the machine. He waves her in. The machine wheezes and churns, struggling to complete the task. "Just give me a second," he puffs at her in frustration.

Eva walks over next to him, looking at the half-printed picture of the waterfall. "Is that—"

"Yep, one of the before shots," Gabe says. "Lighting was pristine that day." The printer suddenly stops. Gabe bangs the side of the machine. "Come on. Not again. He motions to a pile of three other partially printed pictures on the floor. "This nag is on her last leg." He lets go of the picture and walks over to the computer, punching several keys in irritation. The printer activates and spits out the unfinished picture onto the floor with the others. "Guess you won't be buying that one. Probably wouldn't be the best choice anyway, all things considered." He pads to the stacks of framed pictures leaning against the wall. "Pick whichever ones you want from here."

She strolls over and thumbs through the stacks, picture by picture. "Like I said on the phone, I'm really sorry about the gallery opening. I can't believe he went that far." She pulls out a picture that was shot from the ground looking up a redwood tree. The trunk of the tree stretches across the entire bottom of the picture. The sides and thick grooves in the bark along with neighboring trees angle inward toward a central focal point at the top of the picture. Patches of blue sky and light break through the leaves and surrounding trees. "Is this a new one?"

Gabe walks up beside her. "No, that's from a trip I took up north to Humboldt Redwoods State Park last year. I love how the light seems to be coming from all sides and everything is pointing in one direction."

She hands the picture to Gabe. "This one for sure." Gabe sets the picture on the worktable. Eva continues looking through the stacks. She says, "I'm so sorry about the show. Levi has gone completely off the rails." She pulls out another picture and hands it to Gabe. "Have you got another gallery lined up yet?"

"No," Gabe says, stacking the picture with the other selection. "Securing this show took me years, but since reviews were good, I'm hoping that it will go quicker this time."

"You know, as much of a pain as all this has been, it could actually help you. Might not be for what you want, but people know who you are now." Eva's voice softens. "I can probably help you too, if you want. I have some connections with other galleries around town. We'll structure the contract so something like what Levi did can't happen again."

"That's kind of you, but why would you want to help me?" Gabe asks. "Aren't I responsible for getting you fired."

"Not at all. That was all Levi. But let me be upfront. I wouldn't be doing it for free, and as you pointed out, I did just lose my biggest client. I have quite a bit of revenue to make up. Thinking it might be time I diversify." She stops looking through the pictures and turns toward Gabe. What she could make off Gabe would barely be worth her time. She needed about ten Ira's to cover the loss of Levi or one of them to rise to that level, which is where her time should be invested. She says, "But it's not just the money. I also feel terrible about what happened between us." She places her hand on Gabe's.

He slides over to the next stack of pictures, recoiling his hand and burying it in his pocket. "There's some really good night shots in here that I'll think you'll like."

Eva moves over next to him, turning her focus back to the pictures. "More than anything though, I could use a good photographer. I'm tired of dealing with all these scumbag paparazzi. I need someone I know is good and can trust." She stops at a picture of the sun setting behind a single palm tree on a beach, the sky streaked with purple and yellow.

"Moonlight Beach in Encinitas," Gabe says. She hands him the picture. He puts it with the others. "Why in heavens would you think you can trust me? You hardly know me."

Eva leaves the stacks of pictures, following Gabe to the worktable. "Trusting someone doesn't necessarily have anything to do with how long you've known them. She walks along the edge of the worktable, running her hand along the side. "Sometimes you just have to trust your feelings."

"I don't know anything about your world," Gabe says. "And based on the past weeks, I'm not sure I want to."

Eva stops next to him. "There's really not much to it. I just tell you where to go and what to shoot and you'll make several hundred dollars an hour." She nods toward the printer. "Good way to make extra money for new equipment."

Gabe stiffens, again fighting his instinct to decline and tell her off in the process. If it affected just him, he would've done it already. But every time the rage rises in his throat, he steadies himself, remembering Abbie is the one most impacted by his struggles. What he did sell those first few nights and got for the photos, that money was all going toward catching up on bills and the mortgage, most of which he was two months behind on. Abbie also had college coming up. He had saved some of the insurance money from their parents for her education, but not nearly enough. He says, "None of the work you need is illegal?"

"No, and nothing negative either. It's all just to build one of my younger client's career." She removes a business card and pen from her purse and writes an address on the back of the card. "Just go to Chateau Marmont tonight and take pictures of Emily and my client, Ira Bethel. They presented together at the Oscars and are supposedly dating, but it's really just a sham to boost both of their images." Eva plucks a hundred-dollar bill from her wallet and places it next to the card. "Go there at nine tonight and give this to the maître d' along with my card. I'll call him ahead of time so he's expecting you, and he'll let you into the dining room. Tomorrow morning, you can bring the pictures along with the ones I picked out here, and I'll pay you for everything. I should also have some prospects for a gallery showing."

Gabe twists the card in his hand. His eyes fixate on her last name, still a relatively new word to him since she had lied when they met. "Very well, Ms. Florez. I guess I accept."

She holds her hand out to confirm the deal. "I really do hope we can put all the other stuff behind us." Gabe places his hand in hers, their embrace lingering. Eva says, "Well, not all of it."

◆◆◆

LEVI OPENS THE SLIDING glass wall of his bedroom and walks out on the terrace. The smell and bluster of the ocean roll along the treetops and across his lawn up to him. The solitude seethes his emptiness. He can't stay in the house and just wait for something to happen. He knows everything is not going to blow over this time. He's got to get rid of the body stuffed in his freezer, but it's too risky to move it with all the eyes on him. The former frenzy that followed him wherever he went is now a full-on furor. The convocation of media, protestors, and spectacle chasers has tripled outside his gate. His lawyers assured him the personal connection with Marcus and his sister will work in his favor, but it still isn't enough to get the case thrown out. It will help cast him as the victim of a personal vendetta rather than the reckless child predator the court will portray him to be. Their main advice, similar to Eva's in the past, is that he just can't do anything to diminish the positive momentum with any type of incident. For once he heard the message. But he still needs to dispose of the body before someone comes looking for the guy. He knows people who have helped him clean up messes in the past, but this is another level. He doesn't want to involve someone else and make it worse. Unfortunately he fired the only one he can truly trust. He decides to call her anyway and dials her number. She has never said no to him before. The call goes right to voicemail. He dials again. Straight to voicemail. He texts her— one, two, three times—each one more desperate than the one before, oscillating between remorse for how he treated her and anger for her lack of response. The best option is to just go to her place, he concludes. If nothing else, it will get him away from his house, away from everything.

Levi locates the extra key Eva gave him when her place was also the office. Changing his clothes, he sees Hannah crawling from her log into the small pond in the vivarium. Not knowing when he'll come back, he says, "I can't leave my girl behind. You want to go for a ride, baby?" He fetches a large duffel bag and lines the bottom with hot-water bottles covered by a towel. He slides Hannah inside a pillowcase and places her in the bag. "There you go, baby. Nice and cozy." He zips up the bag and hangs it over his shoulder. The bag moves along his hip as Hannah adjusts inside. "Just settle down. You won't be in there long." He goes to his safe and fills a backpack with a hundred thousand dollars in cash, his 9 mm, an extra clip, a box of shells, and an ounce of cocaine—everything he needs for an extended stay away.

On his way through the garage, Levi opens the freezer to check on his guest. A thin white layer of frost covers the exposed skin on his face and arms. The earlobe that Levi had sliced was no longer attached, a bloody scab in its place. The gash on his neck had peeled back as it froze, revealing a rosy mash of flesh and cartilage. His left leg is bent under and behind his back. Concerned about what happened to the piece of the ear, Levi lifts behind the guy's head to search for it, but the frigid body does not budge. He pulls harder attempting to lift the entire mass, but it is too awkward and heavy. The backpack falls from his shoulder onto the body. He picks it up and cradles it against his left side. The lid slams closed. A burst of cold air rushes over. Hannah squirms in the bag on his opposite hip. He pats the side. "I'm sorry, baby. I know you don't like that. Let's get out of here."

He walks over to the Jeep and places her in the passenger seat and the backpack on the floor. He knows better than to drive the Bugatti. It would draw too much attention.

Backing out of the garage, he starts down the long driveway and activates the gate. Lights from the surrounding news trucks flood the entrance. The congregation spills into the driveway blocking his way. Riders jump on their scooters ready to give chase. Levi increases speed wailing on the horn to clear them out. Row by row the rabble roll off to the side, realizing he is not stopping. Levi rests his hand on the duffel bag on the passenger seat, scratching it lightly. "Sorry for all the commotion, pumpkin. Just another few minutes and it'll be smooth sailing."

As the Jeep passes through the gate, the mob folds in behind him. Screams and shouts shoot from all sides blending into an inaudible din. Levi accelerates to escape the encroaching horde as they slap and bang the Jeep. The remaining ones in his path dive into the grass on both sides. Levi takes the corner wide onto the main road crossing over the centerline. An oncoming car swerves to avoid him. He jerks the wheel back to the right, overcompensating and skidding off the road. The Jeep scrapes along a news truck and van parked on the side. Stones and sparks spray in all directions. Levi regains control and steers the Jeep back between the lines. Mounted scooters fall in behind, but Levi has too much of a head start and too much speed for them to catch up. He turns off the PCH and weaves through Paradise Cove until dusk settles and he can travel back on the main roads under the protection of darkness to find an out-of-the-way motel to hole up and figure out his next move.

◆◆◆

At the Hall of Justice, Marcus doesn't wait to be summoned. If the head deputy hasn't already heard about the scene at the detention center, Marcus figures he will first thing when he arrives. Hoping to be the one to break the news, Marcus waits in a chair outside the head deputy's office. The staff trickles in to start the day in reverse pecking order. The lower level clerks followed by their managers then the assistant DAs and finally the head deputy's assistant, which means he's not far behind. She says, "Camped out. This can't be good. Let me check his schedule and see when I can fit you in." She sets her tote on the desk. "But not before my coffee. Can I get you a cup? You look like you can use one."

"No, I'm fine," Marcus says, not moving. His arms wrap around his briefcase and clutch it against his chest like a security blanket.

"Suit yourself. Just to let you know, he still won't be here for another thirty minutes. I can just call for you when he arrives."

"That's all right. It's really important. I'll just wait."

She returns twenty minutes later carrying an extra cup of coffee. Marcus reaches for it even though he declined when she offered. Breezing by, she says, "For the head deputy. He likes it room temperature. Should be along shortly."

Moments later, the head deputy, mobile phone pressed to his ear, streams across the office, triggering the usual feigned busyness his presence typically evokes. Seeing Marcus waiting, he wraps up the conversation. Exchanging morning pleasantries with his assistant, he requests her to reschedule his first appointment then barks "Inside!" at Marcus.

Marcus waits for the head deputy to pass then follows, remaining silent and deferring to him to lead the discussion. Marcus can tell he already knows and clings to the hope that he also hasn't already decided what to do.

Peeling off his jacket, the head deputy says, "I heard it was quite a scene down at the detention center last night. At least I know now why you were so aggressive on this case. I just can't figure out why on Earth you didn't say anything." He picks up the mug of coffee from the desk and veers around Marcus, who is standing in the middle of the room, and continues on to the sitting area with a leather loveseat and two chairs. Sitting in one of the chairs, he directs Marcus to the loveseat. "You've really tied my hands here. If I drop the charges, I look like I'm cowering to a celebrity." Marcus stiffens at the comment but the look from the head deputy conveys it's not his time to speak. The head deputy says, "If I do nothing, the defense will use this to turn the case into a circus. If I remove you, I look like an idiot for not knowing and letting you pursue in the first place. I'm going to ask you this one time and you better be fucking honest with me. If you're not, I'll personally make sure you never work in California again. Is this about you or him?"

"Sir, I'm sorry for not disclosing the connection before. It's just—"

"Answer the question," the head deputy booms.

"Him, sir. He's guilty. No doubt about it. This case is airtight. I've got the pictures and witness to corroborate what's in them."

The head deputy drinks from the mug, holding the warm coffee in his mouth while contemplating the course of action. "Can you pin anything else on him?"

The question confuses Marcus. The interaction has already gone on longer than he expected. He thought he would be cleaning out his desk by now. "Connected to this case?"

"To anything?" The head deputy leans forward, placing the mug on the glass coffee table between them. "We need to double down and raise the stakes. If the defense wants to turn this into a circus, we're going to be the ringmaster. Let's put them on the defensive."

"Sir?" Marcus asks, still not following. But now it's not because he doesn't understand. He's just surprised. It's too good to be true. It's exactly what he has been longing to hear. "Are you saying—"

"Dig up everything you can. What else do you think he was into? Do you think we would find anything with a search warrant?"

"There's definitely a pattern of escalation, but this is the first thing we can prove." Marcus sits up, fully engaged. The head deputy stands and walks toward his desk. Marcus follows, stopping in the middle of the room. "There has been some chatter of a missing photographer who was last seen outside Levi's house, but no one has filed an official missing person's report."

"Find someone and use it to get a warrant." The head deputy picks up his coat and hangs it on the back of his chair, ready to officially start his day with the file laid out on his desk. "Go back to Judge Romans. She'll keep backing you as long as you keep delivering." He looks up from the file. "You thought you were getting fired, didn't you?"

Marcus nods. "Yes, sir. I did."

"Keep thinking that. If you don't find anything, we both will be gone."

CHAPTER 21

IN THE STUDIO GABE lifts a chocolate suede blazer from the back of his chair and slides it on over his blue and brown plaid shirt. He moves to the worktable and packs his camera and several lenses into his bag. Abbie enters from the kitchen. Her oversized T-shirt drapes from her narrow shoulders, contrasting with the tight leggings on the bottom half. She says, "Kind of a nice jacket to be going out for a shoot in, isn't it?"

Gabe fastens the flap on the bag and slings it over his shoulder. "I picked up another gig."

"What excitement are you capturing this time?" Abbie asks. "A fiftieth wedding anniversary party? A bat mitzvah? A retirement dinner?"

"For your information, Miss Funny-Pants, it's some celebrity shots of your hero Emily James and her fake boyfriend Ira Bethel at Chateau Marmont."

Abbie stands motionless, jaw agape. "But, but, I thought," she stammers. "I didn't think you did fluff shots."

Gabe walks by her toward the door. "I didn't. But with everything that has happened, I figured I really can't afford to turn down easy money. Maybe some good can come out of all this mess after all."

"Y-y-you have to let me come with you." She chases after him. "Let me be your assistant or something. Come on. Just this once."

"But I don't need an assistant," Gabe says, stopping at the back door. "Interesting how you never asked to come with me before on any other shoot."

Abbie grabs his hand, swinging it side to side. "Pleeeease. I promise I'll never ask another favor for as long as I live."

Gabe rolls his eyes. "You wouldn't even make it two days."

"I got something," Abbie says, jumping up and down. "How about I work at the stand for two weeks for free? I'll work all the same regular hours, but you don't have to pay me at all."

"I don't know," Gabe says. "It doesn't look too good for me to show up with my kid sister—"

She cuts him off. "They won't even know I'm there."

"It's not that. What I was going to say is, it doesn't look too good for me to show up with my kid sister…dressed like that. This is the Chateau Marmont after all." He tugs at her oversized T-shirt. "I have my image to think about." Now it's Abbie's turn to glare at him, her jaw again going one way and eyes another. He shakes her from her stupor. "If you're going, you better hurry up and change. I can't wait all night."

"I can't believe it. You're the best." She lunges and kisses him on the cheek. "Be back in a flash. I know exactly what I'm going to wear." She runs into the house and returns a few minutes later in a sleeveless olive-green knit dress with a rounded neckline and leather ankle strap heels. A tan leather jacket hangs over her arm with a matching clutch in her hand.

Gabe, not expecting to see her so quickly, had moved over to his desk to do some work while he waited. He looks up from the computer screen. "We're going to work, not have dinner."

She spins to offer a total viewing. "I figured if you were going suede, we might as well match."

An hour later with Abbie at his side, Gabe breezes past a swarm of paparazzi lingering on the Sunset Strip sidewalk in front of the entrance to the Chateau Marmont. He approaches the valet stand and shows Eva's card to the comely twenty-year-old behind the podium. The young charmer flashes a full mouth of bleached enamel at Abbie, who self-consciously looks away. Reviewing the card, he waves them up the tree and shrub-lined drive that serves as the carport for arriving and departing guests as well as the entrance to the parking garage. The Pirelli tires of a glossy black Aston Martin Vanquish squeak against the small, square paving stones as the car pulls out of the garage and turns down the driveway toward the street.

Admiring the well-dressed, polished patrons positioned along the path, Abbie says, "Aren't you glad we spiffed up? Just because we're working doesn't mean we have to look like we are."

Gabe still feels out of place as they walk into the iconic William Douglas Lee-designed property modeled after a French royal retreat. "In and out," he whispers to Abbie. "We're just taking the photos and leaving."

At the maître d' station, Gabe waits for the silver-haired man, who seems to be in charge, to finish directing a svelte young girl to seat the couple in front of them. Still clutching the card with the hundred-dollar bill clipped to it, Gabe presents it to the maître d', who, seeing the name on the card, slides it into his pants pocket. "Ah yes, Monsieur Adams. Ms. Florez informed me you would be coming. May I remind you to please be discreet. We rarely allow photographers inside, but Ms. Florez is a longtime friend of the Marmont, and we like to keep our friends happy." He raises his arm, lightly snapping his fingers. Another tall model-type female approaches. The maître d' says, "Jacqueline, please show Mr. Adams and his companion to Ms. James' and Mr. Bethel's table on the terrace." He shoos her away with a nod, immediately looking past Gabe and Abbie toward the people standing behind him.

Gabe and Abbie follow Jacqueline through a casual dining area with high ceilings and pointed-arch windows. Guests fill padded chairs and sofas arranged to create intimate enclaves in the dimly lit open space. Passing outside to the terrace, the bamboo palms positioned around tables seclude each one, offering brief glimpses of diners as the multiple stems and long, pinnate leaves shift in the breeze. Gabe spots Emily, with someone he presumes is Ira across from her, seated at a small round table under a white parasol. Emily recognizes Gabe and reaches across the burgundy and cream thatched whicker tabletop, grasping Ira's hand.

At the table Jacqueline presents Gabe and Abbie to Emily and Ira and promptly leaves. Uncontrollable excitement effuses from Abbie. Gabe grasps her hand to help her hold it together. "Good evening, Ms. James. Nice to see you again." He lets go of Abbie's hand and shakes Emily's then turns to Ira. "Mr. Bethel, pleased to meet you. Eva just raves about you."

"You brought your sister along," Emily says, mumbling to herself. "That seems professional."

"And who is your lovely friend?" Ira says to Gabe. His politeness neutralizes the momentary awkwardness caused by Emily's boorish reception.

Abbie doesn't wait for Gabe to introduce her. She fires her hand into his. "I'm Abbie, Gabe's sister. I just have to say, I'm such a big fan of yours. It's really an honor to meet you." She lets go of his hand and looks over at Emily. "Of both of you, actually. Nice to see you again, Ms. James."

"Yes, yes, we're all big fans of one another here," Emily says. Not liking the obvious flirting going on between Abbie and Ira, Emily reaches across the table and again grabs hold of Ira's hand, this time to remind everyone it is the two of them on the date. "So, I think five pictures should do it. Take one from the entrance where you just were; one from behind me at him and the other way around; one by that tree over there; one looking back with the arches and columns so people know where we were; and one by those bushes over there." Gabe is silent, looking around at the suggested spots. Abbie's eyes drift toward Ira, then when his fall on her, she looks down with a sheepish smile. Emily says, "What are you waiting for? Let's get this over with. Come back and let me see them before you leave."

Gabe, with Abbie next to him holding his bag, moves around the terrace area, snapping pictures as directed. Emily and Ira feign intimacy, smiling and laughing, always touching one another, eyes transfixed. Abbie says, "God, they're good. Amazing how they can turn it on and off. It all looks so natural."

"That's why you never trust actors," Gabe says, snapping the final shot. "They can become whoever they want to be."

Returning to the table, Gabe accesses the pictures on the camera screen. The warmth and affection evaporate from the table. Gabe flashes an I-told-you-so look at Abbie.

Emily reaches for the camera. "Just give it to me." She flips through the pictures, her face changing in response to each one. "This one is good, fine for these two. This one, you can't even tell it's us. I thought you were a competent photographer. I can do better with my phone. Can't you get more light in it? Last one is all right, I guess. Just redo the one, and we're good."

Ira smiles at Abbie, apologizing for Emily's insolence. Abbie responds with the same demure glance she has worn since their hands first touched.

Gabe doesn't say anything. He just takes the camera from Emily and moves to reshoot the photo. A few steps away he realizes Abbie is not following. He stops, turning back toward the table. "Ab, let's go. We don't want to overstay our welcome."

"Of course," Abbie says. "Really nice to see you again, Ms. James." Emily just nods back with a fake smile.

Ira stands from the table. "The pleasure was all ours, Ms. Adams. I do hope we'll see you again sometime." He takes her hand, leans in, and plants a kiss on each cheek.

Abbie, glowing from the interaction, joins Gabe positioning for the makeup shot. He reduces the f-stop to increase the aperture and let in more light. Looking through the lens, he sees some harsh gesturing from Emily to Ira, then the fake fondness returns. Gabe snaps several more photos. He whispers to Abbie. "What the heck was all that about? You practically climbed on his lap."

"We had a moment," Abbie says. "I think in the business they call that a meet-cute."

◆◆◆

AFTER DINNER IRA DRIVES Emily home to Century Tower. She has been quiet most of the ride, which Ira views as a blessing because all she did through dinner was complain about how stupid and boring people are. He steers his Porsche through the travertine gates and toward the front entrance. Emily puts her hand over his on the gearshift. It was the first warmth she had shown toward him. "You want to come up for a swim?"

"You must be joking," Ira says. He shifts the car in park and looks around. "Or is there another reason we need to keep faking it?"

Emily traces her finger up and down his arm. "Why are you being like this? Don't you like me?"

Ira waves off the approaching valet. "You hardly said ten words to me all night except to talk about yourself or criticize others. Now you expect me to come upstairs? I'm glad we were able to help each other with the photos, but I think it's best if we call it a night."

"I'm sorry," Emily pouts. "I get nervous and ramble about myself when I really like someone. Plus, you made me a little jealous flirting with that other girl. If you like the skittish schoolgirl, I can be that too." She droops her eyes and pushes out her bottom lip.

Ira flops back in his seat. "Who? Abbie? I was being kind because she seemed like a nice person. You might try it sometime. It was refreshing to meet someone normal."

The last word sets Emily off. The simulated sweetness she had been showing subsides. "You're saying I'm not normal? Who the fuck do you think you are to judge me?"

The sudden spite shocks Ira. "Easy. I'm not implying that at all. I just meant someone from outside the business. It was nice."

"Is that where you're going now?" Emily rants. "To meet up with Little Miss Normal? Are you going to take her out for a piece of pie?"

"Are you fucking insane?" He leans away from her against his door. "I just met her. You were there the whole time. Do you think somehow we communicated telepathically and arranged to meet up?"

"I don't care what you say, something was going on." Emily crosses her arms and looks out the window. "Pretty rude to do that right in front of me. I mean, we were on a date."

"A fake date," Ira says. "Arranged by our agents. I'm not sure what you're so upset about. I had a nice time, but it's late and I have an early day tomorrow."

"Fuck you, it's late." Emily pushes open the door and swings her legs outside, looking back over her shoulder at him. "Do you know how many guys would kill for the opportunity I'm giving you? You know what, just forget it." She pushes out of the low bucket seat then leans her head back into the car. "I don't even know why I'm wasting my time with a little boy like you." She steps back and slams the door.

Ira just shakes his head, watching her storm off into the building. He activates the voice command in the car requesting a call to Eva as he pulls away.

Eva answers on the second ring. "How'd everything go?"

"Pictures went fine, but Emily sure is a piece of work." He pulls onto Avenue of the Stars. "She completely flipped out on me when I didn't want to go upstairs with her for a swim afterward."

"I don't think she hears no very often," Eva says. "But the photographer was good?"

"Yeah, he was great. What do you know about his sister?"

"Abbie was with him?"

Ira nods even though she can't see him. "Yeah, attractive blonde about my age I think."

"I only met her once, but she seems really sweet. Why?"

"Do you think you could get her number for me? I'm just so sick of all the drama with these other girls. All they do is talk about themselves or bitch. I don't know. Abbie just seems different."

"I totally get that," Eva says. "If they're not crazy to begin with, this business will turn them that way. Let me talk to Gabe and see what I can do.

◆◆◆

THE NEXT MORNING GABE arrives at Eva's office before nine with the three poster-sized pictures that she selected in his studio. Each is individually wrapped in brown butcher paper. Joelle informs him that Eva is not in yet. Gabe sits and waits, flipping through the pictures on the camera from his morning shoot of early surfers at Pacific Palisades. He figured if he was coming to the west side, he might as well use the opportunity to take some pictures.

Forty-five minutes later, Eva, her purse over one shoulder and computer bag over the other, rushes into the reception area. The straps of the two satchels cross like holsters across her chest. "I'm so sorry to keep you waiting. Had a breakfast meeting that ran over." She waves the to-go coffee cup clutched in her hand toward her office. "Let's go in and review the pics you sent over."

Gabe tucks the wrapped prints under his arm and follows her into the office. "Everything went just as you said it would."

"It should," Eva says, stripping off her leather totes and placing them on her desk. "I pay those guys enough to make sure it does."

Gabe scans the room, noticing all the framed movie posters filling the space on the walls. "I didn't realize all that stuff is so orchestrated."

She takes out her laptop and snaps it into the docking station. "When news gets out, it's usually because someone wants it out. The rest of the stuff is just filler. Then there's a whole other bunch of information that we pay not to be released. The biggest paydays are for the pictures no one ever sees—like your waterfall ones could've been. What did you get for those if you don't mind me asking?"

Gabe shifts his weight from right to left, uncomfortable talking about the money. The business side has never been his strongest attribute. In this situation he knows he should probably lie and drive up the asking price of the pictures he took at the Marmont and could take for Eva in the future, but he decides to stick with the truth. "Ten thousand."

Eva drains the last of the coffee from the cup, which has never left her hand, and tosses it in the trashcan next to her desk. "Could've got five to ten times that amount for deleting them and in the process saved yourself a lot of hassle." She presses the power button on the computer and eases back into her chair. "But what's done is done, right? Onward and upward."

Gabe moves around to her side of the desk. He says, "The extra ones from last night were because Emily didn't like one of the others I took, so she made me do it over. I snapped a few more to be safe. She sure is a handful."

"I'm hearing a lot of that lately. A total pain in the ass, actually." Eva says, shaking her head. "But she's the most popular actress in the twelve to seventeen age group, and my client has a new movie coming out. Being associated with her will boost the opening weekend numbers. Plus, she has an image problem after all the Levi stuff. My client is squeaky clean, so it's a win-win." Eva clicks through the pics. "Yeah, these are all good. I'll leak them to my contacts. Should be out later today." She looks up from the screen with a coy smile. "I hear Abbie went along last night."

"She didn't really give me much of a choice. I hope that's all right. She's been a fan of Emily for years and has always wanted to see the Chateau Marmont. You know how teenage girls are."

"No problem at all," Eva says, walking out from behind her desk. "It seems she made quite an impression. Ira was asking me about her. Wanted me to get her number for him."

Gabe stiffens. "Absolutely not. The last thing Abbie needs is to get tied up with some entitled, Hollywood brat who will just chew her up and spit her out. She's been through too much. I don't want to see her get hurt."

"I understand your concern." Eva leans back on her desk. "But Ira isn't like that. He's the real deal. It's not an act at all. If I thought there was any chance his intentions were less than noble, I wouldn't have even asked. He's a down-to-earth kid and can't stand the typical Hollywood stuff. Why don't you at least meet him in a normal setting? If you don't like him or trust him, it doesn't have to go any further. What do you say?"

Gabe rubs his hand back and forth across his chin, considering the offer. "I guess there's really not much I can do to stop it even if I wanted to. She'll just go behind my back. I might as well at least try to manage it. Go ahead and give him my number."

"That's great." Eva claps her hands together. "I'm telling you, you're going to love the kid. I would trust him with my sister if I had one." Eva stands from the desk and motions toward the wrapped prints. "How much were you thinking for those? I can have my assistant do one transfer for everything."

Gabe retrieves the pictures from the chair he had set them on when he came in. Setting them on the desk, he says, "I can do five hundred a piece." He turns the top one over and pulls the lip of paper to unwrap it. "Or since you're getting three, fourteen hundred will do."

"Fifteen hundred is fine." Eva places her hand on the paper, stopping him from unwrapping. "Don't bother. I trust you." She picks up the phone and calls Joelle. "We need to set up a transfer for twenty-five hundred for Mr. Adams...Yes, he'll give you all that on his way out. Thanks." She hangs up the phone and looks to Gabe. "Just give Joelle your account info, and the money should transfer by tomorrow."

Gabe stands across from her, brandishing a look of surprise. "A thousand bucks just for that little bit of work last night? Only took me about an hour."

"Not everything needs to be difficult," Eva says. "Like I said before, I need someone I can trust. I can't give you access and have you run off and sell to the highest bidder." She removes a pen and tablet from her desk drawer and scribbles down a name and address. "Also, I think I found you another gallery—one Levi can't ruin. I already talked to the curator and she's interested. You just have to go there and show her your portfolio. Should be able to get something set up in the next four to six weeks. In the meantime, I can keep you busy with other opportunities if you're interested in doing more gigs like last night."

Gabe furrows his brow, studying her for a moment.

Eva says, "What? You still don't trust me?"

"No, it's not that," Gabe says. "It's just I still don't completely understand why you're helping me. You lost more than I did."

Eva steps out from behind her desk and walks over to him. Rubbing her hand up and down the side of his arm, she says, "That's easy, silly. I like you, and Abbie too, and just really respect what you've done for her. I want to help."

The truth is, she needs to help to get back in control of something. It's the only thing she lost that she really misses. Another Levi will come along. The world is full of them. It will be so much easier this time. She has the reputation, experience, and most importantly, the money to turn anyone into whomever the world wants.

CHAPTER 22

Ira taps his Tom Ford velvet evening slipper nervously, sitting on the blue-and-white striped couch in Gabe and Abbie's living room. His hands buried in his lap squeeze one another. Gabe sits across from him staring back in silence. The ticking of the antique clock on the wall showing five forty-two reverberates through the room.

Ira wipes his palms on his black chinos. "I really appreciate you allowing me to take Abbie to this awards show tonight."

"Don't make me regret my decision," Gabe says. "Abbie's a sweet girl. She's not used to the fast lane you run in. Have her home by midnight. Is that going to be a problem?"

"Not at all, sir. My parents don't allow me to stay out late either. I have to be home by twelve thirty. They gave the driver strict instructions. We'll leave by eleven and come straight here."

Abbie glides from the hallway into the living room. The solid white sleeveless bodice clings to her fit upper frame. Her black-and-white striped skirt, showcasing her trim waist and burgeoning hips, falls just below the knees. Her hair is parted deep on the side, gathering at the nape of the neck and twisting into a knot held by a rhinestone hairpin. Her eyes are outlined in black with tiny wings extending from the corners.

Silence returns to the room as Abbie's appearance quells the awkward chatter. Both Ira and Gabe stand. Ira bangs his knee into the coffee table. Clutching his leg, he says, "Wow, you look amazing."

Gabe stares with a sappy grin on his face. Abbie reaches over and bats him with the black clutch in her hand. "Don't be a weirdo."

"Wait here. I want to get a few pictures." Gabe darts into the kitchen and through the door to the studio.

"I said not to be a weirdo." Abbie shouts after him. "You're totally embarrassing me."

Ira limps out from behind the coffee table. "It's okay. We have plenty of time. It'll be good practice for later. I guarantee you'll never want to see another camera after tonight."

Gabe comes back with his camera around his neck. "Let's do a few in here then we'll move outside for a couple by the limo." He lifts the camera, motioning toward the window. "Stand together in front there."

Ira and Abbie move into position. Ira straightens the button-line on his white twill shirt and adjusts the lapels of the grey wool-blend blazer. He stretches his arm around Abbie, who leans into him and plants her opposite hand on her hip, arm akimbo.

Gabe snaps two photos then leads them outside for several more in front of the limo and as they climb inside. He bangs on the window to deliver some final instructions. "You got your cell phone? Call me if you need anything. Remember, no drinking. Eva has spies there, so if you try it, she'll tell me."

"Don't worry, Mr. Adams," Ira says through the window. "I don't drink, and the party we're going to following the ceremony is a dry affair. We'll come straight back here after."

"Enough already. You can go back in the house now." Abbie rolls her eyes and raises the window as they pull away. Gabe lifts the camera to his eye, clicking additional shots until the limo turns at the end of the street out of view.

At the Forum for the Kids' Choice Awards, Ira leads Abbie down the red carpet. She doesn't have to smile for any of the pictures because one has been plastered across her face since she left the house. She and Ira approach a mass of photographers huddled around some noteworthy spectacle. One by one, the photographers peel off their previous subject, choosing to photograph Ira and Abbie instead. As the photographers thin out from the scrum, Emily can be seen at the center. She smiles when she notices Ira but immediately sours seeing Abbie. Emily grabs the hand of her date, who appears nothing more than an appointed accessory, and storms off.

Abbie whispers to Ira. "She didn't seem too pleased to see me. I thought you said you two never really dated."

Ira holds up his hand to the photographers. "Please, guys, I think you got enough. We need to get inside." He puts his arm around Abbie's waist and guides her through the crowd, stopping in the first open space. "We didn't. I swear. We only did the Oscars presentation and those photos at the Marmont. Nothing more. That's just how she is. If she's not the center of attention, the world should stop."

Inside the hall away from the press, Emily, with her date trailing behind, approaches Ira and Abbie. Ira clutches Abbie by the hand. "Here we go. This should be interesting." Smiling at Emily, he steps in her direction to greet her. "Emily, so nice to see you. You look lovely as usual."

Emily stops short of Ira not allowing him close enough for an embrace. "Thought you said that was the first time you two had met. You're such a liar. I knew there was more going on.

No wonder you wouldn't come up. At first I thought you were gay. Now I know you just like to bottom feed on scraps."

"Hi, Emily," Abbie says cheerfully, not picking up on the insult. "Nice seeing you again."

Emily just snarls back. "Common and dumb. Quite a winner you have there, Ira. I imagine we can throw in easy and you got your perfect girl."

Ira pulls Abbie closer to him as a sign of protection and affection. "No reason to be rude, Emily. I appreciate you agreeing to do the photos with me, but what you and I had was just business."

Emily's date leans over. "You're upset about this guy? He's not worth your time. Let's go to our table. The program is about to start."

"At least we agree on one thing," Ira says. "This isn't worth our time." He steps to the side and leads Abbie around Emily and her date.

A waiter with a tray of mushroom pate served on baked tortilla wedges walks by. Emily reaches over and grabs two off the tray, one in each hand. "Don't walk away without trying one of these lovely hors d'oeuvres." She smashes them into the back of Ira's and Abbie's heads. "I hear they are just to die for."

Ira spins around, stepping toward Emily. "You really are a fucking nutjob."

Abbie feels the back of her head, picking the pate and tortilla from her hair. The press encircles them.

Seeing the growing audience, Emily plays to the crowd. "What are you going to do, hit me again?"

The comment sets off flashes and questions like lightning and thunder.

Flash "Is that why you broke up with him?"

Flash "How many times did he hit you?"

Flash "Are you going to press charges?"

Emily's date moves between them. "This guy hit you?" He pushes Ira back. "You think you're some kind of bad ass?" Two of the ushers push through the swelling score of spectators and step between them. Emily's date attempts to fight through the security. Emily just stands behind, slyly smiling at the commotion she has caused. The reporters and photographers descend upon her, firing more questions.

Ira immediately backs off, more concerned with Abbie's safety. Wrapping his arm around her, he forces their way through the mob. Once they realize Ira has nothing more to say on the matter, they flock around Emily who has not stopped talking. As Ira and Abbie clear the swarm, more of the ushers arrive to guide them from the melee. Ira keeps Abbie close. "I'm so sorry about this. Your brother is going to kill me."

Abbie looks up at him. "What was that even about? It all happened so fast. She said you hit her?"

Ira looks back at Emily encircled by a mushrooming mass of media as she morphs immediately into a martyr. Her face is strained and her response, emotional. He can't hear what she's saying, but he knows, despite the traumatic theatrical turn, it's those around her being preyed upon. Under the lights and immersed in drama, regardless of tone, is the only way she is happy, and how she will always be.

The ushers lead Abbie and Ira down an empty hallway away from the event to two restrooms not being used. One of the ushers says, "Here, you can clean up and collect yourselves in there. No one will bother you."

"I didn't expect this tonight," the other usher says. "This is crazier than the Laker games…when they were good."

The first usher attends to Ira and Abbie. "Is there anything else I can get you guys?"

"Thanks, gentlemen. No, I think we just need a moment." Ira brushes some of the pate off Abbie's shoulder and leads her into the ladies' room. "I swear to you. What she said, never happened. After we saw you the other night, I took her home. She asked me to come up for a swim, but I declined. After that, I told Eva I didn't want to see her anymore, regardless of the impact professionally. This must be Emily's way of getting back at me." In the bright light of the restroom, he picks more crumbs from her hair. "I'm so sorry you got tangled up in this."

Abbie reaches up and puts her hands in his, lowering them to her waist. "I believe you." She rises up on her toes and kisses him on the cheek. "Let's not let it ruin the night. That's what she wants." She leads him over to the sink. "We need to get you cleaned up. You have an award to accept, and I hate mushrooms."

◆◆◆

Eva returns home after a long day of dealing with questions about Levi's arrest even though her only comment has been that they are no longer working together. To get through the onslaught, she kept reminding herself that the separation from him in the long term will be a benefit, and that she might even be able to get some normal clients, if there is such a thing in the film business. But since the arrest, it's been the opposite, just hassle and stress about Levi. Everything he did and everywhere he went were newsworthy, which meant more questions for her. No matter how many times she told reporters that she no longer represented Levi, the media still came to her for reactions and insight.

Eva assumes by now, Levi probably knows she is helping Gabe, and that he isn't too happy about it. What she doesn't know is what he will do. His actions have cleared her realm of understanding some time ago. All of it makes her question whether she ever really understood, or if she just tolerated and rationalized his behavior because she had to. After all, she created him. If anyone is to blame, it's her. He would've never made it on his own. In her mind, if she hadn't come along and plucked him out of the crowd and brought him to Los Angeles, he most likely would have ended up addicted to meth and opioids in some backwoods town like most of the people he grew up with.

Tired and upset from the stress, Eva trudges upstairs to relax in a bath. Her nightly soaks have become the only remaining peace in her life. She adjusts the water while dropping her tailored crepe pants to the floor. Retrieving a lavender bath bomb from the bottom drawer in the vanity, thoughts of Levi persist. Even alone in her own home, she can't escape him. Dropping the bath bomb in the water, she watches it fizz and twirl while peeling off her remaining clothes. She wants to stay mad at him, but already she can feel compassion, or maybe it's pity, she hopes, swelling within her. But, standing naked in front of the mirror, she remembers how many times he pushed her away for someone or something else and the hateful look in his eyes when he fired her. She doesn't really think he would actually hurt her, but she's not entirely sure he wouldn't either. He looked such a mess in his mugshot, and the ridicule that has come after has had to make him even more desperate.

Flipping on the audio player, she plays seaside ambient music. Sounds of a soothing breeze and resonant waves fill the bathroom. She shuffles across the marble tiling and slides into the low-slung spoon tub. The silky, violet-colored water from the dissolved bath bomb envelops her up to the neck. She pulls her feet back, pushing her knees above the water.

Seagulls squawk in rhythm with the repetitive ebbing and flowing surf through the speakers. She closes her eyes, lolling her head back over the edge of the tub.

The door, slightly ajar, widens. Hannah slithers through the opening onto the smooth, two-tone flooring. Gliding toward the tub, she curls around one of the silver, cast-iron claw feet and disappears underneath.

Eva scoops a handful of water onto her face, massaging her forehead and temples. Slow, deep breaths enter and exit through her pursed lips.

Hannah winds up around the chrome floor-mount hot water faucet. Her mocha head rises above the side at the foot of the tub. She bends over the edge and skims the top of the water along Eva's right side. Graceful and lithe, her movement is undetected. She bows around Eva's knee to above her stomach, which emerges above the water then sinks below with each breath. Hannah stretches further across the water toward Eva's chest and stops just short of her chin. Hannah, her tongue flitting in and out, stares at Eva's exposed neck and jawline.

Eva, eyes still closed, rotates her head in a circle in one direction and then another, leaving her head slumped forward. Hannah remains motionless, her body stretched along Eva's and her tail still outside the tub wrapped around the faucet. Eva lifts her head, slowly opening her eyes. She blinks several times, the lavender oil in the water clouding her vision. Staring directly at Hannah, finally seeing her, Eva thrusts back. Her arms flop and splash in the water. Hannah recoils, frightened by the sudden, frantic movement. Eva slips scrambling to get out of the tub. A wave of water sloshes over Hannah, who hisses back. Eva grabs the side of the tub and flounders onto the floor. Hanna lunges at her, but having the tub to herself, pulls back, her tail releasing the faucet and disappearing below the surface. Clambering to her feet, Eva snags the bathrobe off the hook and slams the door shut on her way out.

A few steps into her bedroom, Eva smashes into the chest of Levi. "How was your bath?" he says, grabbing her wrists and wrestling her toward the bed. The oily water coats her skin, causing his hands to slide off.

Eva drags her nails down his face. "Get the hell away from me." She pushes him and thrusts toward the door. "You've lost your fucking mind."

Levi hooks his arm around her waist and pulls her to his chest. She flails her arms and legs, fighting to get away. He presses his lips to her ear. "You always did like it rough, didn't you?" He lifts her off the ground and flings her onto the bed. She crawls across the comforter toward the nightstand where she left her phone. Levi says, "Looking for this?" He removes the phone from his pocket, pressing a button to light up the screen. "You might as well relax. No one can help you." Despite the warning, Eva springs from the bed toward the door. Levi drops the phone and catches her, throwing her back on the bed and descending on top of her. He pins her hands above her head, straddling her torso.

Eva twists and turns, struggling to free herself. "Let me go, you fucking lunatic." Unable to move her upper body, she drives one knee, then the other into his back. He brings her wrists together to hold them with one hand and reaches behind to thwart the repetitive blows. She rips her right arm away and rakes across his face.

Levi knocks her hand away and swings back through with a slap. "Bitch!" The smack stuns Eva. Her body goes slack. Levi fires his hand to her throat. "Why did you have to ruin everything?" He squeezes tighter, the veins in his forearm bulging.

"Me?" Eva gasps. She stops fighting, wrapping her fingers around his upper arms and pulling him toward her. In between sputtering breaths, she says, "All I've done is love you." Her swinging and scratching become stroking. The sudden change surprises Levi. He loosens his grip. Air rushes into her lungs. She moves her arms up, interlocking her fingers around the back of his neck and urging him closer. "I didn't want any of this. Only you." She pulls herself up and kisses him. "You always knew you could have me at any time. You just didn't care."

Levi pins her back to the bed, his hands again tightening around her throat. "That's not true. You know I care about you. You're the only one I can count on." He moves his lips along her jawline to her neck. "I was just afraid I'd fuck it up. I didn't want to hurt you." His mouth slides to her chest, devouring her in gulps and playful bites. "You've always been there for me."

Eva uses her nails again. This time to scrape the shirt off his back. "Why do you still have clothes on?" She rips at his belt. "Get these off." He stands up, undoing his pants and dropping them to the floor. She wraps her legs around his waist and pulls him back toward her. "Hurry up." Levi kicks his pants off to the side and descends on top of her. His skin, wet from the sweat of the struggle, meets hers, still damp from her interrupted bath. Their bodies slide back and forth as they jostle for a different type of carnal control. Levi reaches and grabs her legs behind the knees, pressing her thighs against her torso. As he tilts back, looking down for the target of his next move, Eva swings wildly, cracking him across the cheek. Levi freezes, stunned from the retaliation. Laughing, she says, "That's for slapping me."

Levi hesitates. "I'm sorry. I couldn't help myself. It was just instinct. What else am I supposed to do? You gouged a fucking piece of my face off."

"I don't care. I loved it. Come here." She drops her feet to the floor and spins around. "I want you behind me." Levi kicks her legs apart, pushing her face into the bed. He guides himself inside her, grabbing a handful of hair and pulling her head back. Her moan escalates to an affirmative yelp. He drives harder and harder. The mattress slides forward with each thrust. She plants her hands on each side and pushes back toward him, arching her back. Looking back at him, she says, "Come on. More. More." Levi bends forward, silencing her with a kiss. She lifts his arm to her chin, burying her neck in the crease of his elbow. "Squeeze harder. I want to feel your bicep against my neck."

Her aggression throws him off. "Are you sure? I don't want to hurt you."

"Just shut up and fuck me." She pushes her hips back into him and angles her torso forward tightening the pressure against her neck. "Don't stop unless I tell you."

Levi flexes cutting off her ability to speak. Her body responds, encouraging him to squeeze tighter. He puts his mouth on her ear, biting the top while announcing the proximity of his orgasm. She presses her body forward, using her body weight to further diminish her air supply. After several minutes of his huffing and puffing and her stifled breathing, he releases her and himself in one motion. She falls forward, filling and emptying her lungs in pleasure. He drops on top of her then rolls off to the side onto his back, catching his breath like he was the one deprived of oxygen. "Holy shit. Where did that come from?"

She rotates on her side toward him. Her body quivers. She presses against him. "I don't know. Fucking adrenalin I guess. Fight or flight. What are you doing here? Why did you bring Hannah over? How in the fuck did you even get in?"

"Came in through the garage. No one saw me."

"Yeah, but the door was locked. How did you get inside my place, not to mention with a seven-foot snake?"

"Hannah travels well. I just line the bottom of a duffel bag with hot water bottles and lay a towel over top. She coils right up inside and sleeps." He strokes his fingers along her side. "Remember, you gave me a key a while back before you had the office? I made an extra copy in case I lost it." Eva sits up on the bed. Levi reaches after her. "Where are you going? Lie here with me."

Eva stands and fetches her robe from where she dropped it on the floor. "I still don't understand why you're here, though. I mean, what were you thinking? What was your plan?"

Levi sits up on the edge of the bed. "Nothing really. I can't stay in that house alone any longer. Just wanted to play a joke with Hannah and talk, I guess. Everything has just been so fucked up lately."

"Whose fault is that? You fired me, remember?" Eva says, adjusting her robe around her neck and cinching the belt. She picks up her phone lying next to Levi on the bed and slides it in her robe pocket. "An apology would probably be the best start."

He stands and walks over to her. The bags under his eyes stretch the full length underneath and curve up the side. He wrings his hands nervously. "You're right. I'm sorry. I really fucked up. I need you to come back."

Eva says, "I don't know. Maybe it's better this way."

Levi steps closer to her, rubbing the sides of both her arms. "But I need you."

"I don't think you do." Eva steps away from him. "What you need is to be on your own and get control of your life. You created this mess. You need to find a way out of it."

Desperation seeps through his panic. "But I can't do it without you."

"I guess you should've thought about that before."

Her rejection intensifies his plea. "I don't understand why you're being like this. I thought you said you loved me."

"I do. It's just we both need to move on," Eva says in a calm and even tone. "I have new interests and clients that would now be a conflict. You need to do the same."

Levi momentarily stops pacing to ask a question. "Like that little shit that's being photographed around town with Emily?"

Eva ignores the comment. "Shouldn't you be more worried about your arrest?"

"Do you mind?" Levi motions toward the bar in the corner of her room. Eva responds with a shrug. He says, "For those trumped up charges? I'll beat it no problem. Remember how I said I thought I recognized that DA? I met him those first few years I was in LA. He was just a teenager then. I dated his sister, Tamara." He fills half of a rocks glass with warm gin. "She was that psycho makeup artist who worked on me for that Thursday night drama *Wish List*."

"That's right. We had to have her reassigned."

"She eventually got fired and fell on some hard times." Levi grimaces, forcing down the straight booze. "Got hooked on H and died. That DA must blame me. Lawyers are going to have a fucking field day with that."

"I don't know," Eva says, turning around one of the bar stools and sitting down. "Seems like with that photographer's testimony they still have a pretty strong case."

Levi gulps more gin. "I heard he was the one who took the pictures of Emily and that little punk at the restaurant. Maybe they're working together. Maybe she set me up at the waterfall."

"Levi, you're fucking obsessed. You have to let this go. It's just a coincidence."

Levi tilts his head, studying her for a moment. "Wait, that douche who was with Emily is one of your clients." Eva remains still and silent in the chair. Levi says, "You set up those photos at the Marmont. You're working with that photographer. You hired him." Levi resumes pacing, his mind racing. Eva just watches, enjoying his melt down. Levi stops and drains the gin in his glass. "Are you behind the waterfall, too?

Eva stands from the stool. "Easy, Mr. Paranoid. He's my client, but I had nothing to do with the waterfall. Why would I ever do anything to sabotage your career? That would hurt me too."

Levi moves toward her. "But Ira was your client before. How is it a conflict of interest now?"

"I'm sorry. I assumed you knew. You're right. I hired the photographer for the Emily and Ira pics at the Marmont." She hops off the stool and walks toward the door. "I've been thinking about adding an in-house photographer to the agency for a while. There's some natural synergy there."

Levi trails after her. "What? How could you do that to me? That guy destroyed everything we were building."

Eva stops and pivots, angling toward Levi, pointing, her voice rising word by word. "No, you ruined it yourself and tried to do the same to him. I'm just trying to undo the damage you did. You know, I think it's probably time you left."

Levi looks down at the floor. The empty glass dangles at his side. "I can't believe after everything we've been through, you're choosing him over me."

"Get over yourself," Eva says. "I didn't pick him over you, and remember you were the one who fired me."

Levi inhales a deep breath, life rushing back into him. "Wait until I get my hands on that guy. He's fucking dead. I'm sick of him fucking shit up for me."

Eva moves toward him. "I can't believe...you know what, I can totally believe it. You just don't even see how you are even remotely responsible for any of this. So typical. I wouldn't even think about retaliating any further with him if I was you. If you do, I'll feed the DA all the stories I've covered up over the years."

The threats deflect off Levi. Regardless of what she has, none of it compares to what is in his freezer. His eyes constrict into a menacing stare. "Not just him. You better also worry about what I might do to you."

Eva removes her mobile phone from her bathrobe pocket, opening the door with the other. "Get out or I'll call the police right now."

Levi roils across the room, stopping in front of her, looking down. "I'll leave, but you never know when I'm coming back." Levi fires the glass against the wall. Shards spray in all directions. Eva swings at him, but he catches her arm, holding it for a moment, then shoving her back.

"You're pathetic." She lifts the phone to her ear. "Last chance to leave."

He doesn't say anything. He just walks to the bathroom, collects Hannah, and leaves.

CHAPTER 23

THREE POLICE CARS AND a City of Los Angeles box truck crawl through the throng of people in front of Levi's house. Marcus, a paper clutched in his hand, exits the back of one of the cars. A voice in the crowd informs him no one is home. Marcus continues to the call box and rings three times with no answer. He waves to the driver, who pulls the truck parallel to the gate and parks. Officers exit the cars in twos moving the curious onlookers away from the gate. The box truck driver alights from the cab and walks to the back, sliding open the door and dropping the ramp. Moments later he is backing a forklift down the ramp and maneuvering toward the gate. Marcus rings from the call box again with no answer then nods to the driver-turned-forklift-operator. Rolling toward the gate, the operator lowers the forks and guides them underneath. The onlookers, still roused from Levi's bracing departure, ooh and ah like a coaxed studio audience. With a pull of the lever, the operator raises the forks. They grab and dig into the wood. Splinters and sparks fly until the door breaks free from the latch and slowly rises on its own. The operator returns the forklift to the truck but leaves the truck parked in front of the gate. Two of the officers stay to keep the crowd from following. The others, along with Marcus, climb back into their cars and drive through the gate.

"Keep your eyes out for any signs of this missing photographer," Marcus says as the cars cruise over the basalt paver stones leading to the house. "Blood, broken photography equipment, anything that looks out of place."

Scanning the trees and bushes along the side, the officer in the passenger seat in Marcus' car says, "Hold on. I think I saw something." The cars stop. Marcus and the officers get out. The officer who called for them to stop walks over to the bushes pointing where Levi chased and eventually drug out the photographer. "Seems to be an opening here." He parts the branches farther. "Looks like someone has been through here."

Marcus pushes in front of him following the matted path. A small clearing swells where the struggle occurred at the base of the fence. Marcus crouches down running his gloved hands over the broken branches and smashed leaves. He picks up one of the ends soaked with red. Standing, he says, "I found blood. Section this area off and call the field investigation unit to process it." He works his way backward, vocalizing the scenario he is building. "So he chases the guy, catches him at the fence, they fight, and he drags him back out." Marcus clears the edge of the bushes looking at the surrounding grass, which the officers are blocking off with police tape. "Then what?"

One of the officers says, "He obviously didn't get away or we wouldn't be here. He had to take him somewhere."

"Maybe that's why Combs tore out of here before. Had the body in the Jeep," another officer offers.

"I don't think so," Marcus says, looking at the house. "Too risky with everyone out there. He'd call someone to take care of it or keep the body here." He points at the two officers who came in the other car. "Call the guys at the gate. Have them canvass the crowd if any other cars have been in and out. You guys work here. We're moving up to the house." Marcus and the other two officers climb back in the car and drive the remaining way.

At the front door, Marcus again follows the knock-and-announce protocol. After no response, he nods to the officer who has retrieved a battering ram from the trunk. In one back and forth motion, the officer splinters the door from the hinges. Marcus steps through the archway, his eyes scanning immediately to the glass wall and expansive backyard. "One of you start out back, and we'll cover the inside."

The officer with the battering ram says, "Let me put this away and grab my kit. I'll take the back."

The other officer moves to the kitchen, spraying luminol on the granite counters and teak flooring.

Marcus walks into the living room, taking a moment to process the scene mentally. He has spent so much time over the years in pursuit of Levi, it's surreal for him to be inside his house. He notices the place hardly looks lived in. It's too clean, and there are no personal effects anywhere. He tracks over to the wall and presses the button to open the glass back wall. The other officer has returned from the car and moves outside. Marcus says, "Start at the fire pit. See if he tried to dispose of anything."

The officer in the kitchen shines a UV light over the sprayed surfaces. "Kitchen looks clean." He works his way backward to the hallway, a spray of luminol followed by a flash of UV light. He stops at the door to the garage. "I got something over here." He sprays the handle again and along the door jam. "Look at this." A florescent blue smear glows from the handle and along the trim. He sprays the floor following the luminescent trail toward the back. "Must've drug him right through here."

Marcus pads over by the door careful to avoid the area that only seconds ago was lit up like the night sky. "So he beats him bloody out by the driveway and brings him back to the house through the garage and out to the yard. But what does he do with the body?"

The officer working the backyard comes back to the house. "The fire pit has definitely been used recently. No traces of bone or tissue though. Only some fabric and buttons. Probably burned the clothes or a blanket or something."

"Come over here," the officer in the living room calls out. He sprays the area behind a chair, which backs up to the walkway from the backyard to the garage. The narrow, straight streaks from the body being drug expand to a circle around the back leg of the chair. He crouches down and sprays the bottom. The whole corner lights up under the UV light. "There was a large discharge of blood right here."

Marcus slides the chair to the side. "Spray it again." The officer complies and points the light. An outline of the chair leg emerges. Marcus bends down examining the chair. "Give me your flashlight." He shines the beam under the chair and reaches under with his other hand. "Grab an evidence bag." He pulls a chunk of dried bloody flesh from the side of the leg. Examining it closer, he says, "Doesn't that look like the bottom of a left ear?" He drops it in the bag. The officer holds it up to formulate an opinion, but Marcus doesn't allow him to respond. "Which means, if it was on this side of the chair, he wasn't dragging the body out." Marcus rushes to the door leading to the garage. "He was dragging it back in." He flings open the door. His eyes flash to the open space between the Bugatti and BMW.

The officer trails behind spraying and shining the UV light confirming his theory. Marcus stands on the top step scanning the garage hoping the body isn't gone with the Jeep. The officer moves around him and follows the trail toward the open space. Marcus's eyes fall on the freezer just as the trail ends.

◆◆◆

LEVI TEARS OUT OF Eva's parking garage onto Seventh and right on Figueroa. He knows he can't go home. With the way he left, he assumes the number of people and attention has probably grown. He doesn't know that Marcus and the police have arrived in between and what they have found. As he continues from the 110 to the 10, heading due east, he realizes the only place he wants to go is Gabe's to settle things once and for all. He locates the address he had provided to the thug and punches it in the GPS.

Not knowing what or who he will find, Levi parks on Del Cerro, the street behind Gabe's. Walking around the block, Levi passes by the front of the house, then at the end of the cul-de-sac, he loops around and travels the full length again, surveying the quiet residence without ever stopping or looking directly at it. Satisfied no one is home, he circles back around to where he parked and cuts between two houses with connecting backyards. Light fans from the neighboring houses across the lawns, fading to black as he approaches Gabe's.

Creeping up to the back of the dark garage, Levi removes a six-inch red flashlight from his pocket. He presses the light against the glass before turning it on to prevent the rays from reflecting back onto him and drawing attention. Flipping on the beam, he sees the framed pictures and photography equipment on the other side of the glass. He turns off the light and pulls his sleeve over his clenched fist, concealing both the light and his hand. A dog's bark from down the block ripples between the houses. He scans the neighboring yards once again to ensure he's alone. Static outlines of swing sets, grills, and patio furniture are silent spectators. He watches the family in the house directly behind through their patio door. They crowd around the dining room table playing a board game. In the home to the right, a couple wash dishes in the kitchen in between sips of wine.

With his wrapped fist, he bangs the window, once, twice, then a third time, increasing the force with each punch. The cracking of glass dissipates through the dormant yards without a response. Several harder taps knock a piece of the webbed glass onto the garage floor. Reaching through the broken window, he unlocks the door and slips inside. Milton scurries by, escaping through the opening.

Directing the beam, Levi views each of the pictures Gabe has prepared for the new show. He sets the flashlight down, angling the beam toward the pictures. He removes his knife from his front right pocket and opens the blade. One by one, he picks up the pictures, smashes them on the ground, and punctures the knife through the center of the prints. With quick, violent slashes, he slices up and down and from side to side.

◆◆◆

IRA'S PORSCHE IDLES IN the driveway. Abbie crosses over the console and kisses him. She wears a black sports bra, tight black high-rise leggings, and florescent green running shoes. "Doesn't look like Gabe is home. You should come inside."

"I'd love to," Ira says, caressing the back of her head. He also sports workout clothes, donning only a gray T-shirt and black shorts and sneakers. Sweat soaks through the shirt and rings around his neck and under his arms along the sides. "But I need to go home and shower."

"You can shower here." She runs her finger over his lips and chin and down to his neck and chest.

"I don't think Gabe would appreciate me being in the house without him here, let alone in the shower."

"He's my brother, not my dad."

"Even still, I think he's just getting over the drama from the awards ceremony and beginning to trust me again. I don't want to do anything to have to start all over again."

"Aw, you're such a good guy." Abbie pecks him softly between each word. "How did I get so lucky?"

He returns her affection, gently rubbing the tip of his nose against hers. "I think I'm the fortunate one. Just glad you didn't let Emily scare you off."

"No chance of that. I guess you're stuck with me." She kisses him again. "Is she still spreading rumors about you?"

"Not since Eva had a lawyer threaten her with a libel suit. Quiet as a church mouse."

"More like a sewer rat. I can't believe I looked up to her for so many years."

"At least she helped bring you and me together. If you think about it, we probably wouldn't have met if it wasn't for her."

"I think I'd rather give Eva credit for that."

Ira glances at the dashboard clock. "I better run. My parents are expecting me for dinner. Thanks for going to the gym with me. See you tomorrow?"

"Let me check my schedule." She kisses him one final time and opens the door to exit. "I think I might be able to fit you in." Sliding out of the car, she removes her phone from her purse and reads messages walking up the driveway toward the house. Ira flashes the lights on her when she passes in front of the car. He waits until she is inside then backs out.

Standing in the living room peeking around the drapes so he can't see her, Abbie watches him through the bay window as he drives away. Even the most mundane activities like going to the gym or grocery shopping or doing homework set her aglow when she is with him. Heavenly is how she describes things when anyone asks her. She digs her headphones out of her gym bag and buries them in her ears. Humming the melody of Taylor Swift's "White Horse," occasionally mixing in the words, she tosses her gym bag and purse on a chair by the door and struts to the kitchen.

She opens the refrigerator and scans the shelves for something to eat. Not impressed with the options, she settles on a leftover takeout box and walks over to the table. Through the sliding glass door, she sees Milton pawing at the glass. Removing one of the headphones, she opens the door. "How did you get out, silly boy?"

Milton trots straight to the door leading to the garage studio and scratches to get in.

Removing the other headphone from her ear, Abbie puts down her phone and the food on the table and shuffles over to Milton. "If you want to be in there, don't leave in the first place." She eases open the door. "Gabe?"

Milton scurries into the dark studio. The light from the kitchen reflects off the chards of glass on the floor from the broken window. Milton scampers through, disappearing into the shadows. Abbie steps into the studio, the glass grinding against the concrete under the rubber sole of her running shoe. Noticing one of the broken frames, she bends down to pick it up. The sight of the sliced-up picture startles her, and she drops the frame. Scanning the room, she says, "Is someone here?" Seeing and hearing nothing, she eases back toward the door and flips on the light.

Levi charges toward her. A scream bursts from Abbie. Levi puts his hand over her mouth, pushing her against the wall. Her headphones fall to the floor. "Sh-sh-sh," he whispers. "Don't fight. I'm not going to hurt you." Abbie struggles, flailing her arms and legs. Levi seizes her throat with his other hand. "Come on. That's not going to help anyone." She drives a knee into his stomach, knocking him back. She lunges toward the door. Levi grabs her around the waist and pulls her tight against his body, securing her with his other arm around her neck. "I'm not here for you. Just relax and everything will be fine." Abbie swings her arms, attempting to land elbows to free herself. Levi fights to hook her arms with the one holding her by the waist. Memories of being in the same position with Eva flood back to him. Tensing, he panics and squeezes tighter around her neck.

Abbie coughs and gasps, fighting more feverishly. Levi doesn't let up. The more she fights, the more force he exerts, eventually leaving her lifeless. Her limp body hangs over his arm. He lowers her to the floor. "Oh, no. No, no, no." Straddling her, he taps the side of her face with his open hand. "Come on. Wake up." He removes his gloves, sliding his fingers to her neck to check for a pulse. "Okay, okay, okay. That's good. You're going to be fine." He stands and looks around, remembering the flashlight on the table by the computer. He retrieves it and heads toward the door to flip off the light. Stuffing the flashlight in his pocket, he pulls out the knife and goes back to Abbie, who remains motionless on the floor. He reaches down and rolls her on her stomach. A whimper flutters from her lips. Levi opens the knife and fetches a roll of tape from the cabinet against the wall. He pulls her arms behind her back and binds her wrists and ankles and covers her mouth. Wearing the roll of tape around his wrist like a bracelet, he returns the knife to his pocket and scoops up Abbie in his arms. She moans incoherently, still too out of it to resist. He scans the room one final time and leaves, staying in the shadows as he navigates through the yards back to his Jeep.

LATER, GABE PARKS IN front of the house and treads up the driveway, glancing at Abbie's Volkswagen then at the dark house. He walks through the door and calls out. "Ab? You home?"

Noticing her purse and gym bag on the chair, he moves to the end of the hallway. "Anyone here?" He tilts his head, listening for a response or the shower or some music, any indication she might be home. He sees Milton eating from the open take-out container on the table. Abbie's mobile phone sits next to the box. Angling to the kitchen, Gabe shoos away Milton. "Hey, get out of there. You know better than that." He walks to the open studio door. "Ab?" Flipping on the light, he sees the broken glass and frames on the floor. "What the—" The backdoor slams shut. More glass from the shattered window falls to the floor. He hurries toward the door. "No! God damn it. Abbie?" He steps out into the backyard, peering into the neighboring yards for any sign of movement or sound. "Abbie? You out here? Abbie?" Hearing and seeing nothing, he charges back inside. He picks up one of the slashed pictures and sees her headphones on the floor. "Please, no." He drops the picture and snatches the headphones, praying nothing bad has happened to her.

From inside the kitchen, Abbie's phone rings. Gabe races to answer it.

In the Jeep, Levi drives with the phone to his ear. Abbie lies in the back seat, her arms, legs, and mouth still taped.

Gabe answers on the other end. "Hello?"

Levi says, "I have your sister. She's unharmed for now."

Panic tightens Gabe's voice. "Let me talk to her."

Levi holds the phone toward Abbie. "Say hi to your brother." Abbie mumbles through the tape. Levi brings the phone back to his ear. "I guess you're going to have to take my word for it."

"What do you want?" Gabe asks.

Levi angles the Jeep off the canyon road onto the dirt trail leading to the orchard farm. "First, what I don't want: police."

"Fine," Gabe says. "But what else can you possibly want from me that you haven't already taken? You ended my show and destroyed my work here. There's really not much left."

Levi says, "Have Eva come over, and I'll call you both back in an hour."

Gabe hangs up and dials Eva. She answers on the second ring. "This is a nice surprise. I was just thinking about y—"

Gabe doesn't let her finish. "I need your help. Levi took Abbie."

"What do you mean he took her?"

"I mean, he just called and said he has Abbie. Judging from the state of this place, it looks like he broke in here and started smashing up the studio. Abbie must've come home and surprised him. He just called and told me to call you and have you come over. You don't think he would hurt her, do you?"

"No way. I know the pending prosecution has pushed him off the rails, but he has no reason to go that far. It's probably like you said. She surprised him, and he panicked. He'll realize he has no move here except to let her go. He's already in enough trouble."

"I hope so. I don't know what I'd do if something happened to her. He said that he'd call us back in an hour. Can you be here? Or I guess I can meet you somewhere if that's easier."

"No, it's fine. I'll come there. Should be about forty minutes."

Unable to sit still while he waits, Gabe gathers the broken frames and slashed prints into a pile. He contemplates calling Marcus for help, rationalizing that technically Marcus isn't the police. Levi never said not to call him, but as desperate as Levi is, Gabe knows it's no time to count on subtleties.

A short while later, Eva knocks at the back door. Her voice travels through the broken window. "I can't believe he went this far. He came to my place earlier and seemed past desperate. We should call the police."

"No police!" Gabe attacks the last word. "Let's see what he wants first."

◆◆◆

PASSING THE DILAPIDATED FARMHOUSE, Levi stops the Jeep next to the barn and shuts off the engine. Chirping crickets and buzzing katydids replace the echo of the rumbling motor. The only light straggles down between the broken clouds. Levi remains in the driver's seat, staring straight ahead through the windshield. The bag with Hannah rests in the passenger seat next to him.

Afraid to move, Abbie lies still in the back seat, her eyes tremoring with fear.

Levi feels around behind the bag for his mobile phone. His movements are slow and methodical, his face devoid of emotion. He presses a button and lifts the phone to his ear.

Gabe answers right away. "Yes, we're here. Eva too. I have you on speaker."

Eva says, "Levi, what in the fuck are you doing? Kidnapping an innocent girl? Really? This is going way too far."

Levi barks back at her. "Don't put this on me. I didn't want any of this to happen. You both brought it on yourself."

"That's complete bullshit. All I've ever done is help you," Eva says. "You never would've had anything if I hadn't pulled you out of your dead-end life."

Levi cuts her off. "Fuck you. You were always in it for yourself. I was happy, living my life, but you couldn't let me do that. You always wanted more, and you needed me to get it."

"But Abbie didn't do anything," Gabe says. "Why do you have to bring her into this?"

"Her role in this is up to you. She'll be fine as long as you cooperate."

In the studio, Gabe and Eva stand on opposite sides of Gabe's desk with the mobile phone on speaker mode between them. Gabe says, "Whatever you want. Just tell us and we'll do it."

"That's the spirit," Levi says. "I want you and Eva to head north on the PCH. Before Malibu you'll come to Corral Canyon Road. Take a right. Stay on Corral Canyon until it forks into Castro and Mesa Peak Motorways. Are you getting all this?"

Eva grabs a pen from the top of the desk and scribbles down the directions on the back of an envelope. "Yeah, we've got it. Then what?"

"I want you to wait there," Levi says. "Once I'm sure you came alone, I'll give you the next instructions."

Gabe says, "What are you going to do with Abbie after we meet you?"

"She can take your car and leave," Levi says without hesitation.

Gabe looks at Eva and mouths, Anything else? Eva shakes her head. Gabe picks up the phone. "We're on our way."

"You have one hour," Levi says and hangs up.

Gabe snatches the phone and hurries toward the door. "Will you drive?"

Eva doesn't follow. "I don't think we should listen to him. He's completely lost it. We need to alert the police."

"Not enough time." Gabe stops in the doorway. "Come on. What are you waiting for? We need to leave now."

Eva walks toward him. "We should at least call them on the way. Or what about that Deputy DA? He'll know what to do."

"I'm not involving anyone. No way am I jeopardizing Abbie. Once she's safe, we'll figure something out."

Eva says what's really been on her mind. "But what about us?"

"If trading us for Abbie is what it takes, then that's what we're doing." Gabe spins around and hurries down the sidewalk along the back of the garage and around the side to the driveway with Eva trailing behind.

◆◆◆

AT THE ORCHARD FARM Levi places the bag with Hannah on the floor and lifts Abbie out of the back of the Jeep and sits her upright in the passenger seat. The wind blows in from the orchard swirling in the open space between the barn, house, and wooded area. Levi removes the knife from his pocket and opens the blade.

Abbie whimpers, her eyes widening.

He lowers the knife between her legs. "Don't worry. Everything is going to be fine." Extending the knife to her feet, he cuts the tape around her ankles. "This was never about you." He drags the blade up over her black leggings along her shin, up to her knee and inner thigh, to her exposed stomach. He traces a figure eight with the tip from the bottom of her expanded rib cage down and across her stomach, circling her navel and continuing up. Her skin bristles over her flexing abdominal muscles. She tries to control her breaths, resulting in stunted, shaky hyperventilating. Levi rests the point of the knife an inch above her navel. "You know, everyone thinks cutting into a person is like slicing a steak, and all you have to do is just rest the blade against the meat and let the knife do all the work." He lowers the flat side of the blade against her taut, quivering stomach. "But it's not like that at all. It's more like cutting a tomato. You have to apply just the right amount of force to break the skin but not too much or you'll destroy the flesh underneath." Levi slides the knife in a smooth motion, leaving a thin six-inch trail of red across her midsection. Abbie pleads through the tape covering her mouth, tears streaming from her eyes. Levi wipes up the blood with his finger. "That's how they taught me for that serial killer role. We used tomatoes." He lifts the knife to her face, resting the point on her chin. "I spent a whole day just slicing tomatoes. Not a single piece of meat." He taps the tip on her chin one final time, then closes the knife and returns it to his pocket. Looking at her, he brushes the hair from her face. "I told you not to worry. This will all be over soon." Levi rests his hand on the side of her cheek. "You are beautiful though. I'm sorry you got all wrapped up in this." He rubs his thumb gently back and forth across the tape covering her mouth. Bending down, he kisses her forehead. "It will all be over soon."

Seeing an opportunity, Abbie thrusts her knee into his stomach. Levi doubles over in her lap. She strikes him on the back of the head with her bound hands and kicks him off.

Sharply inhaling, Levi falls back, floundering on the ground, struggling for his wind.

Abbie unhooks the seatbelt and launches her legs from the Jeep. Her hands still bound, she swings them from side to side as she runs toward the dark orchard.

Levi, still gasping for air on the ground, lunges at her but misses. "You're just making this harder on yourself..." he wheezes. Still fighting to regain his breath, he stands, peering into the orchard. "...and your brother."

Abbie scrambles through the overgrown weeds, stumbling and falling. The coarse reeds scratching against her tights and wrap around her ankles. She crawls to one of the barren trees and huddles around the trunk.

CHAPTER 24

Eva drives her Mercedes with Gabe in the passenger seat. Her headlights provide the only light across the empty road. A sign points toward Corral Canyon Road. Gabe says, "Take the next right."

She conceals the phone between the seat and the door furtively texting Marcus the directions. Glancing at Gabe to ensure he doesn't notice, she says, "We need a plan. If we go in with no leverage, I don't think we're coming back."

"I'm not taking any chances until Abbie is free." Gabe motions for her to turn. "Right here."

Eva guides the car onto the dark, winding Corral Canyon Road. "Then we should at least leave her the phone, so she can call the police."

Gabe opens the glove box, rummaging through the contents. "You got a pen? We'll leave a note telling her what to do."

Eva contorts her arm to the back seat and retrieves her purse, tossing it to Gabe. "There should be one in there somewhere."

Gabe digs out a pen and snags one of the unopened envelopes from the glove box. His hands shaking, he scrawls additional instructions to Abbie on the back of the envelope with the directions from Levi to help her get back.

❖❖❖

IN THE JEEP WITH the high beams on, Levi trolls through the rows of trees, searching for Abbie. The light cuts through the weeds above her, illuminating the trunk of the tree. Her lungs pump as she struggles to catch her breath. The air whistles through gaps in the tape around her mouth. She lifts her bound hands to her lips, working the edges of the tape loose with her fingers and peeling it off. She sucks in several full breaths, releasing them slowly to calm herself. Trembling, she presses her arms against her torso to lie as flat as possible.

Levi stops the Jeep and shuts off the engine, leaving the lights on. The wind rustles through the weeds and trees, wafting the smell of rotting apples. He exits the Jeep. "I know you're out here. No reason to hide. I told you I'm not going to hurt you."

Rambling through the weeds, he listens and watches for a reaction. "Come on, we're going to meet your brother. Then you'll be free." Levi walks by the tree where Abbie is hiding.

She closes her eyes, ready to burst.

Levi stops. "I can hear you breathing."

Abbie finally breaks. A whimper escapes through her clamped lips.

Levi pivots. "There you are. Come on. This little game's over."

Abbie jumps up and flees, running between the trees. She swats at the thick weeds with her bound hands hindering her speed.

Levi easily catches her and throws her to the ground. "You are a live one. I'll give you that." He maneuvers on top of her, pinning her arms above her head. "You almost made us late." He stands up, careful to avoid her kicking legs, and slings her over his shoulder.

Abbie chops her bound hands into his back, screaming for help.

Levi reaches with one arm to hook her kicking legs while holding her in position with the other and carries her to the Jeep. "Relax, relax. No one can hear you anyway." He moves the bag with Hannah to behind the seat on the floor and dumps Abbie into the passenger seat, wrapping several rounds of tape around to secure her against the seat and reapplies a strip across her mouth. "There. That should hold you this time."

◆◆◆

APPROACHING A FORK IN the road, Eva's Mercedes slows down and pulls off onto the berm. With the car still running, Eva and Gabe exit and meet at the front. The headlights cut across their thighs, casting long shadows down the road onto the parting paths. Gabe says, "Should we call him?"

"No point in doing that," Eva says. "He's probably watching." She scans the surrounding woods. Swaying branches and rustling leaves whisper back. She knows she needs to stall. Marcus won't arrive with help for at least another twenty minutes. If they venture too far from the current location, which is the last one she knows and is able to send, he might not find them.

Farther down Corral Canyon Road, Levi's Jeep, the lights off, creeps toward them. Stopping fifty yards away, he flips on the high beams.

Gabe and Eva turn around and walk to the center of the road, both cupping their hands around their eyes to block out the blinding light.

Levi stands in the open Jeep, pointing his gun at Gabe and Eva. "Pull up your pant legs and lift your shirts." They comply, exposing their legs up to mid-shin and bare midriffs

Levi is visible only as a dark silhouette against an even darker backdrop. He says, "Now rotate in a circle so I can see there are no weapons or recording devices." They again follow the directions, pirouetting a complete rotation with their arms raised. Levi says, "Now walk forward to the front of the Jeep.

They shuffle toward Levi as instructed. Gabe says, "Let me see Abbie."

"This isn't a negotiation," Levi barks. "Just keep walking."

Gabe and Eva tread forward, squinting as the headlights blast brighter in their faces.

"And just in case you were wondering, this isn't a paintball gun this time. Levi fires a shot into the side of the road. The sharp, sudden blast freezes both Gabe and Eva. They cower into a crouching position. "Come on, keep moving," Levi says. "When you get to the Jeep, put your hands on the hood."

Gabe and Eva stop in front of the pair of lights. The beams gleam directly on their bare midsections. They place their hands on the hood. Levi dims the lights. Their eyes slowly adjust to the darkness. Abbie, secured in the front seat by the tape, comes into focus through the windshield. Gabe yells out. "Are you all right, Ab?"

Abbie, overwhelmed with fear, nods, tears streaming down her face. Levi exits the Jeep with the roll of tape. He walks to the front and binds Gabe's and Eva's hands. "Kneel down and don't move." He paces behind them. For the first time, Eva is actually afraid. She estimates how long it's been since she texted Marcus. Rotating her head and seeing only darkness in all directions, she knows it doesn't matter. He is not close enough, and Gabe is too focused on Abbie to worry about them and do anything.

Walking backward to keep them in view, Levi moves toward Eva's Mercedes. At the car, he reaches inside for the keys and notices the envelope with the mobile phone. He snatches the instructions and phone and removes the keys from the ignition. Storming back to the Jeep, Levi jams the barrel of the gun into the back of Eva's head. "You always did think I was stupid."

Fortunately, Eva had deleted the messages to Marcus, so even if Levi checks, he won't know Marcus is already en route, hopefully with more help than a paralegal. Eva pleads with Levi to stall for more time. "Levi, this is crazy. The absolute worst case with the pics of Emily is that you'll get a year in jail, and there's no way that's going to happen. Emily won't say anything, and Gabe will withdrawal his statement. But if you keep going with this, there's no turning back."

Gabe turns around to take the focus off Eva. "The phone and note were my idea. Please don't take it out on her. I just wanted Abbie to be able to get away."

"Turn the fuck back around." Levi pushes the gun in Gabe's face. "Don't you worry. I'll be sure to share the punishment between you and your girlfriend here." Levi walks to the passenger side. He tucks the gun in the back of his pants, takes out the knife, and cuts off the tape securing Abbie to the seat. He walks her to the front of the Jeep, stopping next to Gabe and removing the tape from her mouth. "Last chance. Anything you want to say?"

"I'm so sorry, Gabe. This is all my fault. I never should've touched those photos."

Gabe turns toward her. "Ab, no it's not. Don't worry. We'll be fine."

Eva straightens her body in defiance, scowling at Levi. "Don't worry, Gabe. He doesn't have the courage to do any-thing bad. He never could commit fully to anything. Just another empty performance."

Levi walks over and backhands Eva across the head. She crumbles to the pavement. He says, "How else do you think this is going to end?"

"Levi, for God's sake," Gabe implores, "let's just all walk away. We won't go to the police. We'll just forget any of this ever happened."

"Um, let's see." Levi extends his hands, palms up, bobbing them back and forth, mocking as if he's really contemplating the proposal. "Nope. Not going to happen. Because of you and your fucking pictures, I can't walk away. You might be able to, but I can't. You fucking destroyed everything."

Eva says, "Come on, you said yourself, no one is going to see Emily as a victim, and she'll never come forward. This will all blow over."

Levi says, "Not with Ambrose on the case. It's already too late. He's not going to let it go. In his eyes, I'm guilty. No way he lets me off. You think anyone will hire me after all this?"

"I'm not going to say anything," Gabe says. "And the pictures don't show everything."

Eva says, "Yeah, we can say all this erratic behavior is a promotional stunt for your next movie. I'll find a script that backs up the story."

"Just shut up," Levi yells. "Do you ever just listen to the shit that comes out of your mouth? You can't talk your way out of this." Levi grabs the tape off the hood and covers Eva's mouth first then Gabe's.

Levi waves Abbie toward the Mercedes. "Come on. Let's go. March!"

Abbie throws herself toward Levi. "No, please. I'll do anything you want. Just don't hurt them."

Levi pushes her toward the car. "Just walk." He continues behind her, jabbing her in the back to urge her forward as she slows. At the car, he shoves her into the driver's seat. "Put both hands on the wheel. Don't move until I'm gone, or your brother is as good as dead. If you do everything I say, I'll drop the keys in the middle of the road exactly one mile away. You can walk and pick them up and come back for the car."

"Please," Abbie begs. "Just let them go. He didn't even want to send the pictures. I did that on my own."

"Just fucking stop! I'm tired of all your lies." Levi waves the gun back toward Gabe and Eva. "They brought this on themselves. No one else's fault. It's time they pay for what's been done." Levi shuts the door and walks back toward the Jeep.

Abbie drops her head on the steering wheel and sobs.

Levi walks back, stopping behind Gabe and Eva. "See, I told you I wouldn't hurt her. As soon as we leave, she can walk to get the keys." He lifts Gabe by his bound hands. Gabe cooperates since Abbie is still potentially in jeopardy. "That's it," Levi says. "Nice and easy, in the back seat you go." Levi opens the door and lifts the seat. Gabe leans forward into the back. With a push from Levi, Gabe lands face-down on the seat. Twisting and wiggling, Gabe maneuvers on his side stretched across the seat. Unbeknownst to him, Hannah curls in the bag only inches away.

Eva doesn't go as peacefully. She flops on her back and kicks at Levi with her taped ankles as he approaches. "You're such a fucking loser. I never cared about you. I just used you like a plough horse. You better kill me because I'm going to love watching you go down for all this." She knows every moment she can delay, Marcus is closer to arriving. At any second, lights and sirens from approaching police cars could ease their increasing desperation.

Levi says, "Now now, it's too late for that. For once, just try and not be a vindictive bitch." He shifts around to get behind her head before she can rotate to fend him off. Bending down, he lifts her by the hair and slams her into the front of the Jeep. Eva screams as a gash opens on her cheek. He licks up the side of her neck to behind her ear, tasting the fresh blood. "Admit it. You're loving this." Yanking her around to the passenger side, he stuffs her into the seat. "Just like you did before." She twists and kicks, her muzzled screams inaudible. Levi holds her against the seat and fastens the seatbelt. With her hands taped behind her and the belt tight across her waist, all she can do is rock forward and side-to-side. Gabe works his way upright behind them. Levi smacks him back down to the seat. "Don't move a fucking inch. It's not too late for me to go back and get your sister." He walks back to the driver's side and starts the Jeep. "Let's go for a ride, shall we?"

A mile down, Levi drops the keys in the middle of the road between the two yellow lines. A few turns later, the Jeep rumbles down the dirt path toward the house and barn. They speed past both and head into the orchard. Turning the lights off to heighten the fear, Levi weaves the Jeep through the rows of trees in the overgrown weeds. Low branches smack the windshield and swat inside the open cab. Levi flips on the lights. The edge of the canyon is visible fifteen rows ahead.

Eva squirms in the seat, pleading for Levi to stop. He laughs at her begging. "Look at the power-bitch now. Have some dignity. It's better to die dramatically than live in shame."

In the back seat, Gabe has stretched the tape, creating a gap between his wrists and ankles. Rotating his wrists back and forth, he works the tape loose.

The Jeep powers through the decrepit orchard. The rows of trees dwindle. Levi stomps the peddle to the floor. The Jeep bounces along the uneven terrain.

Gabe twists his right wrist and pulls, able to free his hand. He maneuvers his body upright and lunges between the seats at Levi. The Jeep careens off an apple tree and slams into one in the next row. The momentum tips the Jeep and ejects Gabe. He tumbles to a stop, face down in the weeds. He rolls onto his back and sits up. The Jeep slides toward the edge of the canyon. Gabe pulls the tape off his legs and rushes toward the Jeep as it slides into the canyon. A cloud of dust and exhaust pass over Gabe. Coughing, he hurries to the edge and peers over the side.

The Jeep slides down the slope and skids to a halt on a ledge on the brink of falling.

Above on the cliff, Gabe rips off the rest of the tape from his wrists and works his way down to the wreckage.

In the Jeep, secured by her seatbelt, Eva is dazed but unharmed. Levi, his left shoulder and arm pinned between the seat and the door, wails, "I think it's broken." With his right arm he works to free his shoulder. The bag with Hannah is caught under the seat, an eight-inch rip visible along its side.

The tape hangs halfway off Eva's mouth. She extends her bound hands to Levi. "Come on. Cut this off. We can save ourselves."

Levi shifts his weight, rocking the Jeep back and forth. "No fucking way. You're way past saving."

Hannah slithers through the tear in the bag, curling around and under Levi's seat.

Gabe scrambles to the back of the Jeep. "Hey, come on. Work your way back so I can lift you out." Without hesitation, he leans into the back, not concerned with his own safety. The Jeep shifts forward, almost falling.

Eva yells at Gabe. "Just stay back or we'll all three go."

Gabe extends his arm further toward them. "I'm not going to stand back and just watch you die." Hannah stabs out at him from under the seat. Gabe jumps back. "Holy shit! There's a snake in here."

"Hannah is still with you?" Eva shouts.

Levi shifts his weight, urging the Jeep forward. "Stay back! It's better this way."

Hannah retreats under the seat and emerges in the front underneath Levi's legs.

Eva unfastens her seatbelt and extends her taped hands to Gabe. "Here, take my wrists."

Gabe grabs hold of the tape binding and pulls her toward the back of the Jeep.

Levi latches onto her leg but he's too weak from his injuries to stop her. Hannah crawls up his legs onto his lap. Levi says, "Don't worry, baby. Everything is going to be fine."

Safely at the back of the Jeep, Eva turns back toward Levi but doesn't say anything. She just shakes her head and smiles.

Gabe lifts her from the Jeep and sets her on the ground. "We can't leave him. Hold my legs and we'll lift him out."

"No fucking way. He tried to kill us. I'm not saving him. Besides, even if I wanted to, I'm not strong enough. Not to mention the snake on his lap. She'll probably bite you. We need to go for help."

"Not enough time." Gabe removes the tape from her wrists and ankles. "I'll just have to hold you then."

"Fuck that," Eva says, her adrenalin becoming anger. "He deserves to die. He did all this."

Gabe moves toward the back of the Jeep. "I'm going to save him with or without you." Eva reaches for him, but he pulls away, saying, "I have to at least try."

Eva shakes her head in frustration. "Fine. Grab the back of my legs." She climbs onto the unsteady Jeep, which shifts forward from the movement. She sinks her fingers into the top of the back seat. "This is such a bad idea."

"We'll be fine," Gabe says. "If the Jeep goes, we'll fall back on land."

"Jesus Christ," Levi yells. "Hurry up already. This thing is going to go at any second."

"You need to free yourself." Eva asks. "Can you unfasten your seatbelt?"

"I think so." With his left arm still pinned between the door and the seat, Levi moves his right arm toward the clasp, wincing in pain. Hannah remains coiled on his lap. After several attempts, he works free from the belt. "I think I got it."

Gabe says, "Can you get to the phone? I'll call for help."

"No fucking way. You guys will leave me."

"You're going to need medical help," Gabe says, stretching his arm toward him. "Trust me."

Levi maneuvers his hand to his pocket and fishes out Eva's phone, extending it to Gabe.

CHAPTER 25

ABBIE WALKS DOWN THE middle of the desolate road, scanning from line to line for the keys. She glances back toward the car to gauge how far she had come, but it had been swallowed up by darkness long ago. Faint sirens float from the distance. She stops and turns, taking a few steps back toward the car. The subdued sounds strengthen and soon scream toward her with flashing lights. Two LAPD cars and an ambulance screech to a halt down the road. Officers from both cars emerge with guns drawn crouching in the door wells. A command from inside the car orders their weapons down. The officer from the passenger side of the car on the right steps back and opens the back door. Marcus emerges followed by two paramedics from the ambulance. All hurry toward Abbie. She lifts her hands to shield the lights.

"It's Deputy Ambrose," Marcus says. "Are you alone?"

She runs toward him. "I'm so glad you're here." She leaps into his arms. He awkwardly receives her, gently patting her back. She says, "I am now. Levi was here, but he took them. I mean, first he took me, but then he had them come here, and he exchanged them for me. I think he's going to hurt them. We have to do something."

The paramedics stand on each side of them. Marcus steps back so they can examine her. He asks, "Are you hurt?"

She pushes back away from the paramedics. "I'm fine! But he has a gun and was talking all crazy. We have to find them."

"We will," Marcus says. "That's why we're here. Eva texted us to come." Not wanting to worry her, he doesn't reveal the manhunt that has ensued after they found the body at his house. "Any idea where he might've taken them?"

Abbie hurries toward the police cars. "I think so. It's not far. But it was dark. I don't know if I remember the way. It's an old farm."

"Do you remember an orchard?" Marcus asks, taking some folded papers from his pocket.

Abbie stops, turning back toward Marcus. "Yeah, that's right. I got free and ran into a field with a bunch of trees. Smelled like rotten apples."

Marcus unfolds the papers and points to a location on one of the pages that has a map. "It must be here. I found an old orchard farm that Eva arranged the purchase of a few years back by some private company. Had to be for Levi."

"Yeah, that has to be it." Abbie sprints for one of the police cars. "Come on. We already might be too late."

They all follow and get back into their respective vehicles. Predawn light mixes with a morning mist and floats down the road and into the surrounding trees. The police car with Marcus and Abbie leads, sirens blasting and lights blazing.

Careening down the canyon road, the convoy curves onto the concealed course and cruises past the house and barn into the orchard. A thick fog offsets the visibility from the increasing morning light. The cars slow in the thick weeds, which fill the grills and wrap around the tires. The ambulance plows through unimpeded. A piece of wood flies up smashing the windshield of the lead car. The driver slams on the breaks. The car slides into a tree. The trailing car swerves to avoid, spinning into another tree. The ambulance powers on toward the edge of the cliff. The officers spring from the stalled cars, opening the doors to let out Marcus and Abbie. She immediately charges toward the cliff following the tire tracks of the ambulance through the weeds. The officers and Marcus trail after her. The ambulance stops at the edge. A thin trail of smoke rises from just beyond the cliff.

◆◆◆

IN THE BACK OF the Jeep, Gabe stands on the ground holding Eva's legs. She works to free Levi from between the seat and the door. The Jeep rocks with every move.

Levi grimaces in pain. "It's no use. Forget it. Just save yourself."

Eva lowers her voice so only Levi can hear her. "You have no idea how much I'd like to." She pulls on the seat with one arm and latches onto Levi with the other. Hannah slides up Levi's chest around his neck and down the other side. With a forceful heave, Eva finally frees him. The Jeep shifts forward on the verge of plummeting down the canyon. She says, "We don't have much time. It's about to go. Grab on."

Levi seizes Eva's left hand with his right arm. Hannah crawls along his arm toward Eva. He says, "I can't hold on much longer." His grip slides down her arm to her wrist. She wraps her hand around his wrist and grabs his forearm with her other hand. Hannah coils around their joined arms.

"Pull us back, Gabe," she screams. "Pull us back now."

Gabe arches back, pulling with all his strength. Eva and Levi rise slowly toward the rear of the Jeep. Their eyes lock on one another. All emotion fades from her face. Her stare narrows. She lets go with her left hand. Levi slides down. Hannah hisses, slipping back with him. "What are you doing?" he cries. "We're almost there. Hold on."

Eva lets go with her right hand. Levi loses his grip. His fingers claw down her forearm. She says, "Just know, you were right. I was the one who sent him out to that waterfall."

Levi's fingers wrap around her wrist, clinging by surprise at her revelation as much as survival. "What? But how? I thought you didn't know him."

"But I know you," she says, locking her hand around his. "I knew you were taking Emily out there that day and would end up at the waterfall. All I had to do was send someone over to his stand and rave about how he needed to shoot it. You're all so predictable."

Gabe plants his foot on the back of the Jeep for more leverage. With Eva holding Levi by only one arm, the force merely stretches her, barely moving Levi. She yells back to Gabe. "Hold steady for a moment. He's stuck on something."

Gabe eases up, dropping his leg back to the ground. "You better hurry. We're running out of time."

Levi grabs the back of the passenger seat with his free hand and draws himself toward Eva. "Come on. Help me or we're both going to fall."

"I gave you everything and it still wasn't enough." She pulls her arm back. His hand slides over her closed fist, and he falls to the front, taking Hannah with him and forcing the Jeep forward. "This was your choice," Eva seethes. The Jeep teeters for a moment then breaks free, launching over the edge, plummeting wheels-side-up to the bottom.

In the orchard, Abbie, Marcus, and the officers intersect with the paramedics, who had run back toward them. Abbie breezes by toward the canyon. Scant strings of smoke streaming from below thicken to billowing pipes. Seeing the marks from the Jeep, she hurries to the edge. Marcus trails a few steps behind. Peering down the canyon, she sees the Jeep falling. The vehicle drifts from her line of sight over the edge. Abbie plunges down the slope to see farther into the canyon.

Marcus grabs for her, his hand waving behind her back. "Wait for the officers. Let them go first." She doesn't stop. Marcus descends the slope after her, beckoning the officers and paramedics to follow. Instead they stop at the edge and watch the Jeep fall. Marcus yells, "Come on. Let's get down there."

At the next plateau, Abbie scampers to the edge and looks down. On the ledge below, Gabe and Eva lie safely on their backs. She calls to them, but they can't hear her.

Gabe stands and helps Eva up. "Are you all right?

"Yeah. I lost my grip." She throws her arms around him. "I'm sorry. I just couldn't hold on any longer. I can't believe it." Forced tears flow down her cheeks. "We almost had him." They walk to the edge and peer down at the wreckage.

At the bottom of the canyon, the Jeep bursts into flames. They watch the fire devour the wreckage. Gabe says, "No one is ever going to believe this." He takes out Eva's phone that Levi had given him.

"I'm not sure I do," Eva says. She looks at the phone then at him. "This footage would be worth quite a penny."

Holding the phone in front of him toward the wreckage, Gabe frames up the picture. He zooms in to capture the burning Jeep. Hesitating, he looks over at Eva. "I guess they're just going to have to take our word for it." He dials 911 and puts the phone to his ear. "Yes, I need to report an accident."

Farther up the canyon wall, Abbie with one of the officers firmly holding her arm and guiding her down the slope, is finally close enough to get their attention. Marcus and the paramedics shuffle by them. Abbie yells as loud as she can. "Gabe! Eva!"

They spin around. Gabe sees the officers and paramedics and ends the call. He looks at Eva. "You contacted Ambrose?" He slides the phone back in his pocket. Eva stares at him, unsure if he is angry. He grabs her hand. "Thank you so much." They hurry up toward Abbie.

Abbie pulls away from the officer and leaps into Gabe's arms. "When I saw that smoke and those skid marks, I—" Feeling her weight into his sore ribs, Gabe groans, stumbling back a few steps. She jerks back. "I'm sorry. Are you hurt?"

One paramedic races to Eva and the other to Gabe, who waves him off. "Just a few broken ribs I think." Gabe pulls Abbie close. "But other than that, never better."

Eva immediately dismisses the other paramedic and walks over and hugs Abbie. "I'm so sorry you got caught up in this."

Marcus moves toward them. "It's a good thing you texted me. What happened to Combs?"

Abbie steps back. "Did he get away? Is he still out here somewhere? He went completely psycho."

Gabe looks down at the smoldering Jeep. "We tried to save him. Eva had him, but she lost her grip."

Abbie takes the phone from Gabe. "I need to call Ira and tell him what happened. He's probably worried sick not being able to get a hold of me." She dials the number from memory and drifts over to the side, bursting into the story when Ira answers.

Marcus turns to the officers. "Call it in. We're probably going to need a helicopter and some fire support. We don't want that spreading." One of the officers pulls the radio from his belt and barks orders into the microphone. Marcus further directs the officers. "You two wait here." He motions to the paramedics. "You guys come with me. Let's take the ambulance and see if we can find another way to the wreckage. I don't care what's left, we're going through every speck of that wreckage until we find proof Combs died in that crash." They hurry back up the slope.

Down the canyon, Hannah hangs from a tree sprouting from the slope. She drops from the branch and falls to a grass-covered plateau. The backpack lies ripped open in the thick sod. Money flutters through the tear, scattering across the ledge. Hannah weaves between the coarse blades and emerges into a clearing next to Levi's lifeless body. She slides over his right leg and along his groin up onto his stomach. Hundred dollar bills blow across them. Hannah stretches across his chest and stops. Her tongue flits in and out grazing his chin. She extends her head to his lips and hesitates. Smoke rising from the wreckage fills the clearing, continuing its climb up the canyon wall. Hannah curves around Levi's face and curls into a coil on his chest.

Gabe, Eva, and Abbie work their way back up the slope to the edge of the canyon. All three look back over the edge in silence. The sirens from the ambulance with Marcus and the paramedics fade as they speed away.

With Gabe in the middle, they turn and walk back through the orchard. Gabe smiles and puts one arm around each, the sun peeking above the canyon behind them. Eva glances over her shoulder back toward the canyon. The morning light warms her face and strengthens her resolve. A tear wells in her eye but does not fall. Gladness hinders her despair, but the darkness still lingers.

ACKNOWLEDGMENTS

I WOULD LIKE TO acknowledge the following people, without whom this book would not have been possible.

My beloved Christine Kufahl. Thank you for challenging me, exciting me, and most of all loving me every day, every way. Your intelligence, determination, and beauty leave me always wanting more. I'm obsessed with you, monks.

All my Ohio and Michigan family. After living away for twenty-plus years chasing stories and mischief, so amazing to return home and have your love and support accessible on a regular basis.

Bookseller extraordinaire, friend of the author, and one pretty cool and crazy chick, Nancy Simpson-Brice. Your passion for books and zeal for life are an inspiration to all who are fortunate enough to fall into your orbit. I don't always remember everything we talk about (Damn you, Manhattans), but the meaning and motivation never leave me.

My beta reading team: Michael Cotsopoulos, Tammy Flodmann, Beverly Weyer, Matthew Haynes, Kathy Hayes, Rebecca Bodnar, Bryan McCausland, Barbara Weyer, Luke Szabo, Mara Miller, Lisa Houston, and my man Chad Felton (you jumped on the train early and haven't let go). Thanks for slogging through the first draft and answering my exacting questions. Your insight was invaluable and critical to the process.

Ty Harris and Myron Williams. Thanks for the conversation and friendship when I needed to get out of my head and just talk Cleveland sports. We got to celebrate a Cavs championship together. A Super Bowl is next!

Danny Rizk, Francesca Catanese, and the rest of the Beviamo staff. The Dougie All-In smoothies, perfectly-pulled shots, and invigorating banter fueled this project. You're also pretty darn good with relationship advise. Thanks for always being there.

Will, Sully, Amy, Nico, and the rest of the Spotted Owl team. It was amazing…and a bit dangerous to have such an unbelievable cocktail bar in the building. Thanks for hosting my last book release and most of all permitting me to take Sazeracs up to my loft as long as I brought the glasses back. You embody precision, class, and downright old-fashioned cool.

My stylist and friend, Steve Krampf, aka SJK Style, who has had me looking my best for the past ten-plus years. I appreciate you allowing me to fictionalize you and your brand in this book. There's actually no SJK Style store in Beverly Hills like in Chapter 11—yet, but maybe soon. In the meantime, to learn more about him and his clothing line, check out SJKStyle.com.

Carolyn Gardner, Mark Meaden, Barbara Sponseller, Frank Gonet (aka Uncle Frank, as most of the world knows him), Chris Esch, Dave Blackett, Patrick O'Connor, Jeff Goodrich and the rest of my PNC banking family. Thanks for helping me integrate back to Ohio and showing me the parallels between technology development and writing. I am a better writer and person from getting to know you all.

Tyson Cornell, Guy Intoci, Julia Callahan, Hailie Johnson, Jessica Szuszka, and the rest of the team at Rare Bird Books.

My time in LA working on the first two books helped shape the story and your guidance and encouragement lifted it to another level. Thanks for everything.

And finally, my dearest kitty, Maureen. You made it nineteen years and were with me through every move and all the ups and downs of writing three books and me figuring things out. I miss you every day. Just know, Young Louis has stepped in to keep me focused and on task. I wish you two could've shared a can of tuna together.